FIVE SPELLBINDING LAWS OF INTERNATIONAL LARCENY

THE TALE OF BRYANT ADAMS, BOOK FOUR

MEGAN O'RUSSELL

Ink Worlds Press

DEDICATION

For the dreamers who believe in impossible solutions.
Thank you for building a better tomorrow.

FIVE SPELLBINDING LAWS OF INTERNATIONAL LARCENY

1

They can smell panic.

I knew the truth of it down in my very soul, but I couldn't get my heart to stop racing. Hiding my sweaty hands in my pockets, I kept my pace steady and my chin tucked enough that none of my adversaries would think I was looking for a fight.

One of the pack swerved too near me, but the surrounding horde didn't leave me any room to dodge. A letterman-clad monster rammed into my shoulder.

I stumbled, pulling my hands out of my pockets to save my balance.

"Dude, what the hell happened?" The letterman's beta grabbed my wrist, pulling my hand closer so he could get a better look at the charcoal-colored lines that traced my veins and the angry burn that splatted over the black web.

"Cooking accident." I wrenched my wrist free and shoved my hands back into my pockets. I could feel the pack's eyes following me, tracking my steps to see if I would be easy prey.

The glistening gate to my sanctuary shone just out of reach.

Abandoning caution, I dodged through the throng and dove into the safety of homeroom.

I closed my eyes for a moment, willing my heart to slow.

"Are you going to move?" a tired voice asked from behind me.

"Sorry." I shoved my hands deeper into my pockets and slunk to my seat.

Logic screamed that no one in my high school could possibly know that two magical near-death experiences had created the new scars on my hand. There was also no way my homeroom teacher could have discovered I was a teenage wizard who'd, through a series of super unfortunate and very unlikely events, become entangled with the fate of magic.

And, since I hadn't even told my parents yet, the tired girl who glared at me as I sweat through my turtleneck definitely didn't know I was supposed to be flying to Greece in forty-eight hours so I could track down/steal from the thief who'd gutted all wizarding knowledge.

No, the people around me definitely didn't know any of that. All they saw was the seventeen-year-old geek who somehow had the coolest best friend and most perfect girlfriend and totally didn't deserve either.

I sank into my chair and kept my gaze fixed on my teacher's desk.

'Cause, here's the thing—and I don't want to sound like I'm a douche—if I wanted to, if the kids in my class were to actually gang up on me, I could defend myself.

Five months ago, when I found out I was a wizard and went from being plain geek Bryant Jameson Adams to wizard geek Bryant Jameson Adams, I stopped being defenseless.

I could trap my classmates in darkness. I could pin them all to the wall. I could...accidentally light part of the school on fire...again.

But my magic and battle savvy weren't meant to be seen by the regular humans aboveground. Here, trapped in the corridors of teenage angst and swaddled in the unending drama of dating, grades, and cliques, I wasn't a wizard who fate had drawn into the very center of the battle for what the magical community should be. I was just Bryant, the nerd whose mom ran the school drama department.

I'd always been able to almost cope with the strange difference between school Bryant and wizard Bryant, but having visible scars even magic couldn't mend made pretending to be normal during school hours a lot harder to manage.

The bell rang, and I glanced over to Devon's usual seat, ready to see his face and know I wasn't just a freak who had somehow hallucinated the fact that a settlement of wizards lived below the subway tunnels. But Devon's seat stayed empty as the teacher started class.

I gripped my non-magical phone, trying to decide if sneaking it out of my pocket to text Devon was worth the risk of

A) Being caught with a phone in class and
B) My teacher noticing all the damage that had been done to my right hand in the last week and freaking out, therefore sending me to

1. The guidance counselor
2. The school nurse, or
3. Skipping all the in-school steps and just notifying Child Protective Services, thereby forcing my poor overstressed mother into coming up with a logical reason for the two types of brand-new scars.

I dug my hands deeper into my pockets and tried to ignore

the aching in my gut that whispered my best friend could need me to save his life.

Before I'd started hyperventilating, but after I'd managed to get a good start on a brand-new ulcer, Devon breezed into the classroom, beaming like he'd just won a Tony Award and been crowned Prom King on national television.

Devon sauntered right up to the teacher and handed him a slip of paper.

Mr. Ruler of Homeroom read the note before giving Devon a smile. "Congratulations, Mr. Rhodes."

"Thanks, sir," Devon beamed. "I'm really stoked."

"Please don't use words like *stoked* and throw away your shot." Mr. Ruler of Homeroom waggled a wrinkled finger.

"Of course, sir." Devon gave a little bow and slid into his seat, throwing me a thumbs up.

My gut stopped eating itself, but I still couldn't muster the courage to pull my hands out of my pockets as we drifted from class to class.

With random teachers stopping Devon in the hall to wish him luck, it was easier to believe no one knew about any of my weird secrets. Being in the presence of the great Devon Rhodes meant getting seen as wallpaper on a regular basis. Sometimes being ignored sucked. Sometimes it felt like Devon was the best friend equivalent of me wearing an invisibility cloak, which was super awesome.

"You ever going to ask?" Devon set his lunch tray down on the table with a satisfying *thunk*.

"Ask what award you won that's mysteriously taking you away from school starting Wednesday?" I pulled my sandwich from my lunch bag using only my left hand.

"Not an award." Devon took pity on me, opened the baggie, and pulled out my sandwich. "I've been invited to interview for early admission to college. Not bad for a guy who's been disowned."

"And the school is just going with it?"

"Well, after the official-looking letter I turned in this morning and the confirmation call Eric made to the principal, why would anyone doubt me?" Devon winked.

"If you say we're stealing a convertible and dancing in a parade, I'm sending you to Dr. Spinnek." I peered over the heads of the crowd, searching for Elizabeth.

"I haven't seen her," Devon said.

I finagled my normal phone out of my pocket.

No messages.

"What did your parents say?" Devon asked.

"Nothing."

"Because they've suddenly decided letting you leave the country to track down stolen books is a good idea or because you haven't told them yet?"

"Do I really need to answer that?" I shoved my sandwich into my mouth.

"You have to tell them, Bry. We need to book tickets."

I nodded as I chewed, still scanning the cafeteria for Elizabeth. I even dared to glance toward the mural honoring the Lancre lunch lady I'd squished. Elizabeth was nowhere in sight.

"She was fine this morning." Devon joined me in searching the cafeteria. "We walked to school together."

A moment of jealousy pinged in my stomach. I wanted to walk to school with Elizabeth, but as the only one of us who didn't live at the Consortium, and given the fact that my mom had been super freaked out about the tassel-shaped burn on my hand, I hadn't had time to get to the Consortium for my normal *coffee and make sure the world hasn't ended* time with Devon and Elizabeth.

I swallowed the half of my sandwich I'd shoved into my

mouth. "What if she's been snatched? What if her parents came after her? What if there are shadows in the girls' bathroom and she's been trapped just out of reach?"

"First of all, take a breath," Devon said, "I'm sure Elizabeth is fine. Second, if she's in an epic battle against evil shadows in the girls' bathroom, we'll just invade the girls' bathroom. Third, we have enough real problems to stress about. Don't start freakin' out about things that aren't actually a problem."

"When do I get to start freaking out?"

"I'll let you know." Devon shrugged. "For now, just eat your sandwich."

"Sure."

I slipped my right hand out of my pocket, keeping it hidden as I typed two messages.

The first one, I sent to Elizabeth—*Are you okay? I love you.*

The second, I sent to my mom—*I haven't seen Elizabeth today. I don't know where she is. Can you check with the school office? I'm freaking out.*

I tucked my phone and hand back into my pocket and shoved the other half of my sandwich into my mouth.

"You didn't even ask what school I was going to visit about early admissions," Devon said.

"Okay, what—"

My phone buzzed.

I'm fine. Been stuck in the guidance counselor's office all day. I don't need rescuing, but I would kill for a cup of coffee.

"She's in the guidance counselor's office." I grabbed my lunch box.

"So, then she's fine." Devon stayed seated.

"I mean sure, like *monsters and evil people aren't trying to kill me* fine," I whispered. "But she might need emotional support. I'm the boyfriend. It's part of my job."

"Good for you, Bry." Devon winked at me. "You go earn your place as boyfriend."

"I will." I puffed up my chest and strode away with as much confidence and gusto as someone clutching a lunchbox can achieve.

There wasn't a rule about having to stay in the cafeteria during your assigned lunch time, but I still had a gnawing worry itching the back of my neck that someone was going to come barreling down the hall, shouting that I should be anywhere but near my girlfriend.

The door to the guidance counselor's office came into view, as shiny and surrounded by cheerful posters as ever.

I slowed my steps as I passed the cartoon characters standing under skywriting that read *One small change can make a huge difference* and was walking creepily slowly by the time I got to the poster of a kid wearing lab gear with the words *Building a brighter future starts with you!* badly photoshopped around her.

I lingered near the crack in the guidance counselor's door, listening for sounds of emotional distress.

An oddly familiar voice that wasn't Elizabeth's rumbled through the door.

I was just about to go full creeper and press my ear to the crack so I could figure out why I knew that voice, when the ancient biology teacher came toddling down the hall.

Giving him a nod, I picked up my pace, hustling halfway to the end of the corridor before making a U-turn to go back for another eavesdropping pass.

I tried to look cool and calm as I scanned the hall, timing my arrival at the guidance counselor's door so I could press my ear to the crack without any authority figures noticing.

I was so busy making sure the janitor wasn't going to turn down the corridor toward me, I didn't notice the guidance counselor's door swinging open as I leaned in to listen.

"Bryant!"

At the usually non-terrifying sound of Elizabeth saying my name that close to my ear, I screamed and dove away from her, landing on the grubby linoleum with less dignity than a balloon handler during a windy Thanksgiving Day Parade.

"Are you okay?" Elizabeth grabbed my arm to help me up.

"Yeah, I was just pass—"

"Mr. Adams, what happened?" The guidance counselor stepped toward me, her gaze fixed on my screwed-up hand.

"Project for stage makeup class," Elizabeth said. "I think Bryant's found a new talent."

"I didn't know you had a real interest in the performing arts." The guidance counselor furrowed her brow.

"He likes working backstage, just not being near the spotlight." Elizabeth widened her eyes. "Aren't you supposed to be meeting Devon?"

"Yes. Yes, I should go to do that now." Because saying things like that is exactly how you avoid suspicion.

"If you have a moment, we could talk about some very interesting arts opportunities," the guidance counselor said. "Even with the theatre having burned down—"

"I am so sorry to interrupt," the super familiar voice said, "but I'd like to cover just a few more questions before I go on my merry little way."

Lola stepped out into the corridor.

My brain did that weird thing where the entire world seems to blip for a second. Like your mind can't put two things together that should never, ever be together, so it just goes *Nope, I'm out!*

Lola's hair was all curly, and she'd switched out the sparkly romper she usually wore at the Consortium for a deep-blue power suit.

I blinked at Lola, trying to figure out if the last five months of my life had been some sort of weird hallucination.

"We're very excited to be workin' with Miss Wick," Lola said. "But to best serve each of our charges, going over their complete academic record is essential."

"Of course." The guidance counselor bowed Lola back toward her office. "I'm just so thrilled Elizabeth has been given this opportunity."

I kept staring at the door after it shut behind Lola.

"Come on." Elizabeth threaded her arm through mine, leading me away.

"Is that really Lola?" My question sort of came out as a whimper.

"Yep."

"Why?"

"After all the drama with my parents, I've been offered a place with a special teen mentorship program," Elizabeth whispered. "I'll be starting off my time with Steps to Independence with a two-week retreat to make sure I'm prepared to live on my own. Had to get it cleared with the guidance counselor, of course."

"When did this plan happen?" I asked.

"When I was up late last night, researching reasons I could disappear for a bit without your dad's lawyer freaking out." Elizabeth shook her head, sending her blond-with-tiny-black-streaks curls fluttering around her like a shampoo commercial. "Nikki is great, but I have a feeling telling her I'm running away to Greece might make her reconsider whether or not she wants to help me."

"I have a feeling Nikki would help whoever my dad told her to."

"What did your parents say about Greece?" Elizabeth stopped in front of her locker.

"I'm a coward who hasn't told them yet. But I love you." I tried to give a winning smile that probably looked more like a grimace.

"Do you need Devon and me to be there when you talk to them?" Elizabeth reached into her locker, pulling out a green hoodie.

"I..." For a moment, I considered being a selfish prick and making my friends, who'd given up any relationship with their parents, help me with my parents. "I'll be fine. I think I've got a game plan worked out."

By *game plan* I meant *decent lie*, but whatever.

"Let me know if you change your mind." Elizabeth handed me her sweatshirt. "Try it on."

"Isn't this supposed to work the other way around?" I glanced down the hall, waiting for one of the lettermen to come shoulder-check me again.

"We're a modern couple who won't be controlled by the outdated rules of the patriarchy," Elizabeth said.

"Okay." I pulled on the sweatshirt, which was so new it hadn't even pilled up on the inside.

Elizabeth took my hands and pushed my thumbs through the sneaky little holes in the cuffs, leaving enough of the dark green fabric hanging over my hands to hide my scars.

"You're brilliant." I used my weird hand to tuck her hair behind her ear and didn't catch a glimpse of the damage.

"You're welcome."

2

"I'm glad you were both able to join me." I pressed my palms to the kitchen table to keep my hands from shaking.

My parents sat opposite me, filling Mom's tiny linoleum kitchen to bursting. Mom cradled her coffee and looked ready to fall back asleep in her comfy sweater. Dad had arrived in his work suit like he'd been up for hours.

They both stared at me for a long moment until I remembered I was the one who was supposed to be talking.

"I know last week was really rough," I said, "and I want to thank you for being so supportive."

"We love you, Bryant," Mom said.

"I'm finding it hard to be supportive of your coming home with new scars every two days." Dad laced his fingers together with his hands planted on the table like we were in some sort of business negotiation.

"I did start off by saying last week was rough. And"—I pressed on before Dad could pull out some sort of contract obligating me not to get any more scarred up than I already was—"I really think things are looking up."

Mostly true, though not exactly detailed.

"Go on." Dad leaned back in his chair.

"Eric and I found something," I said. "The break we've been looking for."

"Break in what?" Dad asked.

"A way for me to have a higher education," I said.

"A break in you going to college?" A crease formed on Dad's forehead.

"Not exactly college," I said. "Wizards don't have a university accreditation system. But there's a spot in Greece that has more books and knowledge than any other place in the world, and Eric and I have discovered an opportunity that makes this the perfect time to visit."

"Greece?" Mom clutched her coffee even tighter.

"It's the chance of a lifetime," I said. "I mean, I'm learning a ton from Eric, but there's so much in Greece even he doesn't know. And it's the same for Devon and Elizabeth."

"What would Devon and Elizabeth have to learn from a Greek wizard?" Dad asked.

Sometimes having smart parents really sucks.

"So, so much. About the history of magic and how the magical Manhattan we live in came to be," I said. "And there will be no Ladies in Greece. No Beville. No shadows who have our scent. Just a chance for all of us to learn about magic."

"If Greece is so safe, why didn't you go sooner?" Mom said.

"Because the opportunity to go to the place with the books wasn't a thing then." I dug my nails into the table. "And the chance won't last for long. We have an invitation to arrive in Greece the day after tomorrow. If we miss it, we might never be offered entry again."

My parents stared at each other. I could see the silent communication flying between them, but it was in some sort of parent language I couldn't understand.

"It's like getting an invitation to a workshop run by Fosse and Sondheim, Mom," I begged. "This is a once in a lifetime opportunity. This could be my only chance to be really, truly good at something."

Mom took a deep breath and looked at Dad one last time.

"I think it's a good idea for you to go," Mom said. "But there are some conditions. You need to check in at least twice a day."

"I'll have your phone set up to work overseas," Dad said. "And you'll be traveling with a chaperone."

"I can't have a chaperone," I said. "We're doing wizardy things."

"You are not going to a foreign country with only Eric Deldridge as supervision," Dad said. "Your chaperone can drop you off where you're going to study and pick you up at night."

"Okay," I said, "but I need money for plane tickets and hotels."

"You have the credit card. Feel free to use it wherever you like." A devious twinkle filled Dad's eyes.

"Is this some *you'll be watching me* thing?" I shrank down in my seat.

"It's only responsible to keep an eye on credit card transactions." Dad shrugged.

Mom looked at Dad, and she had a little glimmer in her eyes, too. Like she was proud of his stalking parenting skills, or maybe she was just super shocked that when I'd woken up at 6:30 a.m. filled with self-loathing for not having been brave enough to talk to my parents about leaving the country and decided to text Dad to ask if he'd come for breakfast, he'd knocked on our door at 7:15. Either way, she patted his hand when she said, "Well, if that's all settled, we've got to get to school."

Her fingers lingered on his for a moment.

If I had known any therapists in Beville, I would have called to schedule myself an appointment before I'd even left the breakfast table.

But I didn't. So I fled to my room and tried not to imagine my parents sitting creepily close to each other as I pulled on Elizabeth's sweatshirt. I walked to school with Mom, not bothering to say how pointless it was for me to go to class since I would be leaving the country for I didn't know how long the next day.

By the time I sat down in first period, I'd already texted Devon, Elizabeth, and Eric that my dad had agreed to pay. By the time I reached lunch, all I had to do was type my credit card number into a bunch of different pages on Elizabeth's phone to book the trip.

"How did you even find all this so fast?" I asked, trying not to think of how much money I was casting into the internet to buy four tickets to Greece. It was enough to pay my mom's rent for a month. My dad wouldn't even notice the money had been spent.

Except that he was going to be stalking my credit card.

"I've been poking around." Elizabeth took her phone back after I had pressed the purchase button. "I wanted to be prepared. Last one."

She pulled up a payment screen for a hotel.

"I figured I'd only book us two nights in Athens right now." Elizabeth handed the phone back to me.

"And from there, we can try to figure out where a master criminal hid a few thousand books," Devon said. "I'm starting to think we'll be back by the weekend."

"We can hope." I pressed the purchase button and watched more of my dad's money drift away into the ether. "All we have to do is find the books and then figure out how to smuggle them back into the country." I took a long drink of my juice, trying not to panic. "Shipping a few thousand books shouldn't be a big deal."

"We can worry about transport after we find the books." Elizabeth held my hand, and my panic shifted into gleeful *I'm going to Europe with my girlfriend* excitement.

"Now we're just two forged passports away from saving generations of magical knowledge." Devon dampened my glee.

"Eric told me he's got it covered," Elizabeth said.

"Which probably means someone's going to try to kill us before we actually get our hands on the papers." I chugged the rest of my juice. "When are we meeting him?"

"Elizabeth and I are supposed to go right after school," Devon said. "You don't have to—"

"I'm coming with you," I cut across Devon. "I usually really like Eric, but that doesn't mean I trust his sketchy contacts."

"I won't mind the company." Elizabeth leaned over and brushed her lips against my cheek.

"Not in my cafeteria," a grating voice shouted over the chaos of the hungry teens.

I froze, instinct telling me to reach for the phone in my pocket, reason telling me the Lancre lunch lady had been dead for months. Instinct won out, and I slipped my hand into my pocket as I turned around.

A middle-aged woman with a hairnet and scowl weaved through the now-staring students, heading right for our table. "There will be no PDA in my cafeteria."

"Who are you?" Devon looked from her hairnet to the lunch line where the other, nicer hairnet-wearing lunch ladies were still doing their jobs of, I don't know, feeding the students.

"I'm the one in charge," the middle-aged hairnet snapped. "And I won't allow any of this teenage, hormone-fueled lust in my lunchroom."

"Lust?" Heat shot into my face.

"It's fine." Elizabeth packed up the remainder of her lunch.

"I needed to drop by the guidance counselor's office anyway. Maybe she can give me some tips on not showing any emotion or *lusting* after my boyfriend in public. God forbid teenagers form actual attachments. I can kiss my grandma on the cheek, but the school should have something to say about me doing the same thing to a guy."

"I won't take any lip from students." Hairnet sneered as she lumbered closer.

Elizabeth took my chin, tipped my face up, and kissed me. Like full-on *I forgot how to breathe because she tasted like roses and all things good* kissed me. My insides turned to goo, and the whole world disappeared.

And then Elizabeth stopped kissing me, and the world reappeared just in time for the entire cafeteria to start applauding.

"See you after school." Elizabeth brushed her lips against mine, curtsied for the still-applauding crowd, and strode out of the lunchroom.

The lunch lady stood there, sputtering. She said things about write-ups and inappropriate behavior, but people were still clapping and oohing, and the world was still wobbly because the most beautiful girl to have ever existed had kissed me in front of everyone. And the burn of embarrassment from all those people staring at me joined with the fire dancing around in my chest that made it quite impossible to hear whatever the lunch lady was yammering as Devon put my food back into my lunchbox, pressed it into my hands, and yanked me to my feet.

"If you want to write us up, tell the principal." Devon's words drifted through the haze in my brain. "If you just want to take your misery out on someone, find another victim. Or better yet, a therapist."

Devon dragged me to the front of the cafeteria as a renewed round of applause began.

"Where are we going?" I asked as we strode down the corridor and the sounds of the cheering crowd faded.

"Anywhere but in there." Devon's voice had a dark tinge to it, an angry kind of determination I wasn't used to hearing from him.

"Look"—I slowed my steps as we neared our next classroom—"I appreciate you standing up for Elizabeth and me, but as long as Elizabeth doesn't get into trouble, I really don't care."

"I know. I'm just over being treated like a kid when I've literally fought battles to save lives." Devon let go of my arm and ran his hands over his hair in a way that somehow made it look even chicer than when he'd styled it. "I'm not sure if it's because I'm out of my parents' apartment and living at the Consortium, and we're dealing with things the teachers here couldn't even begin to understand. Or maybe it's just that I'm not totally convinced the lunch lady isn't another Lancre come to kidnap my best friend."

The thought of another Lancre hiding in the school brought me crashing back into reality.

"I just couldn't stand her looming over us." Devon ran his hands over his hair again, upping its style...again. "I know I'm not the magical one, but it's starting to feel like existing in this school is tearing away pieces of the person I'm supposed to be. Beville is more real to me than this concrete cage."

"Devon—"

"I think Greece is going to be good for everybody. Get away from New York. Get stuff done. Find the books and restore the Library once and for all. We've just got to get on the plane and everything will get better."

I sat in our next class, not bothering to actually pay attention. I was too busy trying not to stare at Devon while I wondered what would happen once we did find the books. There'd be shipping and customs to deal with. We'd have to restock the shelves, and then find a way to tell the magical population of Manhattan the Ladies were gone. The evil women who had ruled over them for so long were no more. And then...I didn't know what the *and then* was. I didn't know how to tell a bunch of angry wizards there was no longer anyone in charge.

3

I held Elizabeth's hand as we walked from school to the subway stop at Columbus Circle. The crisp winter air stung my cheeks as the wind whipped between the buildings. I took a deep breath and allowed myself a moment to appreciate that, sure, my face would probably be red for the rest of the day, but at least the wind toned down the natural stink of the sludge-filled city.

"How cold is it supposed to be in Greece?" I asked as we weaved through the crowds and down into the subway station.

"Shouldn't you have looked that up before you started packing?" Devon asked.

"Do you actually believe he already started packing?" Elizabeth poked him in the back.

"I didn't want to look suspicious." I took the lead, heading toward the blank bit of wall off to the side where no one ever seemed to want to look. "If my mom found a packed suitcase under my bed and didn't know why I'd squirreled away a week's worth of underwear, I'd be doomed to even more therapy. *Portunda*." I muttered the spell at the wall. An instant later, a door appeared.

Playing it as cool as I am capable of, I opened my newly formed door and let Elizabeth and Devon through before following and closing the door behind us. "*Portundo*." My door disappeared, leaving us with a solid wall behind and the path to Beville ahead.

Elizabeth peered into the shadows along the edges of the tunnel.

I held my breath for a second, waiting for her to say there was something lurking that was going to jump out and try to kill us. But she slipped her hand into mine and started walking toward Beville.

We didn't speak as we headed deeper and deeper underground. The steady sounds of our footsteps dug into my skull in a way that wouldn't have bothered me before the whole wizard thing. Before people wanted me dead, silence meant better opportunities for daydreaming. Post-discovering my wizardishness, silence meant a better chance to hear evil things sneaking up on you. Things like Lancre, shadows, monsters, wizards who want to sell you, wizards who want to kill you...

I shook my head, trying to stop my brain from creating a complete list of all the things in Beville that might want me dead.

It didn't work.

Somewhere between evil spiders crawling up from depths even deeper than Beville and the children of the Minotaur I'd killed months ago, footsteps carried from farther down the tunnel.

I held my free hand forward, ready to attack whatever beast had come for our blood, but it was only Eric, striding up the tunnel like he literally had no concept of fear.

"I thought we were meeting you at your house," Devon said.

"That was the plan." Eric waited until we reached him then matched our pace, continuing down the tunnel.

"But?" I slipped my hand into my pocket, gripping my magical phone as I waited for whatever horror Eric was about to spring on us.

"The forger refuses to leave her lair," Eric said. "I had hoped, with a large enough financial incentive, we might be able to avoid going to her. But she made it clear she will not be coming into my home."

"Wait," Devon said, "which is it? She refuses to leave her lair, or she refuses to go into your home?"

"Does it matter?" Eric asked.

"Of course it does." Elizabeth spoke slowly as she squinted into the shadows. "Not wanting to go into your house is smart. You've trained your house to defend you. The doors chase people. Rooms appear and trap people."

"But not wanting to leave her lair is different," Devon said. "Then we've got to wonder if she's agoraphobic—"

"Or knows something we don't," Elizabeth continued. "And if the forger who deals with all the dark deeds of Beville has a good reason not to want to leave home—"

"Should we be walking the streets belowground?" I let go of my phone and held my non-Elizabeth claimed hand in front of me as subtly as I could manage, ready to shout *Abalata* at the first hint of anyone trying to murder us.

"Would you like the comforting response or the absolute truth?" Eric asked.

"The truth." My voice wavered a little.

"I'm not sure," Eric said. "I can smell something in the air. Change. Dissatisfaction. Revolution."

"But we already did the revolution part," I whispered as we reached the end of the tunnel.

"We did. The rest of Beville did not," Eric said. "The people have always been displeased with the Ladies but too terrified to fight against them. Now that the Ladies haven't tormented or killed anyone in more than two months, the whispers of malcontent have become murmured conversations of dissent."

I let myself look at the base of the giant spire I'd grown during the Battle of Beville. I knew the massive stone reached all the way to Times Square where it rose up with the skyscrapers in a way that defied geologic reason. I knew Thaden's headless body was trapped inside. I knew that battle had weakened the Ladies enough we'd managed to break into the Library, defeat them, and take over.

I couldn't imagine what it was like for the people of Beville who didn't know those things.

"How long does it take to go from the murmur stage to the revolution stage?" I asked as we headed down the street where Eric lived.

"I'm afraid I'm not sure of that either," Eric said. "Throughout the Ladies' rule, there was never a rebellion that survived long enough to truly begin."

"That's not completely true," Devon raised one perfectly sculpted eyebrow.

"As far as we are concerned"—Eric raised a perfectly sculpted eyebrow right back—"it is."

A weird feeling, like I was being watched from the windows of the surrounding houses, nibbled at the back of my neck.

I looked up to the arched ceiling thirty feet overhead. The lights set into the stone gave off an eerily warm glow that did nothing to stop the neck tingle. The weird difference in architecture from one street to the next didn't help either.

The houses changed as we entered what looked more like a suburb than the townhouse-ish vibe of Lark Lane where Eric lived. We passed by some sketchy shops and a few houses that looked like they wouldn't pass inspection aboveground.

I kept waiting for Eric to stop in front of one of the shops—I mean, they definitely looked like illegal dealings would be up their alley—but his pace never faltered.

We weaved down streets I'd never seen before and somehow turned onto a row I definitely remembered.

There were a couple of normal-looking brownstone houses and a log cabin crammed onto the street, just because. But it was the house that couldn't seem to decide what shape it wanted to be that made me forget I was supposed to be walking.

First, it looked like a theme park castle. Then, it flipped to a tropical hut. Then it went all haunted house, complete with wind rustling through the half-dead trees that appeared out front. Then it became a medieval castle, complete with a moat where the sidewalk should have been.

"Come on." Elizabeth tugged on my hand, and we jogged a few steps to catch up to Eric just as he stopped in front of the whitest house I'd ever seen.

The whole thing was built out of some weird, matte metal that looked like it belonged in a sci-fi movie. The front steps were paper-thin strips of white that floated lazily in the air. The windows shimmered in a way that made me not quite sure if they were glass or if I was actually looking at some sort of hologram.

"Here?" Devon whispered. "Really?"

"What were you expecting?" Eric paused for a moment, like he was girding his loins, before climbing the steps.

I held my breath, waiting for the thin strips of white to give under his weight, but the stairs stayed steady as he knocked on the front door.

Maybe I had just gotten too used to Eric's sentient house and the way its front door would just swing open and let people in when it wanted to. Or maybe I was used to how people above-ground peeked through the peepholes in their doors and then decided if they wanted to answer or pretend they weren't home so they could go back to binge watching streaming television. Whatever the reason, I definitely didn't expect the top half of the door to give a weird shimmer and fade away to be mostly transparent.

I also didn't expect to see a girl my age standing on the other side of the door, her arms crossed and face set in an epic scowl as she glared at Eric.

"I do believe we're right on time," Eric said.

The girl tipped her head to the side. Her super red curls bounced with the movement.

"I have brought cash as requested," Eric said.

The girl's lips narrowed into a frown.

"I give you my word as a wizard we were not followed by the Ladies," Eric said. "You will not be risking your security by letting us in."

The girl raised her hand toward the transparent part of the door. For a moment, I thought that would be that. The door would become solid, and we would just have to find a human forger who could make us passports overnight.

But then, with a *hum* so faint I barely noticed it, the whole door shimmered before disappearing.

"We made a deal for two passports, Deldridge," the girl said. "Why the hell do you have three people with you?"

"Raven." Eric gave a little bow. "It is as lovely to see you as ever. My apprentice does not need a passport. He has a legitimate document. However, he is intimately connected with the two in need of papers. Also, finding a way to leave him out of this little errand would have been more trying than I have time for at the moment."

"That's not my problem," Raven said.

"I'm the one paying for the trip." I took a little step forward. "And since I'm funding it, I have a right to make sure the passports we're buying will work. I don't want to have wasted thousands of dollars on plane tickets if these two can't even get through airport security."

"I didn't know you needed a backer." Raven gave an unfriendly grin. "How the mighty have fallen."

"Not fallen," Eric said. "My resources remain steady. However, my humble wealth cannot compete with the accounts to which Bryant has access. Really, you should be thanking me for the introduction."

Raven examined me, from my worn sneakers to my generic, water-resistant winter coat. "I appreciate the unlikely ones." She turned and walked away, going farther into her house.

"Keep close." Eric stepped inside.

For one horrible moment, I thought the door would reappear and trap Eric in the house. We'd be on our own trying to find the books. I'd have to be the one to break it to the people of Beville that they'd really been free of the Ladies for a few months, but we'd been too busy searching for the stolen books to tell them.

But then Devon stepped inside, and Elizabeth dragged me through the door with her.

I gripped Elizabeth's hand as the handle-less door shimmered back into being behind us.

4

The matte-white walls inside the house didn't make me feel better about being locked in with Raven. I glanced back at the door, ready to whisper a quick *Portunda* just to be sure I could make the door reappear. But Elizabeth gave a tiny shake of her head, so I silently followed her farther down the pure white hall.

I'd been in Eric's house often enough that the fact that the hallway was way too long to fit in Raven's house didn't really freak me out. So, as I kept walking down the plain white corridor, it took me a minute to figure out why there was a bubble of panic rising in my chest.

The whole house seemed to be giving off a faint *hum*. It came from the walls, the ceiling, and if I really concentrated, I could even feel it buzzing in my feet as I walked.

"I hate to be rude," Eric said.

"Then don't be." Raven didn't change her pace.

"You give me no choice," Eric said. "Our time is precious these days, and, though I appreciate the theatrics of leading us down an unending corridor, I'm afraid we need to keep our business brief."

"I'm not wasting your time, Deldridge," Raven said.

"So you've moved your work room since my last visit?" Eric asked.

"Nope. Just letting the house do its work," Raven said.

"I'm sorry, what?" I took a few quick steps, dragging Elizabeth forward so we were right on Devon's heels.

"The walls are gathering images," Raven said.

"Wouldn't it be easier to just take a normal passport picture?" Devon asked.

"Sure." Raven stopped and turned around to face us. "But the walls aren't analyzing your faces for the passports. I'm more interested in finding out if your faces match the people I've been looking for."

"What?" My voice cracked enough to make heat shoot up into my cheeks. "Why would you be looking for us?"

Elizabeth squeezed my hand super hard with a grip that quite clearly said *Please don't speak. You're a terrible actor. You will make things worse.*

"I'm not sure if Eric told you," Elizabeth said in a voice that wasn't suspicious, "but Devon and I aren't wizards. So whoever you're looking for, it can't be us."

"Actually, I think it makes you better candidates." Raven tapped the wall, and a portion shimmered and vanished, leaving a doorway in its wake.

She walked into the room, and Eric followed her without any hint of trepidation.

Devon glanced behind to give Elizabeth and me a shrug before stepping up to the door. "Whoa." His eyes lit up like it was Christmas morning as he walked out of sight.

"I hate the going through the doorway into the unknown thing," I whispered as Elizabeth and I took our turn stepping up to the door.

The room beyond was...not what I expected.

"Whoa." I copied Devon's astonished joy as I took in the full wall of monitors, massive bank of computers, and workshop table filled with shiny machine bits like we'd just walked into a superhero's secret lab. "This is the best place ever."

"Yeah." Devon drifted to the corner of the room where a silver coat, which looked almost like a fencing jacket, hung next to a silver shield.

"You're still pursuing your side projects?" Eric leaned over the table with his hands tucked behind his back, peering at the bits of metal and wire that were probably going to be used to build something awesome.

"You're still causing chaos." Raven sat at a keyboard and typed, her fingers moving faster than I could ever hope to achieve. "Well, I guess that's not really true. Even you've never been brazen enough to cause so much trouble topside."

Videos popped up on all the screens. White walls, tall tables covered with electronics, people milling around trying to decide what to spend their money on.

My stomach sank as I recognized the subterranean store.

"There is no need for this display, Raven." Eric clenched his hands behind his back like he was stopping himself from stopping her.

"We're just about the get to the good part." Raven pointed to the top right monitor just as the glass spiral staircase at the center of the white store shattered.

On the next screen over, my shield spell shimmered to life.

Right below it, Devon's sword grew with a red glow.

"The cops have all this footage, of course," Raven said. "They've been careful to keep the decapitated woman off the news. I mean, they have to be. How could they explain to the regulars that a Lancre had been in the store? Long bones, long teeth. The cops aren't stupid enough to call that monster *human*."

"What have they been calling it?" I asked.

"I'm more interested in what the Ladies have been calling it." Raven spun in her chair to look at Eric. "The pipe breaking at that creepy boarding school—"

"It wasn't a boarding school." Elizabeth shivered.

"—I can understand the Ladies ignoring that," Raven pressed on. "Water pipes break. Vandalism happens. The school was filled with juvenile delinquents, so a little destruction makes sense. But that—"

Raven pointed over her shoulder at the largest of the screens.

There was no sound, but from the way screen-Eric's mouth moved, I could tell he was shouting a spell as the Lancre leapt toward him. The tape slowed down for a second, like Raven wanted to be sure we could all see the shift in the air as Eric's spell flew toward the Lancre.

I knew what was coming but somehow couldn't make myself look away as the spell sliced through the Lancre's neck.

The video went back to normal speed as the Lancre's body fell to the ground and her head rolled out of the frame.

"The police are losing their shit trying to figure out how a monster's head just fell off her body." Raven reached behind her and pressed a button. The videos started over from the beginning. "It's not like they can prosecute you, of course. They couldn't explain to a jury how you killed the monster that shouldn't exist. But they have footage, Deldridge."

"And how did you find the tapes?" Eric tented his fingers under his chin.

"Because I'm not like the rest of Beville. I'm not just biding my time underground, fiddling around with magic. I'm a tech girl." Raven spread her arms wide. "Tech starts with topsiders. Monitoring what happens aboveground is in my best interest. That and"—she pointed to a monitor just as one of the Lancre's minions bit into my hand—"it's perfect for my viewing pleasure."

"What do you want?" Devon stepped forward.

"The human asks first?" Raven smiled.

"What do you want?" Devon said again.

"I want to know why the Ladies haven't come after you yet. I want to know where it is you're fleeing to with the very expensive passports you want me to make. And I want to know what kind of awful mess you're trying to drag all of wizard kind into by exposing us to the topsiders, Eric Deldridge."

We stayed silent for a long moment.

I rocked back on my heels as my body begged me to flee from Raven's simmering glare.

Eric took a deep breath. "The Ladies have never been known for their swiftness in carrying out punishments."

"The cops have you on video. Even the Ladies wouldn't take their time reacting to something like that," Raven said. "Lie to me one more time, and you won't get any passports out of me."

I watched Eric thinking. His face was completely still, but somehow I could see all the cogs turning in his head.

"The Ladies are dead," Eric said.

I made a sound somewhere between a whimper and a gurgle.

"I said no more lies." Raven stood, kicking her chair back toward her computers.

"It's no lie," Eric said. "They've been dead for two months. We've taken over the Consortium and the Library."

"Bullshit."

"What you see on that video are the consequences of our trying to stop a Lancre placed in the store in hopes of searching out new wizards to be sold at auction in the horrible settlement far below Beville." Eric stepped closer to Raven.

"There is nothing below Beville," Raven said.

"I assure you there is." Eric pulled aside his collar. "A bone witch gave me this scar when she kidnapped Bryant and me and then tried to sell him. We disposed of most who were indulging in the foul trade of purchasing wizard flesh, but we have yet to deal with Kendrick McDonald. Surely you've heard of him. He ran The Game until we drove him out of business."

"Do you actually think I'm dumb enough to believe this?" Raven stepped so close to Eric she had to tip her chin up to look him in the eyes.

"I haven't even come to the great tragedy of our tale," Eric whispered. "The Library is empty. It has been since long before we were born. The books were stolen, and the Ladies hid the truth of their shame from all of us. We need the passports to try and find the books."

"Bullshit." Tears sparkled in the corners of Raven's eyes.

"We're running out of time, Raven. The knowledge of our ancestors is being sold off on the black market. It drifts further away from our grasp with every lost day. I am asking you to help save the legacy of our people. Anything the police find, any anger from the people of Beville when the truth comes out, it's all meaningless compared to saving the books. Nothing can matter as much as the books."

"You're wrong." Raven spoke so softly I could barely hear her words. "There are books in the Library. The rules of impartment still stand. I won't believe in the fairy tale of the Ladies' death, or any other heroic daydream where you rescue us all."

"Your phone, Bryant," Eric said.

"What?" I gripped my pocket. "No."

"Your phone." Eric held out his hand. "You'll get it back unharmed."

My hand shook as I reached into my pocket and pulled out my one-of-a-kind magical mobile. The black case didn't have a ding on it. After all we'd been through together, the screen hadn't even been scratched. The distance from my pocket to Eric's hand felt like a million miles as I reached forward and laid the phone on his palm.

Eric pressed his thumb to the scanner and started scrolling through spells.

"What are you doing?" Raven shifted to stand beside Eric, peering at the phone.

"Here." Eric stopped scrolling. "Go on. Speak the spell."

"I'm not a kid on the playground anymore," Raven said. "I'm not going to fall for your tricks."

"Try it," Devon said. "What have you got to lose?"

Raven moved her mouth for a moment as though she were soundlessly practicing the word.

I shifted to the side, placing myself between Elizabeth and Raven before she could speak the spell.

"*Viodula.*" A little *whoosh* filled the air as Raven spoke, and then...nothing.

I glanced around the room, searching for whatever it was the spell had done, but everything in the room looked the same.

Except...for the laughter in Elizabeth's eyes. And Devon's eyes. And the slight twitch of Eric's lips, like he was determined not to smile. And the awe on Raven's face as she stared at me.

"What?" I looked between the four of them. "What?"

"Well, I couldn't let her read a spell that might prove dangerous to us." Eric handed me back the phone.

"But what spell did you give her?" I looked at the screen.

For violet pigmentation.

That was the whole damn description.

"What did you do to me?" I shoved the magical phone into my pocket and pulled out my normal phone.

"I think it actually looks pretty nice." Elizabeth giggled.

"What is it?" I turned on the front camera of my normal phone and spent a solid ten seconds blinking at the image.

I looked normal. Pasty skin, brown eyes, casual purple hair.

"Put it back." I rounded on Eric.

"We'll see if there's a counter spell later," Eric said.

"If?" I said.

"How did you do that?" Raven asked. "The Ladies never gave me that spell. I shouldn't have been able to use it."

"The phone is free of the rules of impartment," Eric said. "Thaden created it when he broke into the Library and burned the few volumes the Ladies had left. We took the same path into the Library and found the shelves empty."

"If?" I said again.

"It really looks pretty decent, Bry," Devon said.

"I've told you," Eric said, "the Ladies are dead. The rules of impartment hold no sway over the passing of new knowledge. Their reign of ignorance has ended."

"If!" I shouted.

"After all you have sacrificed to protect magic, are you really making this much of a fuss about hair?" Eric sighed.

"Why didn't you have her magic your hair?" I asked.

"The spell could have chosen to affect any of us," Eric said. "It was purely the luck of the draw."

Elizabeth wrapped her arm around my waist and laid her head on my shoulder. "I like the punk look. It's rebellious."

A happy little squirm wriggled up my spine as I pictured myself becoming an epic revolutionary worthy of posters being hung on bedroom walls in Beville.

"The books really aren't in the Library?" Raven sank down in her chair.

"They aren't," Elizabeth said. "We're going to bring them back. But we have to go tomorrow, and we have to have those passports."

"It shouldn't be up to the four of you," Raven said. "There shouldn't be any humans involved. We should let the people of Beville know what's happened. Send an army after the books."

"And when the information falls into the wrong hands?" Eric asked. "Free knowledge is a beautiful dream, the pursuit of which has nearly cost me my life more times than I can count. But how many people in Beville would take the knowledge of the Ladies' demise and use it for their own gain? To extort, to hurt without fear of punishment, to try and hoard the books for themselves."

"You really are on your own then." Raven buried her face in her hands.

"No, we're not," Devon said. "You just joined the team."

"I'm not on anybody's team." Raven stood and went to a machine in the far corner. "The only person whose side I'm on is me."

"So you're building magical armor for yourself?" Devon pointed to the shield and jacket on the far wall.

"I'm building armor to sell to the highest bidder." Raven pressed a few buttons, and the machine started whirring like a printer. "And trust me, even purple-hair can't afford my creations."

"What's your starting price?" I asked.

5

- *Socks*
- *Underwear*
- *Pants*
- *Sweaters*
- *Shirts*
- *Raincoat*
- *Phone 2x*
- *Phone charger 1x*
- *Wallet*
- *Passport*
- *Sunglasses*
- *Hat to cover my purple freakin' hair*
- *Hipster scarf to cover my neck scar*
- *Toothbrush*
- *Toothpaste*
- *Deodorant*
- *Sunscreen 'cause I'm pasty*
- *And...*

I was up most of the night thinking about the *and*.

I'd traveled before. I'd even been out of the country before. But for some reason, I couldn't stop feeling like I was completely unprepared.

It was after midnight by the time Mom and I realized there was no way boxed dye was going to cover my new purple do. Two in the morning before she'd finished adding thumbholes to my shirts and I finally zipped my suitcase and climbed into bed.

I'm really not sure I actually fell asleep before my dad came with his car to take me to the Consortium.

Mom rode with us. And, even though I could have walked and definitely didn't need two parents to accompany me on the two-second ride, it was nice to have them with me. Almost like they were escorting me to my first day of larceny kindergarten.

When the three of us got out of the car, the lights in the Consortium were already burning bright.

"Right. Well, I guess this is it." I turned to my parents, giving them each as good a hug as I could manage through my winter coat. "You guys go and get some coffee before work." I held the car door open for them to both climb into the back.

"You need the car, honey," Mom said. "Your dad and I can walk."

"No, it's fine," I said. "I know a really great cabbie, and—"

"A cab can only fit four people," Mom said.

"But we only have four people." I pointed to the Consortium window where Devon, Elizabeth, and Eric were all saying goodbye to Lola.

"Five people," Dad said. "You plus four others. That makes five."

"But I bought four tickets." I blinked at my dad, trying to get my early morning brain to figure out if I had somehow forgotten how to count or if Dad thought he was coming with me.

"Don't worry," Dad said. "I added a ticket for her."

"Her?" I looked to Mom.

"Your chaperone." Mom smiled just as a cab pulled up and a woman stepped out onto the sidewalk.

She wasn't the big burly security type, or even the prim protective Mary Poppins type. She looked more like a *just out of Grad school and super happy to intern for next to no pay* type.

"Dad, if we could just..." I pointed to the shadows on the far corner of the Consortium's awning.

"Sure." Dad smiled as I left my rolling suitcase in my mom's care, grabbed his arm, and dragged him away from Miss Chipper Intern.

"What's going on?" I whispered.

"I told you you'd have a chaperone," Dad said.

"I didn't think you were serious. We're going to do magical things. If this lady sees magic, what am I supposed to do? What if she hears the word *wizard* coming out of my mouth and decides to turn me in to Interpol?"

"That's not how Interpol works."

"People can't find out about magic, and the"—I stopped myself before saying *mission*—"studying"—I continued in a not at all super suspicious way—"I'll be doing is all about magic and spells and things regular people aren't supposed to know about."

"You were a wizard for months before I knew," Dad said. "If you kept it from me, you can certainly keep it from Cindy."

"That's entirely different, and you know it," I whispered. "I wasn't riding in cars with you. I wasn't stuck on an international flight with you."

"If you're really concerned about Cindy finding out anything she shouldn't, just be sure Devon and Elizabeth do all the talking." Dad clapped me on the shoulder like he knew damn well he was putting me in a corner with no wiggle room. "Better get going. Don't want to be late for your flight."

I turned back toward the car to find Mom and Cindy talking like they were old friends. No, not friends, coconspirators in my international oppression.

"Are we ready?" Eric led Devon and Elizabeth out of the Consortium. He eyed Cindy. "Did you call a cab, Bryant?"

"Nope." I took my suitcase from Mom and dragged it back to the trunk of Dad's car. "With my chaperone Cindy here, we make five, so we're all going to be riding in Dad's car."

Eric stayed still as stone for a moment. "Perfect. The last thing I would want is to be your babysitter. Being your tutor is work enough for anyone."

I waved through the Consortium window to Lola, who stayed firmly inside in her feather-trimmed dressing gown, and crawled back into the car.

Cindy climbed into the seat opposite mine. "Hi Bryant, it's really nice to meet you." She reached for my hand.

I considered being super petty and refusing to acknowledge her existence, then realized that might only make her watch me even more carefully.

"Nice to meet you." I shook her hand. "Sorry my dad is shipping you overseas to nanny me."

Cindy laughed. "I'm not coming to be your nanny." Cindy paused to greet Elizabeth and Devon as they climbed into the other two backseats.

"Then why are you coming?" A touch of hope flared in my chest as I actually deluded myself into believing maybe we were just giving Cindy a ride to the airport and then she would be heading off on some other errand for my dad.

"Your father hired me as your translator and driver." Cindy waved out the window to my parents as the car pulled away. "From what Mr. Adams tells me, no one in your group speaks Greek or has a driver's license."

"Your dad has a good point." Devon closed his eyes and leaned back like he was actually calm enough to sleep.

My normal phone buzzed in my pocket.

Why did I receive no warning, and how are you getting rid of her? Eric messaged me from the front seat.

I thought my dad wasn't serious, and I have no idea, I messaged back.

I could feel Eric's disappointment radiating toward me from the front of the car.

Sorry, I added.

Elizabeth reached over from her seat beside me and laced her fingers through mine.

I looked to Cindy, waiting for her to say that really her job was translation, driving, *and* making sure I didn't touch my girlfriend. But the chaperone was looking out the window, watching pre-dawn Manhattan speed by and not giving a hoot about my mild PDA.

"By the end of the day, we'll be in Greece." Elizabeth gave me a dazzling smile, and I couldn't tell if she was actually excited to be flying to another country or just putting on a show for Cindy.

I focused my gaze on Elizabeth, trying to pretend there wasn't a stranger sitting opposite me and the fate of magical knowledge didn't rest on my incompetent shoulders. "It's gonna be great." I was so wrapped up in how sparkly Elizabeth's eyes were, it actually came out in an almost convincing manner.

We didn't hit much traffic as we made our way out of the city and to the airport. It was too early for most people, and we were heading against the commuters anyway.

Before the fact that the next time I slept in a bed I'd be in a different country than my parents really sank in, the driver pulled up at the departures terminal and got out to unload our bags.

Five rolly bags, three backpacks, one purse, and one douche

wizard who probably had so much hidden in his pockets he didn't need a bag.

Everything was going fine as we checked in, handed over our rolling suitcases, and headed to airport security. It was easy, like we were just regular people going on a nice international trip.

Until we got in line to get our IDs checked to go through security. That's when my sleep-deprived brain freaked out.

"Ma'am, you need a passport to get on your flight." The ID checker had about as much compassion/enthusiasm as a hired princess at her third preschool party of the day.

"This is a special kind of license," no-passport lady said. "I can get through. I promise."

"Your promise doesn't have any sway over the law."

The law.

What an abstract yet firm construct.

Because people had drawn lines on a map, the law said we needed fancy printed papers to leave our part of the game board. The absurdity of it brought a laugh to my throat, just before the reality of having two illegal passports in our party shot panic through my veins.

The line moved forward, inching us closer to the ID checker.

But was having faux passports really that bad? They had all the right information on them...I hoped. I hadn't checked.

But Raven had seemed like she wanted to help. So she wouldn't have done anything weird to the passports...probably.

But did she actually care about obeying the human-style laws? Did she care about any laws?

I mean, now that the Ladies were gone, technically there weren't any laws governing the wizards in Manhattan.

Which on the one hand was very cool. Wizards didn't need the Ladies doling out spells like a miser who has yet to be visited by the spirits of Christmas past, present, and future. We didn't need arbitrary lines on a subterranean map telling us where magic could be used and where it was banned.

Except, maybe we did.

What if, without the Ladies, all the wizards of Beville just decided to hop right on up into Manhattan. Whether they meant to or not, they'd cause chaos. There would be too much magic flying around for anyone, even the normally oblivious Manhattanites, not to notice.

First, the reporters would panic.

Then, the police would panic.

Then, everyone would panic and start calling wizards freaks and we'd end up locked in weird magic-proof cages where they would do experiments on us to find out if they could make us into mutant super soldiers.

But some wizards would stay free.

And they'd have to fight back.

They'd be declared evil for standing against the human government, but all reasonable wizards would know they were vigilantes, fighting for the freedom of magickind.

My daydreams of epic magical battles waged in Times Square wouldn't be daydreams anymore. The whole city, maybe even the whole world, would be dragged into an existence where wizards were creatures to be used or feared.

The only thing protecting us from that awful fate was the laws put in place by the evil Ladies we had overthrown. And as soon as the people of Beville found out the Ladies were no more, the laws would dissolve like cotton candy dipped in a puddle by a sad raccoon.

And it was our fault. We had started the beginning of the end. We'd been trying to help, but leaving a void where laws should be would make things worse in an unforgivable way.

"It's wrong." My words came out as a strangled whisper. "It's all wrong."

"Is he okay?" The ID checker stared at me. She held Devon's fake passport in her hand, and Elizabeth already had hers out and ready.

They were both breaking the law. They were going to be dragged away and locked up and I was going to be put in a research facility by some secret branch of the human government and I wouldn't be able save my friends.

"No." I shook my head so hard the airport went blurry. "No, no we can't do this. It's too dangerous. We can't trust Raven." I reached for Elizabeth's passport.

"Sure we can." Elizabeth moved her passport out of my reach as the ID checker grabbed her walkie-talkie.

"He's terrified of flying," Devon said with a hint of humor in his voice I in no way appreciated.

"I am not—"

"I don't think *terrified* quite covers it." Elizabeth looped her arm through mine, squeezing tight. "We've been through this—planes and birds are both built to fly."

"He had a raven attack him when he was little." Devon took his passport and ticket back. "He's been afraid of flying things and Edgar Allan Poe ever since."

"He's been seeing a really great therapist." Elizabeth passed her papers over. "And as soon as we get him to the gate, he'll be taking a nice dose of Dramamine. The drowsy kind."

"Yep," Devon said. "Just enough to calm him down."

"We don't want a fuss in the airport." The ID checker set her walkie-talkie down and returned Elizabeth's passport like it wasn't fake at all.

"No fuss." Elizabeth lifted my hand, making me give the checker my papers. "Just a phobia and some early morning brain fatigue."

"Right." The lady scanned my passport, made a few marks on my paper ticket, and passed everything back. "Have a nice flight. And remember to stay calm or they can and will remove you from the airport."

I answered with a weird sort of guttural whimper.

"Breathe, Bryant," Elizabeth whispered in my ear as we joined the post ID checker, pre x-ray belt line.

"We never should have gotten involved with someone like Raven." I wrapped one arm around Elizabeth's waist and rammed my other hand into my pocket. Neither actually hid how badly my hands were shaking.

"It worked," Devon said. "Raven didn't almost get us tossed by security, you did. So just relax. We'll be napping on the plane in no time."

"But she—"

"Mr. Adams didn't mention that you have a fear of flying, Bryant," Cindy said.

"I have a feeling there's a lot my dad forgot to mention."

With Cindy standing so close, I couldn't even tell the others that Raven might be the crack in the dam of secrets that could ruin the lives of everyone in the world.

6

When flying internationally, if the chaperone your dad hired decides to upgrade all of you to business class, you go with it. That way, you can pretend to sleep while actually panicking about the fact that you've quite possibly destroyed both the magical and non-magical worlds in comfort.

During take off, I was still super worried about Raven outing the death of the Ladies to everyone in Beville/having added a code to Devon's and Elizabeth's passports that made them look like criminals so they'd be arrested the moment we landed in Athens.

By the time we'd gotten solidly over the ocean, I realized that, like it or not, I was going to have to find a way to preserve the secrecy of the magical world to:

1. Make sure Manhattan didn't end up looking like a casualty of the latest, large-cast superhero movie.
2. Not let wizards decide to sneak into human politics and slowly take over the world.
3. Keep Beville from becoming a subterranean tourist trap.

4. Avoid being locked in a secret government facility before finishing high school.

Sometime after the last round of snacks but before the plane actually started to land, the first awkward steps of a semi-ludicrous and potentially catastrophic plan started to form.

Of course, I couldn't say anything because Cindy was sitting in the seat right behind me, and for all I knew super hearing was on her special skills list right next to translator and driver.

"You feeling better?" Elizabeth rested her head on my shoulder.

"Umm." I tried to think of a way to tell her my plan without using any words like *magic, seizing control of the government,* or *uprising.* "Yeah. We're really doing this. It feels good to be on the move."

"I hope we can find a second to see some of the sights."

I could hear Elizabeth's smile in her voice.

"If we don't, we'll just come back another time." I shifted so I could wrap my arm around her.

"I'm a soon-to-be emancipated minor. I don't have money for vacations."

"Completely untrue. You're a soon-to-be emancipated minor with a boyfriend who has a father who would gladly pay for the trip as long as he approves all sight-seeing expeditions."

"I'm not dating you for your dad's money." Elizabeth leaned away enough to look into my eyes.

"And I'm not dating you because you're the most gorgeous girl to have ever lived. But those are the packages we came in."

Elizabeth leaned in and brushed her lips against mine. "Your dad paying Nikki to deal with all the legal stuff is a really great boyfriend bonus."

"Yeah, Nikki can be useful."

And just like that, the wheels in my head were spinning like a whirling dervish as we touched down in Athens, Greece—stop one on our quest to save the books.

Even though I was exhausted, hungry, and desperately in need of a shower, a weird kind of energy filled my body as we collected our luggage and got in line for customs.

I had plans. Big, save the world kinds of plans, and I was one cup of coffee and some decent cell service from starting on the project that would save the world.

Dogs sniffed around the customs line, and a little pang zinged through my chest. I wished we could have brought Sniffer McDeadDog with us. The kid deserved some globetrotting. I smiled as the dog came closer to us and sat down, staring right at Devon's suitcase.

"What a good boy." I beamed like an idiot.

The guard said something I couldn't understand to Devon.

"Sorry?" Devon said.

"You, come with me." The guard reached out and grabbed Devon's arm. "Bring your bag."

"What?" Devon said.

"Why?" I said.

"This boy is a minor under my care," Cindy said.

The guard examined our party. "All of you come."

He didn't loosen his grip on Devon's arm as he stormed a path through the rest of the crowd waiting for customs, leaving us to scramble along in his wake.

"I sometimes forget how inconvenient air travel can be." Eric frowned as the guard hauled Devon to a section of tables off to the side of the space. "So much security packed into one tiny place."

"I don't mind being patted down." Devon spread his legs and lifted his arms for one guard to pat him down while another searched his backpack and a third unzipped his suitcase. "I don't know what your dog scented on my bag. I mean, I live with some rare bred canines"—not really an adequate description of Lola's guards, but whatever—"but I don't think any of them went near my suitcase."

The guard searching Devon's rolly bag flipped open the top and started digging through Devon's socks, pants, and toiletries. Everything looked normal until the bottom layer where the security guard reached a metal tube, a blue and orange foam dart blaster, a tub of gray capsules, a shiny jacket, and a metal disk the size of a tea saucer.

I don't think I've ever mentally sworn so much in my life.

"What is this?" The guard lifted the metal hilt.

I held my breath, waiting for the red glowing sword to blossom to life and drive through the guard's face as she squinted into the dangerous end of the tube.

"It's for school," Elizabeth said at the same moment Devon said, "I like to photoshop," I added "LARP!" and Eric sighed and looked to the ceiling like he'd given up all hope.

"It's a LARP school project, and we're using photoshop," I said.

Devon and Elizabeth both looked to me with fear in their eyes like I'd just stepped into a shadow monster's lair without any hope of using magic.

"We're in a drama club back home, and one of the projects we're working on is Live Action Role Playing, LARP, as a way to get really into character and develop traits that fit our roles." The words spewed out of my mouth. "We're going to be missing some school, and to make up for being gone, we're doing extra credit by taking pictures as our characters during our trip. We couldn't bring our whole costumes because the luggage weight would have been way too much, so Devon's going to photoshop in a light saber for his character. The foam blaster and jacket are for me. I'm portraying a futuristic cop, but obviously real-looking weapons are a huge no-no."

"And her?" The guard pointed to Elizabeth.

"Alice in Wonderland," I said. "The disc is a saucer for a teacup at the Mad Hatter's party."

The guard pointed to Eric.

"Don't involve me in this. I'm merely here as the tutor," Eric said.

"I'm the chaperone," Cindy said.

"What are these?" The guard held up the tub of gray capsules.

"Stool softeners," I said. "Devon's a nervous traveler. Can't let nerves hurt the bowels."

Deep pink tinged Devon's cheeks. "I have a temperamental stomach."

"Right." I dug my hands into my pockets, clutching my magical phone and wondering how much damage I would be doing to the fate of the world if I had to use magic to escape the Athens airport.

"Be sure to respect the monuments and temples in your photoshopping," the guard said. "They weren't built for tourists to play in. They were built to honor the ancient gods."

"We will be sure to respect all the things," Devon said. "Promise."

The guard muttered something in Greek I'm pretty sure translated to *stupid American tourists*. She tossed Devon's stuff almost into his suitcase and handed him the unzipped mess. "Enjoy your time in Athens."

"Thanks." Devon took his suitcase and knelt on the ground, shoving what had been neatly folded clothes into a wad so he could zip his bag.

"Mr. Adams didn't mention any photo project to me." Cindy took Devon's backpack from the other guard.

"Dad's never shown much interest in my homework," I said. "As long as I get A's he doesn't actually ask."

"Right," Cindy said. "Well, if I can get a list of your lesson plans tonight, I'll look around and see what nice photo ops we can squeeze in."

"I think Eric can get the schedule to you." I looked at Eric, because clearly as the *tutor* he should be the one who had that sort of information.

"Absolutely," Eric said. "I haven't made a schedule for tomorrow yet. Young Bryant tends to become violently ill at the drop of a hat. I wanted to see if he was capable of leaving his room before making any firm plans."

"I'll locate the nearest hospital, too," Cindy said.

"Thanks." I glared at Eric's back as the guards led us to a special place where we could cut part of the line since they'd gone through the trouble of tearing apart Devon's bag.

"I'm not sure if I should be mortified or impressed," Eric murmured when Cindy had stepped forward to have her passport stamped.

"That you're going to have to turn in a written schedule to Cindy the chaperone?" I whispered back.

"That you managed to tell an absurd yet somehow very convincing lie."

7

Getting rental cars sucks. Driving through a city way older than your country is cool. Finally getting to hop into a hot shower after being in recycled air for so long you might be patient zero for the plague that starts the zombie apocalypse—priceless.

I tried not to let myself think too hard about the epic disaster I might be causing as I messaged my dad.

Landed safe. At the hotel. Also, would it be okay if I asked Nikki to help me with a project? Nothing big, I swear I'm not in any trouble. It's more like an academic theory I want to run past someone who knows about law.

I set my phone down, assuming Dad wouldn't answer since it was the middle of the workday in Manhattan.

I started looking for my toothbrush, and my phone dinged.

Glad you got in safe. As long as it's purely academic, I'm happy to have you chat with Nikki. She's an excellent resource. I'll call her tomorrow and tell her to expect you to contact her.

I let myself feel a moment of triumph and began to set my phone back down before it dinged again.

If you're considering law as a career, I have a friend in the depart-

ment at Yale. *We should drive out and have lunch with her when you get home.*

I rubbed my hands over my face. My fingers grazed my hair and, even though I know I couldn't *feel* the purple, it reminded me I still had the do of someone way cooler-with-a-hint-of-punk than I'd ever be.

I pulled my shirt on and tucked my thumbs through their little sleeve holes before I could catch a glimpse of my scarred hand and add that to my freak out over the pile of ways magic had left its mark on my body.

"Bryant," Elizabeth called before knocking on the door, like she knew a random knock would make me panic but her voice would send me to the gooey place where I'm not really capable of worrying.

"Coming." I grabbed my boho scar-covering scarf, crammed everything I needed into my pockets, and ran to the door.

I'll be the first person to shout to the whole world that my girlfriend is glorious, but there was something about her standing in a hotel hallway in an ancient city wearing a pale blue cardigan that made me wonder if maybe Elizabeth wasn't human at all. Maybe she was a goddess and I'd just always been too smitten to see through her ruse.

"Are you ready to go? I'm starving." The goddess reached for my hand and led me out for a night in Athens.

———

I'm not a travel writer. I'm a barely competent wizard who's trying to preserve magical knowledge and maybe not have world order crumble if I can swing it.

I'm not qualified to tell you about the economics that made it so Athens is filled with graffiti right next to, or even on, fancy marble buildings that are way older than anything in Manhattan. I don't know enough about art to tell you why some of the graffiti should really be considered street art and is so cool there ought to be a way to move it into a big art gallery.

I have no clue why the plaza with the big fountain was important, what the random super-old columns in the middle of a field were for, or what the street we walked down to find dinner had been before it was taken over by gift shops and restaurants that catered to tourists.

But, as a person with a reasonable amount of experience with magic, I can tell you that walking through a chilly evening holding the hand of the girl you love, listening to the people you pass speak in a language you don't understand, all while surrounded by architecture so foreign to my Manhattan-raised bones I might as well be in a movie—that is a truly magical experience.

Cindy got us a table on the sidewalk with one of those weird little gas torches in the middle to keep us warm, and by the time we'd eaten, all of us were laughing while gazing up at the ruins of the Acropolis high on the hill with lights beaming on them like it was the end of a quest in a video game.

Eric and Cindy discussed our schedule for the next day while I snuck bits of my meat to the three stray cats hiding under the table and decided I wouldn't mind traveling overseas more often.

The happy adventurer daze carried me all the way back to my hotel room where I was ready to tumble into bed and dream of bringing Elizabeth back to Athens someday when we were old enough that my dad wouldn't be able to demand we have any chaperones. I was just about to crawl in between my bliss-fully not over-starched sheets when a knock sounded on my door.

I rammed my feet into my shoes while grabbing my phone from the nightstand.

"Who is it?" I called. I didn't sound at all calm. Apparently, I had burned through all my acting skills at the airport.

"Your tutor," Eric said.

"Right." I tried to tuck my phone into my pocket before remembering I was wearing pajamas. "Sorry." I kept the phone in my hand as I opened the door.

Eric, Elizabeth, and Devon waited in the hall. Eric pressed a finger to his lips and led them all inside, then clicked the door quietly closed behind them. He murmured a spell at the door and I felt a whisper of magic fly past me.

"Do you think we're going to be attacked?" Devon sat on my bed. His pajama pants had pockets, and there was no mistaking the presence of his sword's hilt.

I suddenly felt a lot less weird about gripping my phone for dear life.

"I have no reason to believe we'll be attacked," Eric said. "However, with the unexpected added complication of a chaperone, I thought it best to make sure she didn't hear any voices coming from Bryant's room."

"When did the whole chaperone thing happen?" Devon asked.

"When Dad agreed to pay." I ran my hand over my hair, remembered it was purple, and cringed. Not that purple isn't a great color for hair. I just wasn't the kind of guy who could pull things like that off. "Sorry, I thought he didn't mean it."

"It'll be fine." Elizabeth eased my phone out of my death grip. "One human chaperone doesn't even rank on the list of top twenty problems we've encountered."

"It does cause a rather large headache for the tutor who is supposed to have a lesson plan," Eric said.

"Sorry," I said again.

"So what's the schedule for tomorrow, Teach?" Devon asked.

"We have a rather long day visiting the Acropolis Museum

and the Acropolis itself," Eric said. "Both of which are located conveniently near the only wizarding contact I have in Greece. I'm hoping once we're thoroughly ensconced in the history of ancient Athens, Cindy will allow us to wander away."

"And what's the lesson plan from there?" I asked. "We don't know where the woman who was shipping the books to New York to be sold might actually be."

"I've informed Cindy that Bryant's father arranged this trip in the hopes of Bryant gaining a deeper understanding of non-U.S. cultures. To instill the greatest appreciation in Bryant, we're going to be following his interests," Eric said.

"What does that mean?" I asked.

"Get ready to lie some more, because you're going to be in charge of convincing Cindy to drive us wherever we need to go next," Devon said. "It's a perfect plan. What could go wrong?"

"Thanks." I punched Devon on the shoulder.

"Best to get some sleep. We're beginning our studies early in the morning." Eric muttered another spell at the door before slipping back out into the hall.

"It's almost like he doesn't want me to know that one," I whispered.

"Is it weird if I sort of hope the books are hidden near Mount Olympus?" Elizabeth sat on my bed next to Devon.

"Is it weird if I hope the books are on a beach?" Devon asked.

"Not unless it's weird that I hope we find them tomorrow and get to play tourist for a few days while Nikki figures out how to get them through customs." I sat beside Elizabeth.

"Am I the only one who feels less prepared to fight bad guys here than in Manhattan?" Devon asked.

I looked to Devon, searching for a crack in his usual bravado.

"Nope," Elizabeth said. "I'm telling myself it's the language barrier and lack of home-field advantage."

"Sounds good." Devon stood up. "We'll just go with that and

hope Eric's one Greek contact happens to know someone who's been hoarding a mound of priceless books. See you kids tomorrow."

He winked at me before slipping through the door, leaving Elizabeth and me alone.

My heart fluttered in circles in my chest as she reached up and touched my forehead. Then I remembered my purple hair again and winced.

"Do you think it would be better or worse if I just shaved my head?" I asked.

"I like it purple." Elizabeth gave a sly grin. "You're a rebel. Why shouldn't you look like one?"

"But—"

"I have black streaks, you've got scars and purple hair. Think what a perfect pair we make."

A pair. Like two halves of the same thing. Like two pieces of a really easy-to-solve puzzle. Like a couple drawn together by fate herself.

"Yeah," I said. "It's not so bad." And then I leaned in and kissed her.

8

As a native New Yorker, I do my best to avoid tourist hotspots. Times Square, Rockefeller Center at Christmas, the zoo on free days. I just don't go near them. Heading to the Acropolis Museum reminded me why.

It's not just that there's a ton of people all wanting to be in the exact same five-foot square to get the best picture. It's the school groups with the teacher walking backward, not caring if she steps on you, just as long as none of her students go AWOL. And the mom who forgot that if she didn't pack a juice box, her kid was going to have a meltdown, and now the kid's realized there's no juice box in sight so its DEFCON five tantrum time.

Then there are the retired dodderers who can't seem to remember that anyone could be on a schedule, so they just meander while somehow blocking everyone around them from actually moving at a pace suited for getting anywhere within a reasonable timeframe. The social media influencers who are going to spend twenty minutes in everybody's way taking the same picture over and over again. The ones who talk super loud like they want to prove they have a voice even though they don't speak the local language. The people who drank too much the night before and look like they might spew on your shoes if you step too near them.

And, worst of all, the chaperone your dad hired who decides she'd like to see the same museum you're going to, making it impossible to give her the slip.

"Do they sell coffee here?" I whispered to Elizabeth as the entrance attendant scanned my ticket.

"I really hope so." Elizabeth spoke through her yawn.

The ticket taker eyed my hair for a moment before letting me through the turnstile.

I puffed my chest out, attempting to look like a badass as I sidled through the barrier, trying not to let the rotating bars knock into me in any unfortunate places.

"So, Bryant, what would you like to see first?" Eric didn't bother hiding his frown as he glanced from me to Cindy, who looked like a kid in a candy store as she stared through the glass floor to the excavated ancient settlement beneath us.

"I don't know." I bit my cheeks to keep from smiling. "You're the Greece expert. What are the most fascinating bits of the museum?"

Eric's eyes darkened from their normal creepy bright blue to an angry dusky blue. "This expedition is to be led by my students' interests. Take a look around and see what strikes your fancy."

"This is pretty neat." Devon headed away from the mini replica of the Acropolis and to the glass walls filled with artifacts.

I kept close on Devon's heels, hoping that, if we moved fast enough, we could ditch Cindy right away and head straight to Eric's contact.

But Cindy was not to be dissuaded so easily. We hadn't even made it to the end of the hall before she caught up to us, giving a little wave as she kept to her side of the exhibit.

"Should I text my dad and ask him to tell her to leave us alone for the day?" I whispered to Eric. "I mean, Dad knows we're supposed to be meeting people Cindy shouldn't know about."

"The problem is the address," Eric said. "She'll want to follow us. To know where to pick us up."

"Would that be so awful?" Devon said.

"I think we can all agree the time will come when we can no longer tolerate Cindy following us." Eric led us up the glass steps to the next level. "When we are forced to part ways with Bryant's chaperone—"

"I think she's really here for all the teenagers on this trip," I said.

"—the last thing we'll need is for her to show up at the door of my contact looking for answers," Eric said. "There are very few I trust in this world, and I will not betray Zoe by leading a human anywhere near her doorstep."

"So let's give Cindy the slip and catch up to her at the hotel," Elizabeth said.

I started looking around the gallery for an easy exit that wouldn't require magic or cause any security footage that might come back to bite us in the butt.

"Stay near the stairs," Eric said, "when Cindy wanders to the far side of the gallery, we'll casually walk back down to the lobby and be on our way."

"I love a good meander." Devon headed toward a statue of a woman who had lost both her arms, though I couldn't tell if time or violence had harmed her.

"It's actually a really cool museum." Elizabeth held my hand as we wandered to a statue that gave us a great view of Cindy coming up the stairs and heading right to where she could keep an eye on me.

"The statues are cool." I actually looked at one of their faces for the first time, and a weird shiver shook my spine. Not like fate had come for me, or the museum held some sort of magic my body was sensing. The shiver was a pure human reaction to remembered terror.

The cut of the statue's chin, the pure white of her stone hair, all of it just screamed *Lady* in my brain.

I wanted to crack the statue apart, destroy the piece of ancient art just to prove it wasn't really a Lady and they hadn't come back from the grave to kill us.

"You okay?" Elizabeth squeezed my hand.

"I don't think I'm a fan of all-white art," I said.

"They didn't used to be like that." Elizabeth pointed to a sign in front of one of the other statues.

That woman had bits of color in her hair. Not coating it, just in the crevices of her curls.

"A long time ago, most of the statues had bits of color," Elizabeth said.

I tried to picture it. Not being surrounded by white statues that gave me flashbacks to some pretty traumatic near-death experiences, but instead, having vibrant color filling the room.

"I wish they were still that way." I studied the lines of a man's stone beard, deciding where I would add pigment.

"Time wiped it all away."

"I wonder..." I looked back to the lady with the color creeping out of her curls. She had color in her eyes, too. There were even places where it looked like there should be vibrant hues on her dress.

"Yeah?" Elizabeth prompted.

"I wonder if it's all a metaphor." I rubbed the center of my forehead with the knuckles of my non-Elizabeth claimed hand.

"I think it's really a statue." Elizabeth nudged me with her elbow.

"I know that. I just mean, what if the Ladies, like *capital L*

Ladies, used to be all vibrant and lifelike, too? What if they were like us when they started? Full of hope. Wanting to save knowledge. Wanting to create a peaceful and prosperous life for the people of Beville. And then their humanity got drained away as magic leeched the color out of them so when we finally met them they were no better than bleached stone."

"I don't think their humanity got syphoned away." Elizabeth twisted our wrists so she could kiss the back of my scarred hand. "I think they got greedy, and they forgot it was their job to protect the people in their care. Being in power makes some people want more power, and the Ladies fell so deep into wanting to stay in control, they forgot about everything else."

"I don't want to end up like them." The truth of my words stung in my chest like someone had popped the balloon that held my thin resolve to stand at the center of the web of fate as we put right the wrongs the Ladies had started. "Someday, years from now, when I'm dead—hopefully of natural causes—I don't want some teenage kid looking at my life and wondering how I got to be so evil. I don't want to be in anyone's nightmares. I don't want to be so hated people won't even be mad or sad that I'm gone."

"That's not going to happen, Bryant." Elizabeth took my face in her hands. "You are a good person. You would never let that happen."

"But what if the Ladies started off as good people, too?"

"This isn't going to work." Devon stepped up next to us, stopping me before I could confess my half-formed plan to Elizabeth.

"You as the third wheel?" Elizabeth said. "It wouldn't feel right without you around."

"Ha." Devon flicked one of Elizabeth's curls. "We're not going to be able to ditch Cindy. Not when she glances up from every plaque she's reading to make sure she still has eyes on Bryant."

"Do I call my dad, or do we try and magic our way out of here as subtly as possible?" I asked.

"Neither," Elizabeth said. "Get Eric, and head out front. I'll meet you there in five minutes."

"Why?" I caught hold of Elizabeth's hand. "What are you going to do?"

"I'm going to abuse the girl code all women must obey and beg her to come help me in the bathroom," Elizabeth said. "I'm probably going to get some nasty karma for this."

Elizabeth let go of my hand and headed toward Cindy. She glanced over her shoulder and winced before leaning close to whisper something to our chaperone.

"Let's grab Eric," Devon said as Cindy led Elizabeth toward the bathroom. "Don't want to waste Elizabeth's violation of the girl code."

9

I f wandering around the city the night before had felt like we'd left New York a world away, following Eric through the winding streets around the base of the hill where the Acropolis itself stood seemed like we'd fallen into a different time.

In the little neighborhood built of uneven alleys and super old houses, where there were stairs set into the street so there was no way a car could follow you, it sort of felt like we'd stepped into a fairy tale.

A clowder of cats lay in a sunny patch between houses, not even bothering to look up as Eric stopped beside them, examining the sapphire blue door of the yellow house on our right and the blood red door of the pale blue house on our left.

"Hmm." Eric tented his fingers under his chin.

"What?" I asked.

"Don't tell me we're lost," Devon laughed.

"Not lost," Eric said. "Simply still searching."

"Is there anything I should be looking for?" Elizabeth kept hold of my hand as she stepped closer to the yellow house, studying the trim-like graffiti someone had painted along the bottom of the wall.

"Use your gift as well as you can," Eric said, "but I'm afraid I don't know what to tell you to look for, only that I shall know when I find it."

"Do you have an address?" I asked. "I could look it up."

"Zoe never gave me her address." Eric headed down the narrow street, ducking below branches that would have dripped with fruit during the summer. "I don't believe she ever intended for me to visit her."

"Are you telling me we're going to drop in on someone who doesn't actually want you visiting them?" Devon asked.

I ducked below the branches, almost tripping over a cat who'd decided that while I was bent double was the perfect time to wind between my ankles.

"We are in pursuit of a great and noble cause," Eric said. "Is one unexpected house call too great a price to pay for saving the books?"

"No." Devon dodged around Elizabeth and me to walk beside Eric. "But it does change my expectations for how knocking on the door is going to go. I mean, the whole Raven thing worked out well in the end, but if this is going to be the same sort of deal, I'd like to be ready in case screaming and spell throwing start to happen."

"It's not at all the same." Eric stopped at a fork in the road, taking a moment to study each path before heading downhill. "There are no previous entanglements between Raven and me."

"Wait"—Elizabeth dragged me along with her as she ran a few steps to walk right behind Eric—"are you telling me we're paying an unexpected call on your ex?"

"Not an ex," Eric said. "A former entanglement."

A mixture of laughter and exasperation sparkled in Elizabeth's eyes. "This should go well."

We headed down another set of stairs where each cat in the

clowder—and yes, that really is what you call a group of cats—had claimed a different step.

Mwarr. The cat who had tried to trip me earlier darted right under my foot as I went to step down. I wobbled and would have fallen and smooshed a cat if Elizabeth hadn't grabbed my arm.

"Careful, kitty." I tried to step around the cat, but it dug its claws into my shin and gave an awful *yowl*. "I didn't step on you! Why would you hurt me when I didn't step on you?"

With another *yowl*, the cat headed back the way we'd come, stopping at the fork in the path where Eric had chosen to go down. The cat turned to make eye contact with me and yowled again.

"Eric, can cats be like Lola's guards?" I said slowly.

"That really looks like a normal cat," Elizabeth said.

"Okay, but can a normal cat be magical?" I said. "Like a familiar, or a guide to lead you on a side quest in a videogame?"

Devon climbed back up the steps to stare at the cat.

The cat yowled again.

"That is a little weird," Devon said.

The cat hissed.

"I have heard rumors of select felines being trained as companions with skills far beyond that of a normal cat," Eric said, "but I've never seen such a thing put into practice."

"Okay." I nodded like I could somehow take that as an affirmation I hadn't lost my mind. "I think we should follow the cat and see what happens."

"Because the cat seems to know more of where it wants to go than Eric?" Devon asked.

"I mean, yeah," I said. "That, and it just feels right."

"Then we'll follow the feline." Eric looked to the cat. "Lead on."

The cat gave a satisfied little *merp* before walking down the path Eric hadn't chosen.

"I don't want to be the naysayer," Elizabeth said.

"If there are shadows creeping in around us, please just tell me." I held her hand tighter, determined not to allow any monster to rip her away from me.

"No beasties." Elizabeth stepped in front of me as we reached a road too narrow for us to walk side by side. "I just wonder if following a cat to see someone who probably really doesn't want to see Eric isn't some sort of a trap."

"Oh, it very well could be," Eric said from the front of our feline-following parade. "But it would be a trap of magical making, and that would definitely lead us closer to the right direction."

"So, the good kind of trap," Devon said. "Sounds great."

The cat/possible bait for a magical trap led us onto a wider street, up an alley between houses I wouldn't have been brave enough to cut through on my own, past a café where a couple sat outdoors sipping wine and staring up at the hill where the Acropolis lay, through another alley, and out into a courtyard surrounded by four houses.

The cat turned to give us another *merp* before heading toward a house with a violently pink front door.

"Looks promising," I said. "Not pure white. No weird markers."

"I'd prefer Elizabeth's assessment." Eric crept closer to the door.

With a final *yowl*, the cat walked into the bushes and disappeared from view.

"It looks like a house." Elizabeth tipped her head to the side. "A cool house, but there's nothing strange about it."

I agreed with the cool house bit. Aside from the bright pink door, the place looked like somewhere you'd find a Greek grandma busy making you dinner. You'd sit around a lace-clothed table with fresh-cut flowers in the middle and be overfed while she told you stories of all the young men who flirted with her when she was a girl.

"Once more unto the breach." Eric knocked on the door.

"No *cliaxo*?" Devon whispered.

"It might not be Zoe's house," Elizabeth said.

"And if it is," Eric said, "I don't want to give her any reason to turn us away."

We waited a full minute before Eric raised his hand and knocked again.

The moment his knuckles touched the pink wood, the door swung open with a *squeak* straight out of a horror movie.

"Lovely," Devon said.

I watched Elizabeth as she peered through the door. She furrowed her perfect brow but didn't look scared.

I turned my gaze to the inside of the house. It was a little darker than the bright morning suggested it should be but otherwise looked like we could walk into my Greek grandma food fantasy— a pretty painting on the wall, a carefully swept stone floor.

"After me." Eric stepped through the door.

I held my breath, waiting for disaster to strike as Devon followed.

The house didn't grow teeth and eat them, so I wrapped my arm around Elizabeth's waist, keeping her close to my side as we crept through the doorway together.

I dared to take another breath. The faint scent of old books mixed with the aroma of something baking.

Devon looked to me and opened his mouth to speak just before everything went to Hell.

With a jolt like I'd been launched out of a cannon, gravity shifted, and I fell toward the ceiling.

I tried to keep ahold of Elizabeth, twisting in hopes of my

body cushioning her fall, but the new freaky gravity had different plans for her.

She tumbled sideways, landing on the pink door with a *thump*.

The air I was going to use to shout "Elizabeth!" was knocked out of my lungs as I hit the ceiling. I tried to push myself up to my knees, but my brain's understanding of gravity wasn't meshing with the reality of my situation. I swayed and flopped sideways like a dying fish.

Devon had fallen to the far end of the entryway and was trying to stand on the painting of flowers that hung on that wall.

The only one who hadn't been cast aside by the laws of physics was Eric. He stood on the normal floor, not even fighting as the stone twisted and curled as it wound up his legs and wrapped around him like cartoon bandits were going to tie him to the train tracks.

"Well done, Zoe," Eric said once the rock ropes had stopped moving. "I expected security from you, but training the house to have more than one response to unwanted visitors is quite impressive."

I looked at the doorways around us, trying not to vomit from the super weird vertigo, waiting for Zoe to saunter out and purr at Eric that she'd been waiting for him to arrive.

"Zoe," Eric said, "I know we didn't part on the best of terms, but I'm not here for a personal call. I've come to discuss some very important business. I need information."

"Based on this greeting, I really don't think she's going to want to tell you anything." Devon had managed to get to his feet, clinging to what had become his wall for support.

"She won't want to give me information," Eric said. "I would never be naïve enough to believe that. But once she hears who I'll use the information to eliminate, that might be interesting enough to entice her."

"Entice me?" A woman stepped through one of the door-ways. Her black hair shimmered around her shoulders, and her green eyes shone with loathing as she glared at Eric. Though she had an accent, her words were perfectly clear as she stalked closer to him. "I have you trapped in my house. I have your friends, too. I can't think of any pleasure in this world that would keep me from hurting you, or a prize that would be worth my helping you."

10

"Zoe, it's a pleasure to see you again." Eric smiled.

Zoe took two steps forward and slapped him across the face.

"Come now," Eric said, "you can't possibly hate me more than you loathe anyone else in the world."

She slapped him again.

"What did you do to her?" Devon asked.

"None of your damn business." Zoe rounded on Devon.

"Okay." Devon nodded, paying for moving his head with a stumbling wobble. "I don't doubt you have every right to slap him."

"I'm looking for books." Eric pulled Zoe's focus back to him.

"I'll kill you before I let you near my books," Zoe said.

"I don't blame you," Eric said. "After what the Ladies did to you, I don't think a person with any empathy would speak ill of you for hoarding your collection away from the world."

"Do you want me to believe the great Eric Deldridge can feel compassion?" Zoe pursed her lips. "I'm not that foolish. Hunt for books somewhere else. You aren't welcome here."

"It's not your books I'm interested in," Eric said. "And if I succeed in my mission, the Ladies will fall. Their time in power will be over. So which do you prefer? Petty vengeance for a love affair that ended badly, or a hand in the destruction of a regime that stole everything you truly cared for?"

Zoe chewed the inside of her lips before speaking. "There's not a book in the world that can end the Ladies' rule. Whatever spell you find, they'll have something more powerful. Whatever weakness you think you've discovered, they will find a way to trap you. I would have thought you were smart enough to know that, Eric."

"A single book could never topple the Ladies," Eric said. "But a few thousand books, stolen from their Library, hidden away for years...if someone were to find that trove of knowledge and expose that the Ladies had concealed the theft for decades, all the people of Beville would rise up. And with the wisdom of the lost books on the people's side, even the might of the Ladies would crumble."

Zoe lifted her hand. For a moment I thought she was going to slap Eric again, but she just fiddled with the pendant on her necklace. "Even if you were right. Even if there were such a masterful thief and the books really had been saved from the Ladies, none of the books I have would help you find the missing volumes."

"As I've said, I have no intention of going anywhere near your books. I'm simply seeking information."

"My father didn't steal the Ladies' books, and neither did I."

"If you wouldn't mind reaching into my right pocket. There's a picture on my phone. I want to see if you recognize the place or perhaps even the handwriting."

With a twist of her finger, the stone coils around Eric shifted, leaving his pocket exposed. Zoe pulled out Eric's phone, then stretched the bindings so she could press his thumb to the scanner.

"This?" Zoe turned the phone enough that I managed to get a glimpse of a torn shipping label.

"Some of the books were mailed to New York," Eric said. "That is the information from the box."

"So you have nothing?"

"There's got to be the name of a city," Eric said.

"Yes, and?" Zoe said.

"How many wizards and witches are there in Greece?" Eric said. "One thousand, maybe two?"

"Not quite two," Zoe said.

"That's a fairly small community, all things considered," Eric said. "I simply want to know if any wizards live near the city from which the box was shipped. A name would be lovely. An address, most appreciated."

"You're a fool." With another flick of her finger, Zoe shifted the ropes enough to shove the phone back into Eric's pocket.

"Do you want me to beg?" Eric said. "Do you want me to tell you I'm sorry for being a cad who broke your heart?"

"You give yourself too much credit." She clenched her fist, tightening Eric's bonds.

"Don't hurt him." I raised my hand to start a spell, but the gravity on the ceiling/my floor doubled, pinning me to the ground.

"Nothing I say will make a difference to you." Eric's words came out strained. "You wouldn't give me water if I were dying of thirst. I understand that, and most would even say I deserve it."

Zoe gave a bitter laugh.

"But what the Ladies did to you, to your father..." Eric dragged in a breath. "Your vengeance against them is worth far more to you than your loathing of me."

Zoe waved a hand, and the stone bindings froze.

"You're looking for Meteora." Zoe looked down at her hands as she spoke, like she didn't want to admit to herself that she was helping Eric. "I don't know the names of any people, but I did visit there with my father when I was young. The area isn't only sacred to the unmagicked. The keepers of our books used to live up there, hidden amongst the rocks and monasteries. When the airport came, the books moved to Athens, but some of the book-keepers stayed behind.

"They were old men when Father and I visited them. They stayed in their home, studying the few books they'd kept for themselves. If I had to guess, all that's left in that place are the bones of old men who died hunched over dusty volumes."

"Where in Meteora are they?" Eric asked.

"I don't remember much." Zoe furrowed her brow. Her gaze traced the lines on her palms like she was looking over long-forgotten terrain. "We walked through the woods to get there, and I was afraid. I begged my father to carry me, but he said I had to make the journey on my own feet. There was a path, and light all around me. But shadows lurked, too. Shapes I tried not to understand. There was a building perched high up on the stone. It's not on any map. They designed it that way, a secret not to be shared or easily discovered. I'm honestly not sure I could find it again."

"That's all right," Eric said, his voice lacking its usual bravado. "You've given us more than I have any right to ask for."

"I have," Zoe said. "And if you die chasing your dream of dethroning the Ladies, I won't feel even a prickle of grief."

"That much, I am sure I deserve." Eric gave Zoe a nod.

A sudden feeling of overwhelming awkwardness sent heat to my cheeks. Not because I was still pinned to the ceiling in a super uncomfortable position. It felt like I was spying on them. Seeing Eric in an intimate and vulnerable way that I had never wanted to see him. And that was completely apart from the fact that I'd only ever known him when he was with Lola. Well, maybe not *with*, but the *we don't talk about it but it just sort of is* equivalent.

"Would you like me to tell you when our task is complete?" Eric asked. "Knowing the women who killed your father have been washed away might allow you some closure."

"Closure is a myth," Zoe said. "My grief doesn't end, and neither will my watch. Still, tell me if you survive to see the Ladies burn. My father never got to finish his work. Once the Ladies are gone, I'll do it for him."

"As you wish," Eric said.

"Now get out of my home before I decide to kill you and let your apprentices finish your task." Zoe stormed away.

The door closed with a *click*, and gravity went back to normal. I fell with a shout and hit the ground hard enough for stars to swallow my vision.

"Ow." I rolled onto my back, wondering if I should do a healing spell just in case any of the twenty-odd bones that felt broken actually *were* broken.

"That went well." Devon stood and brushed himself off while Elizabeth came to steady me as I wobbled to my feet.

In my defense, I had fallen much farther than they had.

"We should go." Eric shook his shoulders, and the stone ropes that had bound him shattered and fell to the ground.

I watched in awe as the floor reabsorbed the debris.

"Can your house do that?" I asked.

"I hope to never find out." Eric opened the door and stepped back out into the courtyard.

I herded Devon and Elizabeth in front of me as I scampered outside before gravity could go all weird again.

Eric looked around the tiny square for a moment.

"Are you going to tell us?" Elizabeth asked.

"Once I know which direction we should go, I will certainly enlighten you." Eric studied the way we had entered the square.

"I mean about Zoe," Elizabeth said. "What happened to her father?"

"Her father was the official librarian of Greece." Eric stared at the pink door as he spoke. "It's a small collection, but valuable nonetheless. As much as I hate to speak ill of the dead, her father was an optimistic fool. He brought some of his precious books to Manhattan, hoping to compare them with the Ladies' texts."

"Let me guess," Devon said, "they killed him and kept his books?"

"Right in one." Eric led us down a narrow path, heading toward the Acropolis hill.

"No wonder she wants revenge," I said.

"It's her place, both as a daughter and as the new librarian of Greece," Eric said.

"She's the librarian?" I turned to look back at the house with the pink door.

"Indeed," Eric said, "and you've just been inside the library."

———

When we met Cindy back at the hotel, she was so freaked out about having lost us, I didn't even have the heart to tell her it wasn't really her job to follow us around all the time. So, I just gushed about my newfound fascination with religious structures built on top of rocks and asked if she could drive us to Meteora.

Elizabeth picked a new hotel for me to book, Devon picked where we should eat dinner, Eric brooded his way through it all. Really, it was almost like we were on an actual educational tour of Greece.

But I couldn't get the cycle of worry in my brain to stop.

We were getting closer. I could feel it. Like the strings of fate that had been wrapped around my being were tightening their hold, determined not to let me go before I found the books.

When I finally got back to the hotel after dinner, I typed out my message to Nikki.

The request was absurd. Any decent lawyer would have laughed and said *No, you nerdy freak. I want nothing to do with your shenanigans. Even a pair of natural 20s couldn't persuade me to help you.* But before I'd brushed my teeth and hopped into bed, I'd gotten a message back.

> *Hi Bryant,*
>
> *Sounds like an inventive project. Let's start by making a list of specific items you want to address. What are your top concerns? Once we get those hammered out, we can get into building a more detailed structure.*
>
> *Nikki*

Top Concerns

- *Magic must remain hidden from non-wizards for the safety of all*
- *No noticeable spells in human territory*
- *No telling humans about magic*
- *Freedom of knowledge must be established*
- *The Library of Magic will be open to visitors, free of charge*
- *Penalties for injuring people or property with magic , be set*

Other crimes that need set penalties

- *Buying and selling wizards*
- *Kidnapping wizards*
- *Death matches*
- *Grave robbing for the purposes of bone magic*
- *Grave robbing in general*
- *How TF are we supposed to enforce the laws if there are no cops, jails, or anybody in charge?*

11

There are a lot of things in life growing up in Manhattan totally prepared me for. Dodging through tourists. Eating sketchy food made in carts where there's clearly no way for the food preparer to wash their hands. Navigating broken subway systems. Judging when a street performance is going to drift into railing against society so you know when to run for it.

What Manhattan didn't prepare me for—long road trips.

Greece may not look huge on a globe, but if your driver insists on going the speed limit even though there are no cops in sight, it's still big enough to make it a four-hour car ride between Athens and Meteora. Which is just as bad as trying to get from Hell's Kitchen to Brooklyn when the MTA decides not to run... I'm almost kidding.

For the first part of the trip, Cindy taught us all a few words in Greek.

Δεν προσπαθώ να είμαι αγενής, απλά είμαι αδέξιος.

Which gave me a totally new appreciation for the Phoenician alphabet.

Then, Elizabeth read us some facts about the soaring monasteries of Meteora.

The more Elizabeth told us about the monasteries, the more ravenous the worry gnawing at my stomach became.

The regular, human monasteries had been built on soaring columns of rock starting in the 11th century. The monks had used ladders and scaffolds and nets to get to their homes perched high above. The pictures on Elizabeth's phone were amazing and awe-inspiring and...if human monks managed to build in such hard to reach places, where had the wizard bookkeepers built?

Elizabeth laid her hand on my knee as she read to us about the raids on the monasteries during the 17th century, like she knew my mind had started to creep to the panicky place where remembering to breathe took a lot more effort than normal.

By the time we got our first glimpse of the soaring monasteries, I was basically convinced I should become a hermit and live in a cave on the side of one of the stone pillars because there was no way we were going to find the secret hidey hole of the probably deceased bookkeepers. But there was something soothing and empowering about the monasteries floating high up near the sky.

That's when I decided I would be a real asshat to give up and hide, because if 11th century monks could build those monasteries without the help of the internet or magic, then I needed to buck up and find the damn hidden books.

We got into our second hotel and I took a moment to hide and check my email for a message from Nikki.

Bryant,

If your primary concern is maintaining order, you need to consider retributive vs. restorative justice. Take a look at both options and see which you think works better for your world building.

I'd love to see your campaign notes when you're done. I used to dabble a little in my pre-law days.

Nikki

Retributive or restorative.

The two words swirled around in my head as I devoured some really good food for lunch.

A cat wound around my ankles in the restaurant as I ate, but I think it only wanted a bit of my cheese, not to answer any philosophical questions or even give me directions to the book-keepers.

Retributive or restorative. Two little words that could remake the world.

"You okay?"

I blinked at Elizabeth and realized I had somehow daydreamed my way from being inside a restaurant to walking down the street beside her.

"I'm fine." I kissed the back of her hand and wrapped my arm around her waist.

"When Zoe told us the bookkeepers had a hidden place here," Devon said, "I had sort of hoped there wouldn't be quite so many good places to hide."

Devon was right. The stone columns stretched out to the side of us as far as I could see. We could spend years hunting through every crevice and not find anything.

"Our first order of business is to get rid of the chaperone," Eric said. "Once we no longer have a human pretending not to follow us—"

"Don't diss the humans," Devon said.

"—we'll begin our search in the only way possible—asking the locals," Eric finished.

"You're kidding, right?" I dragged Elizabeth forward a few quick steps to walk beside Eric so I could actually watch his face for any hints that he was joking.

"Not at all." Eric raised an eyebrow at me. "This is a very

serious matter, Bryant. We are talking about the accumulation of centuries of knowledge. I would never be so crass as to joke about it and would hope for better from you as well."

"Who's on ditch-Cindy duty?" Elizabeth asked before I could say I knew damn well the fate of magic rested in our hands, thank you very much. "I took care of it yesterday."

"I can do it." Devon reached into his pocket.

For one terrifying moment, I thought he was going to pull out his glowing sword, but instead, he pulled out his foam blaster.

"Right over here, if you will." He stepped into the little space between two restaurants like he wanted to look over the dinner options on the menus out front.

Cindy kept walking toward us, looking at the buildings like she wasn't stalking us.

Devon let out a long breath and pulled the trigger. With a little *dhoomp*, a tiny gray thing shot out of the blaster and hit the sidewalk.

"What are you—"

My question was cut off by Cindy's squeal as she tipped forward, leaving her shoe stuck to the sidewalk behind her.

"I think we should call that the Cinderella maneuver." Devon led us down an alley and out onto the next street over.

"How did you do that?" I asked.

"Remember two years ago when the props shop figured out how to fill blood capsules and shoot them out of foam blasters for the barricade scene in Les Mis?" Devon asked.

"I remember my mom banning it," I said.

"Well, I got ahold of one of the guys who figured the capsules out, asked him how it was done, and made some tiny doses of the sticking potion." Devon beamed as he winked at me. "Thus the sticky blaster was born. It's not as showy as the water gun technique, but I figured the capsules would be safer for air travel."

"Devon, I mean this with absolutely no derision," Eric said, "I am thoroughly impressed."

"Thanks," Devon said. "I'm pretty proud of the sticky blaster concept. Now let's hope we can get back to New York without me needing to use any of my other toys."

"Wouldn't that be living the dream?" There was a tiny touch of worry in Elizabeth's voice as she laughed.

"Where are we supposed to find a local who might know about the"—I stopped myself from saying *magical bookkeepers* as a group of tourists passed by—"what we're looking for."

"By reading the signs," Eric said.

Reading the signs.

I started searching the sidewalk for any hint of a stray cat wanting us to follow it. Or a door appearing where it shouldn't be. Or words shimmering into being at the exact right moment.

"This should do." Eric stopped in front of a building with wide widows.

A sign hung in the glass.

Monastery Tours! English speaking guides! Snacks and bottled water included!

"Oh," I said, "that kind of sign."

Giving me a pitying frown, Eric pushed open the door to the little shop.

The scent of some really good kind of food that I couldn't quite pinpoint, but definitely made me want to curl up in front of a fire binge eating bread, filled the air.

The man behind the counter said something I couldn't understand before smiling and starting again. "Are you looking for a tour?"

"At the moment, we're just shopping around." Eric stepped

forward with a smile. "We have some rather unique interests and are hoping to find a guide with knowledge to suit."

"Ah, Americans." The man gestured toward my purple hair. "I should have known."

"Thanks?" I said.

The man didn't acknowledge me. "Our guides are all very knowledgeable on the monasteries and the history of the hermits in the area. If you are more looking for the geology, we have a tour that examines the rock pillars—"

"We're more interested in the myths of the area," Eric said.

"Myths." The man leaned his elbows on the counter, a slight furrow creasing his brow. "What myths are you looking for? Our history in Meteora is written on the stones you see rising toward the sky. There is no myth involved."

"The stories I've heard haven't been presented as fact," Eric said. "Unless, of course, there truly were men possessing other-worldly powers who were drawn to Meteora. From the tales I've been told, they were rumored to be scholars, keepers of books that held great power."

The wrinkles on the man's brow faded as he smiled. "Ah, I see. Why would you want to hear children's stories when the truth of the monasteries offers more adventure?"

"It's for a school project," Elizabeth said. "We're collecting local legends from all over the world."

"That's quite the project," the man said.

"It's an arts-based school," Devon said.

"Ah." The man frowned like he was just as confused with Devon's lie as I was with how Eric thought we were going get good information from the tour guide. "We don't go near those things on our tours. I can promise you, none of the companies you will find here talk about that. We look at the history of this place. Not strange stories that change with each telling. Sorry. I cannot help you."

"I know it wouldn't be right to ask you for the stories for free." I stepped toward the counter. "But, is there some sort of private tour rate? You could charge us for the whole thing and just tell us the legend here. I mean, I know it's not true, but it would be really helpful for our project." I pulled out my black credit card and slid it across the counter. "It wouldn't take more than a few minutes of your time."

"I suppose not." The man took the card and started punching things into his computer. "The stories used to be told as truth even when I was a boy. They would say there are men in the woods who are not monks. They hide in the forest behind the monasteries, deep in the trees where no sane person would dare go on purpose. But if you were foolish enough to stumble into the territory of the shadow men, you have found a place where no one with a soul belongs."

A shiver twitched up my spine.

The man shoved my card into the scanner. "If you are unfortunate enough to find the shadow men hidden behind the stones and trees, the best thing to do is pray for a swift death."

"The shadow men kill people?" I whispered.

"Some." The man set a receipt on the counter and handed me a pen. "Some are found dead in the woods with no hint as to what killed them. Some are never found at all. The ones that do make it back, they tell stories of horrors hidden in the darkness. Bear marks of the torment inflicted upon them. Strange scars and deformities."

I signed without looking at the total and stuffed my scarred hand into my pocket.

"Wings like a dragonfly growing from their backs, webs of white scars that cover their bodies, images of terrible monsters burned into their minds so they can't close their eyes without screaming from fright." The man looked down at his own hands on the counter.

"But if the shadow men are hidden," Elizabeth asked, "how did so many people end up running into them in the woods?"

"The path that leads into the darkness is said to hold beauty beyond compare." The man shook his hands out and shrugged. "Some found the path by accident and didn't have the strength to turn back. Others went looking for it, wanting to see whatever splendor had lured so many, and foolish enough to think they could resist. When I was very little, my grandmother told me not to worry. The monks of the hidden monastery had learned how to scare the shadows away. I used to believe it was true."

"And now?" Elizabeth asked.

"Now I'm old enough to know a bedtime story told to keep children from wandering into the woods when I hear one."

12

I leaned against the wall in the men's room, trying to get through checking for messages from Nikki quickly enough they wouldn't send Devon in to make sure I wasn't stress puking.

I had a text from Dad.

Check in with your mother, and don't forget you have a session with Dr. Spinnek this week. I expect you to take her call.

I had a text from Mom.

I hope you're learning a lot. Stay safe, and call when you get a chance. Don't forget to message your dad. He worries about you.

I had an email from Nikki.

Hi Bryant,

 With the format you're talking about, your best bet would be a council. Think a not-for-profit board but incorporating the best parts of the Knights of the Round Table. Keeping it small would maximize getting things done quickly, but having multiple members would prevent one bad actor from spoiling the system. Laying out duties depending on the council size would help decide who would be best for membership by choosing a candidate for each particular role.

How many are you including in the campaign? Would you like a council seat assigned to each of them?

I'm excited to see your maps when they're ready.

Nikki

Maps. I hadn't even thought of her wanting to see maps.

I dragged my hand over my purple hair, warring between keeping up the story versus calling the whole thing off to protect the truth I was dancing around so hard I might as well have tried out for the New York City Ballet.

I didn't have a clue as to how many council seats would be a good number. Or how council members should be chosen, or... what the hell I thought I was doing lying to a lawyer about creating a hypothetical framework to govern a community of wizards.

"Stupid, stupid, stupid." I knocked my head against the wall behind me.

I typed a quick message to Nikki, tucked my phone back into my pocket, and looked in the mirror. "I am Bryant Jameson Adams, sidekick to the great wizard Eric Deldridge." I fixed my scarf to cover the burn scar that circled my neck. "And I have no idea what fate wants from me."

I carefully removed the look of mingled resignation and angst from my face before stepping back out into the restaurant. Two men sat together off to the side, playing guitar while occasionally singing but mostly just talking and laughing with each other.

Self-loathing curdled in my stomach as I realized I was jealous of the men. Not because I didn't like my life. I just wanted the decisions I had to make to be as easy as what song to play next, not if taxing wizards was a feasible concept and would I get murdered for suggesting it.

"The boys make bets with each other sometimes." Our

server leaned close to Devon, tipping her torso in a way that displayed her ample cleavage. "They climb up behind the cliffs and see who can last the longest in the woods alone. They all come home, but the funny part is watching for which ones come out crying."

"Have you ever gone into those woods?" Devon gave the girl a grin as he spoke, like he wanted her to know he knew she was trying to show him how low the front of her shirt was, but he wasn't going to take the easy bait.

"I've been to the cliffs at night but never into the woods." She filled Devon's water glass. "I like an adventure, but there are limits."

I waited until the server walked away to take my seat.

"That's the third confirmation of the story we've received," Eric said.

"No two people have told the exact same story," Elizabeth said.

"But there are enough similarities to make me certain there is something in the woods the locals cannot explain." Eric studied the leftover food on his plate like it might somehow form a map to the bookkeepers' lair. "What awaits us in the woods might not be exactly what we're looking for, but it most definitely seems worth exploring."

"So we go into the woods people have been avoiding at night and see if Bryant gains a pretty pair of dragonfly wings?" Devon asked.

"Absolutely not. Magic has done enough weird things to me lately. You get the wings." I shoved the rest of my stuffed leaf into my mouth.

"Not to mention that wings could be really helpful if they were sturdy enough to hold your weight," Elizabeth said. "Between being able to fly and all your other new toys, you'd be ninety percent of the way to being an actual superhero."

"I guess you're right." Devon tossed a bit of his Souvlaki to the cat begging from under his chair. "A cool name, and I'd be at ninety-five percent."

"Shall we begin our climb now?" Eric asked. "Or do we need to wait for Devon to design his costume?"

"I could finally answer Cindy's voicemails and ask her to give us a ride," I offered.

"And have me goop her shoes on a cliff at night to get rid of her?" Devon asked.

"We'll walk," Eric said. "It will do Elizabeth good."

"Excuse me?" Elizabeth glared at him with a forkful of dessert halfway to her mouth.

"While I have every confidence in the education Lola has been giving you, there are some things only experience can teach." Eric pushed away from the table.

I frantically waved my black credit card at our server like a noob who'd never paid in a restaurant before.

"Think of the shadows, shimmers, and monsters you've seen in New York as the local flora and fauna," Eric said. "You are used to the squirrels, pigeons, and elms of Manhattan. There are some species, like cats for example—"

Devon's begging cat gave a well-timed *meow*.

"—that can be seen both here and in Manhattan, though admittedly in vastly different quantities. Then there are the types unique to our current environs such as a white-toothed shrew, or perhaps a mountain goat. While the aim of our trip is not to expand Elizabeth's education, we would be remiss to ignore the opportunity. Especially as the alternative would require petty deceit or intervention on Devon's part."

"Technically, it's Bryant's turn to ditch the babysitter." Devon pointed at me.

"I don't mind waiting for my turn."

The server scanned my card and I tacked on a tip and

signed, all while trying not to think through how much money we'd actually spent in Greece so far.

"Better start walking." Elizabeth pulled on her sweater like she was donning some sort of armor against whatever might wait in the shadows growing outside.

"I may not be as comforting to have around as Sniffer McDeadDog, but at least you won't be alone," I said.

"Ha ha." Elizabeth nudged me with her shoulder before lacing her fingers through mine.

I could tell from the way she held my hand, clutching it as though wanting to make sure that even if the earth cracked open and tried to swallow her she wouldn't lose her grip, that she did not at all like the idea of the magical seer equivalent of finding a white-toothed shrew. Still, she didn't argue as we headed for the road that wound up toward the monasteries.

The setting sun left strange shadows slanting away from the massive stone columns.

I tried not to stare at Elizabeth as we climbed up the steep road. I wanted to know if she was seeing anything lurking around us as the darkness deepened, but I also knew my watching her like she might spook and bolt at any moment wasn't going to help the situation.

None of us really said much until we passed the first monastery.

"Anything yet?" Eric asked as we crammed ourselves against a stone guardrail to let a tour bus pass.

"Not really." Elizabeth chewed her bottom lip for a moment.

I fought away the sparks in my stomach that made me want to have a turn with her bottom lip.

"It's wobbly," Elizabeth said.

"I'm sorry, what?" The sparks in my stomach fizzled away.

"Like frosted glass." Elizabeth tipped her head, examining what looked to me to be completely normal shadows around a strangely twisted tree. "It looks like there might be something moving on the other side of the glass, but I can't tell what it is or if it's really there."

"That doesn't sound so bad." I took a bracing breath and started up the hill. For once, all the others actually followed me.

"Hmm." Eric made that awful noise before we'd walked ten steps.

"What *hmm*?" I picked up my pace, climbing with the determination of a kid at a birthday party trying to get to the front of the food line because he knows full well there aren't going to be enough slices of cake to go around.

"On the one hand," Eric said, "the lack of aggressive presence lurking around us is extremely fortunate. We are on a mission to find a place that could very well be guarded by unknown magic."

I started walking even faster, like I could somehow outrun the needle of fear that wanted to pop my courage bubble.

"On the other hand," Eric said, "we are in a place that has been inhabited by humans for centuries. And not only humans, but humans who are devoted to things beyond the mundane and easily visible. I would find it extraordinarily odd if no shadows or creatures had found their way to this remarkable place, and odder still if none had been birthed here."

"What are you actually trying to say?" By that point, I was jogging up the mountain, dragging Elizabeth along behind me.

"If Elizabeth is correct, and there are shadows kept just out of sight, as though trapped on the other side of a pane of glass, the necessary questions become more difficult," Eric said.

"What's so bad it's been hidden behind glass?" Elizabeth said. "And where does the barrier between them and us break?"

13

The *crack* of the branches beneath my feet was somehow as frightening as the *snap* of stepping on unknown bones in the tunnels on the outskirts of Beville. I kept my shoulders relaxed and didn't let my hands shake. I don't know why, but admitting that being in the forest at night freaked me out seemed somehow worse than being scared under normal circumstances.

Of course, from the way Elizabeth kept flinching, I was probably right to be scared.

The sun had gone down before we'd reached the top of the hill where a sketchy bridge and obscene number of stairs allowed visitors to access one of the monasteries.

In a way, the fact that we were creeping into the woods in the dark was a good thing. No one could see us, so what chance did Cindy have of finding us?

On the other hand, we hadn't seen the terrain in the daylight, so even Eric couldn't pretend he knew where he was going as he led us through the woods.

I gripped a sphere of light in one hand and kept my other raised, ready to shout a spell if anything leapt out of the trees to terrorize us. Elizabeth gripped my arm for dear life as she stared into the shadows. Devon gripped his sticky blaster like he was ready to star in an action movie. And Eric led with a little less confidence than I'd grown used to.

In New York, it always seemed like Eric was just storming through the world, knowing exactly where he was going even when I was pretty sure he was as lost as the rest of us.

Apparently, that Eric superpower didn't extend beyond the Tri-State Area.

"I still don't see anything different," Elizabeth said when Eric paused on the edge of a dark precipice. "There's the same wobbly darkness but nothing beautiful and enchanting to lure us to the shadow men."

"I think I spotted another trail a ways back," I offered. "Or we could go back the way we came and wait to hike around in the daylight. Get the lay of the land, then come find the shadow men at night."

"We're not leaving these woods until we find the bookkeepers' lair." Eric headed left, in the opposite direction of the perfectly good trail I had spotted.

"Whelp, I'm glad I ate a big dinner." Devon followed Eric, staying close on his heels to take advantage of Eric's magically made light.

"I don't like the feel of these woods." Elizabeth loosened her grip on my arm as we picked our way across a patch of rocks jutting up through the dirt of the trail.

"Under the circumstances, I don't know if that's a good thing or a bad thing," I said.

"I think it depends on if we're all still breathing come morning," Elizabeth said.

"Right." I nodded like an idiot. "That would shift the point of view."

The path Eric had chosen—if you can call a thin strip of

semi-worn dirt a path—cut farther down the slope, away from the town of Meteora, all the monasteries, and any hope of someone finding our bodies before we'd been eaten by wild animals.

The farther downhill we went, the closer together the trees grew, their thick branches hanging over the path like nature was trying to trap us in some sort of weird wooden cave.

Or casket.

I tried really hard not to let myself think *or casket.*

Something rustled in the trees overhead.

I grabbed Elizabeth, pulling her close to me, ready to shout a shield spell to protect us from whatever monster was attacking.

The rustle of wings and a high squeaking carried to my ears before I could speak the spell.

"Bat," I panted. "It's just a bat."

At the time, it didn't occur to me that it was strange that no one laughed and said *Of course, Bryant* or *Take a breath, Bryant, nothing's going to swoop out of the sky and attack us,* or even better, *Bryant, we're perfectly safe here. There's absolutely no reason to think we'll be murdered tonight.* They stayed silent as we all just turned back toward the not-really-a-path path and kept heading downhill.

Three more bats and one woodland mammal terrified me before a hint of light caught my eye.

I squinted against the glow of my spell, trying to see if I'd lost my mind or if my eyes had gone funny. But as hard as I squinted, the light didn't disappear.

The tiny glimmer wasn't anywhere near us. It was way off through the trees.

"Guys," I said, "I think I see a thing."

"A thing?" Devon asked.

"How descriptive," Eric said.

I tucked my light behind my back, but I couldn't see the gleam any more clearly. "Is that a building?"

"Maybe." Elizabeth let go of my arm and cupped her hands around her eyes to shield them from our magic-made lights. "I mean. It looks like a normal light to me. I don't see anything magnificent or magical about it."

"Then we shall find a path toward the light." Eric looked around for a moment before giving up the not-really-a-path-but-better-than-nothing path we'd been on to bushwhack through the trees.

"Are you sure about this?" I pushed a branch aside for Elizabeth only to have the dumb thing smack me in the face as I tried to duck beneath. I sucked air in through my teeth and touched my cheek. My fingers came away red. "Great. *Sinato*." I gritted my teeth against the bite of my own healing spell.

"I'm not sure if it would be pure comedy or cruel irony if we die falling over the edge of a cliff in the dark," Devon said.

"I'd call it solid dark humor." Elizabeth flinched, ducking away from me.

"What?" I raised my palms toward the tree branches above us.

Elizabeth screamed and covered her head, cowering as though a thousand bats were attacking her.

"*Primurgo*." I wrapped my arms around Elizabeth, protecting her from the invisible things as my shield spell blossomed over us.

"Elizabeth, what are you seeing?" Eric spoke calmly even though he'd cast a shield spell of his own to protect himself and Devon.

"I..." Elizabeth's breath came in shaking gasps as she moved her arms away from her face and looked up. "I don't know. It's things."

"More detail." The light in Eric's hand vanished.

I hesitated before letting the orb in my palm fade.

"Not quite human." Elizabeth leaned closer to me, like she really thought I could defend her against the darkness. "Not like Charles. Not people coated in shadow. More like memories. Faded and distorted. But the worst memories. The things that come back in your nightmares." A tear ran down her cheek. "I think they were people once."

"Ghosts?" Devon reached into his pocket and pulled out the hilt of his sword. "Are you seeing ghosts?"

"I don't know." Elizabeth yelped and pulled herself closer to me.

"What do we do?" Devon said.

"That depends on what we are facing. Have the spirits of the dead somehow been trapped in these woods, or are the woods themselves trying to tell us a tale of their own?" Eric trailed his fingers along the inside of his own shield spell.

"Was I supposed to understand that?" My voice came out all whimpery.

"Elizabeth, do these seem to be the same sort of figures you saw near the monasteries?" Eric asked, his tone calm like it was a simple, academic question.

"Yes, but those were contained and hidden, these aren't." Elizabeth flinched as a weird shimmer zinged across the top of my shield spell like something had just crashed into it.

"Aha," Eric said.

"Tell me you have a plan." I looked to Eric.

"It's more a theory," Eric said, "but it does mesh with the history of this place."

"Do we get to hear the theory?" Devon asked.

"I don't believe what Elizabeth is seeing are individual spirits," Eric said.

"So we're not surrounded by ghosts?" The panic constricting

my lungs eased enough I could almost take in what counted as a breath.

"I fear our predicament may be far more troubling," Eric said. "I believe we have walked into a forest filled with phantasms."

"Phantasms are more troubling than ghosts?" I slid my hand into my pocket to pull out my magical phone.

"If these aren't spirits or creatures," Eric said, "then someone or—the more tragic possibility—this place is deliberately manifesting the phantasms."

"You're really not helping with the panic," I said.

"Terrible things have happened near the soaring stone columns. We read the truth of it all over the brochures in town," Eric said. "The tourists don't understand the raw horror of it, but the woods remember. Pain, fear, panic, grief, all etched into the trees themselves. The overabundance of humans at the monasteries would block such things—too much petty worry and greed oozing out of the hordes. The memories the forest holds can't hope to break through. But out here, where people are not meant to be, the trees remember."

"So what exactly is the protocol for dealing with tree memory phantasms?" I asked.

"Keep walking, stay together, and pray to whomever you think watches over you that we will have the fortitude to hear what the woods want to tell us, the courage to push forward until we meet the light, and that the memories held within these woods have not been twisted to a darker purpose." Eric waved his hand through the air, reconjuring his light as his shield faded away.

I shoved my fear down, cramming it beneath my need to protect Elizabeth. "You ready?"

"Sure." She trembled in my arms as her eyes tracked the movement of something I couldn't see.

"I promise, I'll stay right beside you," I whispered. "I won't let anything hurt you."

"Okay." She slipped her hand into mine. "Just don't leave me."

"Never." I let my shield dissolve. "*Heliono.*" My orb of light reappeared in my palm.

Eric kept his pace slow as we headed toward the light in the distance, making sure our little pack stayed close together.

"It's really not fair, you know." Elizabeth's voice wavered as she spoke. "Seers should be given some sort of defense mechanism."

"Want my sticky blaster?" Devon asked.

"Thanks, but that's not what I mean." Elizabeth flinched and tightened her grip on my hand. "I don't think a sticking potion would help with dive-bombing forest memory spirit things."

Eric paused at the top of a rocky slope. He peered into the darkness before leading us sideways, cutting along the incline. "What sort of defense would you prefer?"

"Some built-in badassery to go with being a seer," Elizabeth said. "Porcupines get quills, bees get stingers, even skunks get stink sacks. I should have something."

"Have you ever mentioned this to Lola?" Eric asked.

"Yep." Elizabeth clung to my arm. "We have to move faster. There are more of them here."

"What did Lola say?" Eric picked up the pace, walking quickly enough to knock stones down the slope.

The sound of the rocks clattering away into the darkness felt like we were sounding an alarm, telling everything in the forest that might want to torment, haunt, or kill us exactly where we were.

"That life has never been that kind to seers," Elizabeth said. "At least society has progressed enough that I hopefully won't be institutionalized for being hysterical or burned because people freak out and think I'm a witch. So, that's something."

The ground leveled out in front of us, offering a better view of the light I'd spotted.

A single candle glowed through a window partway up a cliff. As we moved through the woods, the window came in and out of view, but it wasn't until we reached the edge of the trees and stood at the base of the stone pillar that I realized there was more to the structure on the side of the cliff than a single lit window.

A whole two-story building clung to the side of the rock, though how it stayed stuck to the pillar, I had no idea. There were two little chimneys and a set of carved stairs leading up to the entryway. If it hadn't been dark, and Elizabeth hadn't been shaking like she was facing an orc army without even a Halfling-size sword to defend herself, it might have been a charming hideaway in the woods.

But Elizabeth shouted, "Eric stop!" right before he reached the stairs, and all my feelings of awe for the little structure clinging to the side of the rock in a completely illogical way vanished.

The woods seemed to still for a moment, like the trees and their weird memory spirits/phantasm things had all paused to see what had frightened Elizabeth so badly.

"What do you—" I never finished my question.

The air around me seemed to solidify, pressing against my skin. But the pressure wasn't even. It shifted and lurched like I was being jostled in a crowd.

"I don't think they want us to go up there." Elizabeth reached out, running her fingers across something I couldn't see.

14

"Don't!" I yanked Elizabeth's hand back, terrified that whatever it was she was touching would devour her.

"Why are they here?" Elizabeth said. "Why do they have substance?"

"We need to get into that building." Eric slogged toward the steps like he was shouldering his way through Times Square on New Year's Eve.

"The seer just said no to going into the building," Devon said even though he was already shoving his way forward in Eric's wake.

"We are looking for a hidden place that at the very least contains invaluable information." Eric gripped the wall by the stairs and dragged himself forward in a way that would have been super comical if it weren't for the invisible—to me—things holding him back. "The place we are being prevented from going is the most likely candidate for being the place we seek."

"Love it." Devon reached for the wall but could barely graze the stacked stones with his fingers.

Eric grabbed Devon's wrist, wrenching him forward.

"Stay right behind me." I shifted to stand in front of Elizabeth, knocking my shoulder into something that felt like a linebacker. I clenched my jaw against the inevitable bruises and shoved another foot forward.

"They really don't want us to go into that building." Elizabeth wrapped one arm around my waist, keeping herself tucked to my back as I stepped forward. "Bryant, they look desperate."

The night pressed against me as I squeezed between two invisible things. I would have thought I was back in Athens with the weird gravity pressing me to the ceiling, but whatever beings/spirits/woodland memory phantasm things I was shoving between had enough substance that my sleeves shifted on my arms like the material had caught on other people's clothing.

I gritted my teeth and plowed another step forward.

"Has it occurred to you," Elizabeth said, "that maybe we're being kept from getting to the building for a good reason?"

"We must assume the reason is to protect whatever secrets wait inside," Eric said.

"I meant a *good* reason." Elizabeth pressed on my back, steering me a little bit left. I couldn't see why, but my next step was slightly easier. "Like maybe they're trying to protect us."

"What makes you say that?" My voice came out all strained as I pushed through what felt like a wall of rubber to get to the base of the steps.

"If the bodies of the phantasms can make it harder for us to walk, couldn't they do other things to us, too?" Elizabeth said. "If they wanted to hurt us—"

"Let's not give the creepy things ideas." Devon grabbed my wrists while Eric reached for Elizabeth.

I have no memory of being birthed, but Devon dragging me onto the steps was way closer than I ever wanted to get. Something between a groan and a yelp sprang involuntarily from my throat as my body was compressed like Devon was trying to drag me through a tube. As soon as the pressure was gone, I stumbled forward, knocking face first into the rock wall. Dragging air into my lungs, I looked back to try and help Elizabeth, but she was already standing next to me, her hair barely out of place as she stared into the woods.

"I just think some things are hidden for a reason," Elizabeth said. "And if the phantasms are trying to protect us, then whatever's inside could be a lot worse than what's out here."

"If the phantasms you see mean to help us, we will thank them after we've seen what waits inside." Eric started up the steps. "We cannot be dissuaded from our cause."

"Do you really think the things you're seeing want to help us?" I wrapped my arm around Elizabeth's waist, not only because I wanted to make sure the shadows didn't drag her away. I also just needed to feel her safe and solid beside me to maintain my ever-slipping attempt at remaining calm. "You don't normally seem this freaked out by the things you see."

"Of course I'm scared," Elizabeth said. "I don't want those things flying around me, and I like them being solid enough to block our path even less."

"But?" I whispered as Eric reached the door of the building.

"I just can't get it to make sense," Elizabeth whispered back. "If Eric's right and it really is the woods projecting a visual memory, what reason would a memory have for solidifying to block us? And if they're individual spirits, what common goal could they share that would make them stand in our way?"

"I have no idea." I kissed Elizabeth's temple. Partly because I was in love with her and wanted to offer a bit of comfort even though I had literally zero comforting things to say. The other part was me wanting to sneaky smell her hair to give myself an aromatic bravery booster as Eric reached for the latch on the door.

The bar moved up with a sharp metal-on-wood *clack.*

Eric extinguished the light in his palm, and I did the same. He pushed the door open and stepped into the shadows.

I much more reasonably pulled out my normal phone and turned on the flashlight before stepping up beside Devon.

Elizabeth shifted away from me, peering at the shadows Eric had so casually walked into.

"I don't think there are any phantasms inside," Elizabeth said. "At least none that I can see."

"There won't be," Eric said. "I doubt they can exist on consecrated ground."

I inched forward enough to be able to see Eric standing in the entryway, staring up at a glittering mural that looked like it belonged in a cathedral.

"The hidden monastery where the monks learned how to scare the shadow men away." I stepped inside, and the air changed, growing colder and damper within a few feet.

"Well, they're keeping the phantasms out, but what about the shadow men?" Devon shined the light of his phone up at the paintings that looped around the top of the wall.

"This way." Eric beckoned us toward the only other door in the room.

The bolt moved with another *clack*, but the stone of the walls seemed to amplify the sound, making it bounce around the enclosed space.

I held my breath, listening for any hint of angry monks coming to chase us back out into the horde of phantasms.

Nothing.

Making sure Devon and Elizabeth stayed right behind me, I stepped through the door and into the corridor beyond.

A row of doors took up the side of the narrow hall closest to the rock face, and on the other side, a single door opened into a dark room overlooking the woods.

"Where's the candle?" I whispered as loudly as I dared.

Eric pointed forward where another closed door blocked our path.

I shook out my free hand, trying to convince myself I could not only move my fingers, but was also capable of creating a spell to defend us.

Eric paused in front of the door, studying the light drifting through the tiny cracks in the wood. He reached forward to touch the bolt, but before his fingers even grazed the metal, the door swung silently open.

Devon pressed his sticky blaster into Elizabeth's hand and pulled the metal tube of his hilt from his pocket.

"I'm so sorry to interrupt your evening unannounced." Eric spoke calmly and cheerfully, like he'd spotted an old friend in the white-painted, candlelit room beyond, where there was definitely no person in sight. "We're here on some rather urgent business that couldn't wait until morning. If you have time for a quick word, I'd be very grateful for your assistance."

He was so smooth, so unafraid, if I hadn't been on the spooky walk through the woods with him, I might have believed we were just dropping by the monastery for a chat. And that chill-under-pressure definitely ranked in the top ten reasons why I would always be the sidekick to Eric Deldridge, wizarding hero.

Eric stepped into the room.

I attempted to walk with a calm swagger as I followed him. I'm pretty sure it just looked like I was sore from too many squats in gym class.

I glanced around the room. The rock face of the cliff had been used as one of the walls. Candles had been set into the crevices, though none of them were lit. The other three, man-made walls had all been painted the same pure white without any of the fancy murals from the entryway. A single candle burned in the window.

"We're seeking a place that should be near here." Eric turned in a slow circle as he spoke, like he was addressing a gallery full of people instead of an empty room. "I was told by an old friend that I might find the bookkeepers in these woods. You may have a different name for them. Perhaps you call them the shadow men, though I believe that local legend might come from the entities outside."

"Eric," Elizabeth said.

I spun toward her, ready to shout a spell to defend her. But she was still and calm as she pointed toward the corner where a man was slowly materializing out of the white wall.

The man was old with a weathered face and bright white hair to go with his bright white robes.

I fought against my urge to shout a spell to knock him back into the wall as my instincts screamed *Lady.*

"The men you're looking for are gone," white-hair wall-appearer said. "They all died years ago."

"I'm very sorry to hear that," Eric said. "I was hoping they might be able to help me. I'm looking for some very particular books."

The man shook his head. "They are gone. Their home is gone. The path to their home is gone."

"How?" I asked. "What happened to them?"

The man studied us all for a moment before moving.

He took a step forward, and for one awful moment, I thought he was going to attack Devon. But the man just walked through the door and waved for us to follow.

I held back, staring at the place where the man had appeared out of the wall, as Devon and Eric followed him.

The wall was just a wall. No hidden cubby I could see. No marks where he'd done some creepy camouflage thing.

"Where did he come from? Did you see any weird magic?" I asked. "Are your eyes fuzzy? Is he using bone magic?"

"I don't think so." Elizabeth took my hand, leading me after the others.

Electric lights had been turned on in the big room opposite the wall of doors.

Elizabeth and I arrived just in time to watch the man push aside a super old tapestry to reveal a little kitchen, complete with a stainless-steel fridge.

He pulled out four bottles of water, giving one to each of us. "Even when the weather isn't baking you, it's not an easy path to get here."

"Thanks." I tamped down the voice in my head that railed at me for touching single-use plastic and took a drink of the cold water.

"We don't get many visitors to our monastery during the day," the man said. "We get fewer at night. I try not to count the time between those who stumble to our door as they seek the other men hiding in the woods."

"Because they're dead?" Elizabeth asked.

"More than a decade." The man sat on one of the spindly, wooden chairs. "They were nice men, for the most part. We weren't supposed to know what they were doing out in their corner of the woods. But you can only see so many strange things before you start to guess.

"I would watch them sometimes when they were out walking in the woods. They were as friendly as one can expect of recluses. Some of their visitors would end up at our door by mistake. Some of ours would get lost in the woods—it didn't go so well for them. We have stone stairs leading to our monastery, but the path to their home was filled with unnatural things."

"Did you ever see it?" I sat down in front of the man.

"Once." He stared at the wall like he was seeing the path all over again. "One of theirs came to our door. She was badly wounded but insisted there was nothing a doctor could do to help her. I had never been near the other place, even though I'd lived in this monastery for twenty years by then. I'd been told which direction the other place was when I first came here, as a warning not to venture to that corner of the forest. But I couldn't let the woman die, so I went to find the men.

"I walked in the direction everyone had pointed." He tapped his chin like it was a nervous twitch as the wrinkles on his brow deepened. "I hurried through the woods, calling for the men, praying they would find me."

"And did they?" I asked when he hadn't spoken in a few moments.

"No," the man said. "I had almost given up hope. Then faint lights began to glimmer all around me, like the dust in the air had learned to shine. I followed the glow, keeping to the bright path. Up ahead, darkness swallowed everything, like I was staring into the mouth of a great beast. The light around me grew, everything gleaming with more beauty than this earth was meant to host, even as demons I cannot name surrounded me, trapping me in a place I did not belong.

"I was sure it was the end of my life, so I shouted to the other men, trying to make sure they would know to hurry to our monastery and help the woman. One of the men stepped out of the darkness and took my hand. In that moment, all the things I had seen vanished. I led the man here and watched as he used his powers to heal the woman. It was a miraculous thing."

"Thank you for being willing to help one of our kind," Eric said. "And for accepting the differences between us."

"The peace we shared was a good one." The man nodded.

"But what happened?" Elizabeth asked. "How do you know they're dead?"

"One came to visit years ago. He said he was the last. Said the way the path to their home was created depended upon his life. And when he was gone, their home would go with him. He warned me I would hear whispers in the woods. That his fellows had been keeping the trees quiet, but the silence would end with the rest of it.

"It wasn't more than a week later that I woke to find six books by the door. The man left a note. He said it was his time. Asked me to keep the books. Said one day someone would come looking for them, to please keep the volumes safe until I could pass them on. That night when I tried to sleep, the whispers in the woods woke me."

"I'm so sorry." I didn't really know what I was sorry for, but it was the only thing I could think to say as childlike fear filled the man's face.

"I'd grown used to the whispers," the man said. "When she came, she dampened their sound. Made things easier for me here in thanks for my having kept the books safe while I waited for her."

"This *she*," I said, "do you know her name? Or where we could find her?"

"Iliana?" The man finally looked back toward me with a mixture of fear and grief in his eyes that made me want to run. "I don't know where to find her. But now that she knows you're here, she'll come for you."

I set down my water bottle and stood, wondering if the rolling in my stomach was from the man having drugged me or just plain panic.

"How would Iliana know we're here?" Eric asked. "Did you send her a message?"

"No. I don't know how, but she always knows when one of your kind enters our sanctuary." The man stood and went back to the fridge. "But now that you're inside the monastery, the whispers in the woods won't let you out. Don't worry. I have enough food to keep us all alive until she comes."

"And once she gets here?" Devon said.

"I have never been brave enough to ask." The man froze, his back still toward us. "But when the screaming starts, part of me misses the whispers."

15

I 've been told more than once that my self-preservation instincts need to be honed. I'll panic when things are fine and not even notice when death is flying straight at my face.

However, I can say with complete certainty that when I grabbed Elizabeth and Devon by the arms and dragged them out of the monastery sitting room from Hell, my self-preservation instincts were working just fine.

"Bryant, wait," Eric said just as I was about to throw open the outside door and run down the stairs into the phantasms/shadow people I couldn't see but could definitely feel as I'd shoved my way through them just a short while before.

"Wait to find out exactly what Iliana is going to do to us to make us scream?" I grabbed the door latch.

"I have no intention of waiting here," Eric said. "But if we are going to force our way out of this place, it should be me who leads."

"Right," I panted, letting go of the latch and stepping aside. "I can see the logic in that."

Eric tossed open the door. "*Heliono.*" A glowing orb burst into being in his hand. He strode down the steps toward the things we couldn't see with as much confidence as a varsity quarterback in a JV game.

"*Heliono.*" My light flickered and dimmed in my hand as my magic wavered.

You will not panic. You are not allowed to panic.

The orb buzzed as the light shone bright.

"Let's go." I took Elizabeth's hand and stepped out into the night.

A cold wind touched my cheeks as I walked down the stone steps. I tried to tell myself the sounds I was hearing were only an unfortunate combination of the wind rustling through the trees and my heart thumping so loud I might as well have installed subwoofers in my ears.

But Elizabeth said, "Eric. Eric, I don't know if we can get through," and the fear in her voice shot ice down my spine.

"We don't have a choice." Eric stopped at the bottom of the steps.

The sounds of the whispers surged and fell like waves trying to drag us under.

"Bryant," Devon said.

"Yeah?" I fought against my instinct to reach for my phone, unwilling to let go of either my light or Elizabeth's hand.

"I think this would be the time to freak out." Devon's red sword voomed to life.

"Great. Good to know." I swallowed the knot in my throat before my fear could choke me.

"If we're separated, head back toward the road. And know I will not rest until I've found you." Eric stepped off the stairs.

To my normal eyes, it looked fine. Like he'd just stepped down onto the forest floor.

But Elizabeth screamed, "Eric!" as the air around him seemed to shift and a giant tear appeared on the arm of his coat.

"Get away from him!" Devon leapt off the side of the stairs, slashing his sword at the things he couldn't see. A deeper *hum* vibrated through the glowing blade as it met his invisible foe.

I hesitated on the bottom step.

We needed to escape.

But I had to protect Elizabeth.

I had to help Devon and Eric, who were both fighting like they were penned in by a pack of demons.

But I had to protect Elizabeth.

Devon shouted and stumbled back. Blood oozed from a cut on his cheek.

"Stay right beside me." I wrapped Elizabeth's arm around my waist. "*Aarantha!*"

The wind of my spell surrounded us, the vortex picking up dirt and debris from the forest floor as we stepped down onto the ground.

Elizabeth clung to me as I moved toward Devon.

I kept waiting for something to block my path, making each step forward a fight. But I didn't feel any resistance as I reached out to grab Devon's arm. If I could get him into the funnel of my spell and then grab Eric, I could keep the spell going all the way out of the woods.

Even as my brain formed the plan, I knew I wouldn't be able to maintain the magic for that long.

"Devon!" I grabbed his arm and wrenched him through the vortex.

Elizabeth let go of me to steady him.

"Stay close." I headed toward Eric.

Even if I couldn't keep the spell going for the whole hike back to the road, Eric could. He could keep the wind going. I just had to get to him.

"Eric!" I reached forward, trying to grab his arm as a stream of crimson haze flew from his palm.

The haze didn't rush through the air and dissipate. It solidified, forming the outline of a person.

The phantasm's mouth opened in a soundless scream as it swung its arm down as though preparing slice through Eric's neck.

The haze lengthened, growing around the outline of a sword as the blade neared Eric's flesh.

"No!" I dove forward, out of the safety of my own spell, grabbing the misty form around the middle and tackling a very real-feeling body to the ground.

"*Exci.*" I tried to pin the form down as my spell pummeled it in the face.

The mist that had surrounded its head poofed out in an almost beautiful way.

I rolled to the side, and scrambled to my knees, trying to stand so I could get back to Elizabeth.

A stab of pain cut through my side. Like I'd been struck by lightning, or stung by the world's largest wasp, or stabbed.

I looked down to find lots of blood on my stomach.

"Oh, shit." The pain quadrupled as I realized I'd literally been stabbed. "*Sinato.*"

The agony of my healing spell seared through me, and the whole world went wiggly and dark. I could feel myself tipping toward the ground. I put my arms out, trying to stop my fall, but somehow I hit the ground on the side where I'd been stabbed.

A scream tore from my throat as I rolled onto my back, digging into my pocket for my magical phone, desperate to find a better healing spell.

A horde of people surrounded me, blocking Devon and Elizabeth from view, keeping them from seeing how badly I needed help.

But the figures looming over me weren't made of red mist. They were people with faces and clothes and weapons.

A *rustle* and a faint sound like a long-forgotten scream came from nearby, but I couldn't see who had cried out.

"*Telinto.*" I felt the magic rush from my body, like I'd tried to topple a city instead of casting a simple slicing spell.

The shimmer of my spell flew toward the man closest to me. He grunted and stumbled as my magic met his very real-looking flesh, but he didn't bleed or fall.

He screamed words I couldn't understand, his filthy, bearded face twisting with a kind of loathing I'd never seen before.

"I haven't hurt you." I tried to push myself up, but the pain in my side shocked through my body, making it impossible to stand. "*Primurgo.*" I barely managed to say the spell. Still, my shield blossomed around me, blocking the bearded man's blade.

His face shifted from loathing, to awe, then to fear.

He shouted something to the other warriors.

As one, they all stepped toward me, crowding around like they wanted to squash me to death.

"Who are you?" I coughed, and something that tasted horribly like blood flew from my mouth. "*Sinato.*" The sting of healing came again, but it already hadn't worked once. "Eric." I coughed more blood.

The men, and they were literally all men, loomed over me, pushing against my shield like they didn't care about the horrible way my magic should have been stinging their flesh.

I pressed my hand to the blood on my stomach, making myself breathe instead of scream in pain. The world wobbled for a moment, but when I could see clearly again, the men were still standing over me.

"What do you want?" I asked.

One of the men pulled his spear back and stabbed at my shield. A horrible *hum* vibrated my bones, but my spell held.

Another man, this one wearing armor, slashed at my shield

with his sword. Metal met magic, and the man let out a ferocious scream as my shield flashed.

And that's when I realized none of the men matched. It was like my mom had decided to do a Shakespearean play, but the costumer didn't know what concept Mom had chosen. There were old school warriors, a guy who looked like he could be a Victorian duke, and a guy who looked like he was trying to be a 90's PI.

"Why are you all here? Why is she making you do this?"

The 90's dude raised his pistol and pointed it at me.

"I'm not here to hurt anyone. I'm trying to help find the books."

Books.

It was like the trees had started whispering the word.

Books. Books. Books.

The shapes of the men around me shivered and reformed.

Books. Books.

"We want to protect them." I tried to take a breath and gagged on my own blood. "Someone stole them. We have to find the..."

Everything started to fade into darkness. I thought it was the end.

"...the books."

I would die in the woods in Greece. Eric would have to tell my parents. Cindy would have to arrange to ship my body home.

But death didn't come for me, and the darkness didn't swallow me whole. It shifted and twisted, turning into a different scene.

Green leaves hung from the trees like we'd leapt through time to the beginnings of summer, and the Monastery glued to the rock face disappeared. The whole stone column vanished like I'd moved to another part of the forest.

A light, like glowing shimmer powder, filled the air as the

men who had tried to kill me faded away, leaving a girl my age standing on the gleaming path, speaking to an older man.

I couldn't tell what either of them was saying, but I could read the look on the girl's face. She thought the man was lying to her. She was suspicious and livid.

The man kept his voice calm, but his eyes were filled with authority tinged by fear.

The girl shouted something at the man and turned away. As she stalked past me, she muttered in perfect English, "His lies will get him killed someday."

The scene twisted, the glow twirling around me, blocking everything from view before a new scene reformed.

The older man limped toward the darkness at the end of the gleaming path, pausing for a moment before stepping into the black and out of sight. The darkness did nothing to dampen his terrible scream of pain.

I tried to push myself up so I could go see if the man needed help, but I couldn't get my body to move.

I'm sorry. I couldn't even make myself speak the words.

Another, younger man stepped out of the black. Blood coated his cheeks and hands. But there was something about his face that seemed familiar even through the gore.

Thaden.

Terror joined the pain still zinging through my stomach as Thaden walked past me and faded into the darkness.

The glow that filled the air shifted, dimming as everything went bone-chillingly cold. The light vanished, and my teeth started to chatter as the ground beneath me turned to ice.

A *crunch* of frost under feet came from beside me. I looked up to find the girl from the first scene standing next to me. But she wasn't a girl anymore. Time had passed since she'd shouted at the man.

She looked around the woods for a few moments before calling out.

I held my breath, waiting for someone to answer. The forest stayed silent without even the wind or phantasms whispering through the trees.

She called out again as she walked toward the place where Thaden had been in the scene before. Moving slowly, she crept through the spot where the darkness should have eaten her.

She buried her face in her hands before letting out a horrible scream. Lightning streaked down from the sky, striking the ground around her. She let her hands drop and looked back to where the man had stood years before. "I'll find them myself. Rot in Hell, cowards."

The trees shifted, moving me back to the forest right beside the monastery. The mismatched men surrounded me again, their weapons raised, their gazes locked on my face.

I opened my mouth to try and talk, but my body didn't seem to be able to rally the strength to speak.

The 90's-looking dude pressed his palm to my shield. "They were never here." He spoke with a British accent. "They decimated the keepers in their search. But the books you seek were never here."

How do you know?

I wanted to ask the question, but the world started fading. No monastery, no trees, no creepy mismatched phantasms, no beauty from the shimmering path made of light. Just darkness creeping toward the center of my vision as everything faded to black.

"You've died for nothing," he said.

You're wrong.

16

Y*ou're wrong.*
    You're wrong.

The words kept churning through my head over and over as the blackness spun around me like I'd fallen into a bottomless pit.

You're wrong.

There was pain in the blackness. A sharp, white-hot pain in my stomach.

I hoped the others were alive and Eric would heal me. Or, if they were dead, I hoped their deaths had been less painful than mine.

You're wrong.

You're wrong.

Eventually, the spinning changed into a sort of bouncing that made the pain in my stomach worse. Then the blackness became less complete as sound broke through my shroud.

Panting. Footsteps, panting, and a little cough like someone was choking on tears.

Elizabeth.

I tried to get my mouth to form the word, but all I managed was a weird cough.

"It's okay," Devon said. "You're going to be okay, Bryant. Just hang on."

Devon sounded so confident I didn't mind when the blackness started to swallow me again.

I knew that dude was wrong.

———

I may not be the most knowledgeable world traveler, but here are some tips for creating a joyful international escapade.

- Don't go into hidden monasteries at night.
- Don't forget to run as soon as a monk materializes from a wall.
- Don't get stabbed by a forest phantasm.
- Don't wake up on the side of a cliff with the taste of your own blood still in your mouth.

I mean, maybe those are just things I personally don't enjoy, but if there were a way to leave a negative review for a morally questionable monk hiding in a forest filled with tree memories of death, I would have some nasty things to say about that whole night.

On the plus side, I finally managed to make my eyes flutter open to find Elizabeth kneeling beside me, holding my hand, Devon alive and with his face already healed, and Eric looking more worried than disappointed. So, it could have been worse.

"Careful." Elizabeth wrapped her arm around my back as I sat up.

The terrible agony in the side of my stomach from being

stabbed had morphed into a clenching pain like I'd gotten a cramp from running for too long.

"I'm okay." I managed to speak without coughing up any blood.

"Shit, Bry." Devon rubbed his hands over his face. Some of the dried blood on his cheek flecked away. "I really hate it when you do the near-death thing."

"I'm not such a big fan of it myself." I tried to laugh. It came out more like a death rattle.

"We should keep moving." Eric stood, brushing imaginary dirt off his pristine clothing.

"He needs to rest," Elizabeth said.

"I agree," Eric said. "But he'll rest better at the hotel, and the more distance we put between us and that vile monk, the better. I'd prefer to be far from here when Iliana comes."

"Are you sure?" Devon grabbed me under the arms and hoisted me to my feet.

"A woman who managed to manipulate phantasms to trap people in the monastery until she could make them scream?" Elizabeth wrapped her arms around me, holding me steady as my legs wobbled. "I don't want to wait in the dark for her to show up."

"But we need to talk to her," Devon said. "If she knew the bookkeepers, she could be the next step in finding the books."

"I agree," Eric said. "We will find Iliana, but we will not wait near the woods she's contaminated. I will not give her that advantage."

"I hope we can find some food in town." Devon started down the steep slope of the road.

"Let me help you." Elizabeth kept her arm around my waist, helping me balance as new shocks of pain zinged through different parts of my body with each step. "We don't even know if Iliana has any more books than the six the monk gave her."

"But we're not the only ones to have thought the books stolen from our Library ended up here," I said.

"What do you mean?" Eric asked.

"Thaden was here." I started to take another step down, but the rest of them had frozen.

"What?" Elizabeth said.

"Thaden was here. I assume he was looking for the books. I don't know why else he'd show up in a forest in Greece to kill someone," I said. "And there was a girl looking for the books, too."

"What are you talking about?" Devon wrinkled his brow as he studied me, like maybe I'd lost my mind when I'd been stabbed.

"When I was on the ground, coughing up blood, and the weird whisper phantasms looked like real people, I saw where the entrance to the bookkeepers' lair was," I said. "Thaden killed a guy and walked away, and a woman visited twice. I know she was looking for the books, so I think it's safe to assume Thaden was, too."

Everyone stared at me.

"Am I the only one who saw this?" My shoulders crept toward my ears as a need to hide from their gazes tightened in my still-throbbing stomach.

"You were the only one who was dying," Eric said. "The phantasms may have recognized you as one on the brink of joining their ranks, balancing on the bridge that joins our world and theirs."

"That's not good," I said.

"You went down, and then you got really rigid and started twitching." Elizabeth's fingers dug into my recently stabbed side. "I didn't know if you were having a seizure or being tortured by something I couldn't see."

"I'm sorry." I kissed her temple, pretending her gripping me as she remembered being terrified of losing me didn't feel like she was shoving a hot poker into my flesh. "I didn't mean to scare you."

"Don't apologize." Elizabeth thankfully eased her grip as she started walking down the hill, guiding me along with her. "It's not you who needs to be sorry. It's Iliana the psycho witch who decided using phantasms to attack people was a good idea. She's the one who's going to be sorry."

"If she's that determined to murder wizards who show up at the monastery, she must have a good reason." My sentence was punctuated with odd grunts as my organs rearranged themselves back into their pre-stabbing positions. "What better reason could there be than the books everybody's been going into the woods to try and find?"

"Great," Elizabeth said, "then I don't even have to feel guilty for wanting to track her down tonight. Eric, can you get ahold of Raven from here?"

"I'm sure I can," Eric said.

"Have her find us a witch named Iliana," Elizabeth said. "Hell, have her find every witch who's ever been named Iliana. Bryant's dad can pay her for her work."

"Elizabeth," Devon began.

"Do not tell me to calm down, Devon Rhodes." Elizabeth's voice had a dark quality to it that was both terrifying, because she sounded like she would be willing to burn Iliana alive, and exhilarating, as she would be doing the burning on my behalf.

"Okay, no calming down." Devon held up both hands. "Just remember to bury your rage enough that you won't be caught unawares if Iliana comes to find us first. Also, maybe don't let Cindy see the murdery vibe, either."

Elizabeth took a deep breath. "I watched my boyfriend bleeding out on the ground, and there was nothing I could do about it." Her hands started to shake. "I've gotten used to seeing horrible things and not being able to do much to defend myself from them. But what Iliana set those phantasms up to do to us, what they've done to other people...she's a murderer. And we're going to make her pay."

"Indeed, we are," Eric said.

"Good." Elizabeth started down the hill again.

It took me a while to figure out what words I wanted to say, and then a little bit longer to be brave enough to say them.

"I love you," I whispered, counting on Devon and Eric to at least pretend they couldn't hear me. "And I'm sorry for all the terrifying things you have to see."

"It didn't even help." Tears glistened in Elizabeth's eyes. "I knew we were walking into shadows, and it didn't help anything. I should have been the one to get stabbed. Seeing is the only thing I'm good for."

Fear that I somehow hadn't felt when I'd been stabbed shot through my whole body. "That's not even a little true."

"Yes, it is," Elizabeth said. "Otherwise, I wouldn't have felt so helpless."

I tried to think of comforting words to say as we made our way into town.

No, not comforting, that wasn't what I wanted to be. I wanted to be honest about the real value she held, make sure she understood that her bravery, and intelligence, and relentless determination had saved us all more than once. But I couldn't think of a way to say it that wouldn't risk sounding patronizing.

"You should clean your clothing." Eric stopped in front of the door to our hotel.

"*Nudla.*" With a *hiss* and a *pop*, the blood and dirt disappeared from my clothes. "*Nudla.*" I cleaned what I could only assume was my blood off Elizabeth's sweater.

"We should rest," Eric said. "I'll send a message to Raven.

Hopefully, she'll have some information for us by the time we wake up. Then we can be off to our next destination."

"Iliana is supposed to be on her way here," Devon said.

"All the more reason to move quickly," Eric said. "I would very much prefer to search Iliana's life for any sign of her knowing the whereabouts of the books before she gets home from her mission to murder us."

"Great idea." I nodded. "First, we sleep."

We all entered the lobby and headed toward the polished wooden staircase that led up to our rooms.

Elizabeth kept her arm around my waist as we reached my door, and a little bit of joy flitted circles in my chest as I wondered if she'd insist on coming into my room so she could sleep in my arms and feel that I was safe and breathing.

"A moment, Bryant." Eric stopped right beside my door.

The flitting stopped.

"Get some rest." Elizabeth brushed her lips against my cheek and headed toward her room at the other end of the hall.

Eric didn't speak until Elizabeth had closed her door. "I know what you did."

I froze as my mind raced back through the woods to the monastery, back to town, and into a bathroom where I'd sent a potentially catastrophic email.

Nikki.

My newly healed stomach clenched itself into a super painful prune of fear.

"The blow that nearly killed you was meant for me," Eric said.

My stomach expanded out of its fear-prune state only to start shaking around my gut in weird, nervous embarrassment. "I mean, the thing was swinging for your neck. I had to do something."

"No Bryant, you didn't. In fact, many wouldn't have. You

could have stayed in the safety you'd created for yourself and hoped I would see the sword in time to defend myself. But you didn't. You put your life at risk specifically to protect mine." Eric held my gaze for a long moment. "I am very grateful."

"Oh." Heat burned my cheeks. "It's no problem. It's not like you haven't done the same for me."

"But I am the teacher. I hold a burden of care when it comes to the life of my apprentice. You have no such obligation."

"Yeah, I do." I patted Eric on the arm. "It's called having friends. *Cliaxo.*" I ducked into my room before I could say anything that would make my embarrassment complete enough for my face to actually catch fire.

I dug my fists into my eyes for a few seconds, letting the spots dancing in my vision block out the images the forest had shown me.

There was something about it that didn't make sense, but I couldn't quite figure out what bit of the puzzle I'd put in the wrong place.

I tried to sort through it as I changed out of my clothes. My shirt and sweater both had holes slashed through them. I thought about searching the phone for a mending spell, but honestly I didn't want to wear either of them ever again. I wadded up my stabbing attire and shoved it into the trashcan.

I didn't check my phone for a message from Nikki. I didn't even shower. I just climbed into bed and lay staring at the wall, trying to put the pieces into an order that made sense.

17

F act one: The books used to be in the Library in Manhattan.

Fact two: The books were stolen from the Library a long time ago.

Fact three: There used to be men who lived in the woods in Meteora. They had books, but NOT the books from the Ladies' Library.

Fact four: Zoe now has the bookkeepers' texts in her home/library in Athens—except for a few the bookkeepers kept for themselves then gave to the monk who gave them to Iliana, the woman who made the forest phantasms all evil and murdery.

Fact five: Thaden came to Meteora—probably looking for the books from Manhattan once he found out they'd been stolen.

Fact six: Phantasm vision lady wanted the books from Manhattan but they were not in the woods.

Fact seven: I'm still massively confused.

I stared at the notes I'd written on my napkin while Elizabeth and Devon tried to run interference with the now very angry Cindy while Eric paced on the street outside the dining room window, talking on his phone to who I really hoped was Raven.

Fact eight: Vision lady and Thaden both found some evidence that made them believe the books were in Meteora.

Conclusion: At least we're not the only people to think the books are in Greece.

Post-Conclusion Statement: None of this actually tells me where the freakin' books are.

"Isn't that right, Bryant?" Elizabeth said.

I clapped my hand over the notes on my napkin and looked up. "Yes, absolutely." I had no idea what I was agreeing to, so I kept my gaze locked on Elizabeth so I could real smile at her instead of trying to fake smile at Cindy.

"It was such an amazing time," Elizabeth said. "The history behind the monasteries is so fascinating. I don't remember the last time I felt so immersed in history."

"Yeah, it was like I was being sucked into a vision of another time." An involuntary laugh rumbled in my throat as I appreciated my own grim joke.

"Well, I'm happy to drive you wherever it is you want to go today," Cindy said. "And since your phone seemed to have such problems yesterday, I'll make sure I stay nearby so you can get a ride back whenever you're ready. After all, your father is paying me to make sure you get where you need to go, and to translate for you. I can't translate if I can't find you."

A little, tiny pebble of guilt sank in my stomach. Cindy seemed nice enough, and I couldn't blame her for being miffed that the rich guy's teenage son was making it impossible for her to do her job.

At the same time, it's not like I was running away with my friends to drink Raki. I was on a mission, and the knowledge of generations of wizards hung in the balance.

"I'm not used to having access to a car," I said in a way I

hoped sounded self-deprecating instead of condescending and ungrateful. "Back home, I take the train or walk most places. Sometimes, I take a cab if I need one. But a driver? I've only ever had one pick me up when Dad wanted to send me somewhere specific."

Cindy's shoulders relaxed a little. "Well, since there's no public transportation to run you where you want to go, and you can't read the signs to try and find your own way, how about you let me do what I was hired for? I promise, you'll learn a lot more if you aren't spending half your time wandering around lost."

I wasn't sure I completely agreed with the sentiment, but I gave her a nod anyway. "My legs are too tired to do much climbing today anyway."

"So you want to go back up to the monasteries?" Cindy asked.

"No!" Elizabeth, Devon, and I all said at once in a way no one could deny was completely suspicious.

"Bryant's monasteried out," Devon said.

"Too much iconography for me," I said.

"Then where to next?" Cindy sipped her coffee. "Do you need any help with your photoshop project for school?"

I glanced out the window. Eric was still pacing on the street.

"Eric's working on it." Devon swept in and saved me. "He's talking to some of his contacts about where our next stop should be."

"Great." Cindy sounded like she did not at all think the situation was great. "A spontaneous European trip. What a thrill."

I slid my written-on napkin off the table as we all went back to awkwardly eating our breakfast.

I set my napkin on my leg and scrunched in one more line of writing.

Fact nine: Zoe's dad became the librarian for Greece. If the bookkeepers had ever known where the stolen books were they would have told him. He wouldn't have gone to Manhattan, and he wouldn't have died.

I crossed out my old conclusion and wrote in:

New Conclusion: Whoever sent the package from Meteora left us a breadcrumb trail leading to stabby near-death and failure.

I shoved the napkin into my pocket.

I almost died because we were tricked into coming here.

My breakfast turned to lead in my stomach as I remembered the searing pain of almost dying less than twelve hours before.

"You okay?" Elizabeth squeezed my hand.

"Yeah. Just tired." I threaded my fingers through hers, needing to have something to hold on to so I wouldn't start screaming at the top of my lungs. "I might sleep on the ride to wherever we go next."

Devon cleared his throat and nodded toward the door as Eric strode into the dining room like he was first in line for a Black Friday sale.

"We're going to Crete," Eric said. "Get your bags. We can book a ferry on the drive south."

"Okay." I stood and headed for my room before Cindy could argue.

———

Normally, in regular life and with magic stuff, I try to pull my weight. But since I had been stabbed and nearly bled to death the night before, I didn't feel too bad about falling asleep in the car and not waking up until we were all the way back in Athens.

I probably could have slept even longer if Eric and Cindy hadn't been grumbling at each other in the front of the car.

"We don't need to be on a tight timeline."

I think it was the unfamiliar snappishness in Cindy's voice that dragged me out of sleep.

"We can contact Mr. Adams, ask him if he prefers we fly," Cindy said.

"The flight would get us in later than the ferry," Eric said. "We're taking the boat."

"Why are you in such a hurry?" Cindy asked. "We can get an early flight out tomorrow."

I shifted to sit up, realized I'd been leaning on Elizabeth's shoulder, saw the drool-covered napkin she'd draped over her shoulder, then died a little inside as embarrassment surged through me.

"Perhaps I've misunderstood," Eric said. "I was under the impression your job was simply to be the driver and translator. Has something in this arrangement changed?"

"I can't be the driver if you all keep running away so I can't find you," Cindy said. "I also can't be the translator if you hide from me."

"No one's hiding," I said.

Elizabeth gripped my leg, apparently not so disgusted by my drool she never wanted to touch me again.

"Exactly," Eric said. "We are following Bryant's academic interests."

"Bryant," Cindy said, "exactly what academic interest has us racing to a ferry right now?"

"As I've said—" Eric began.

"I asked Bryant." Cindy turned off the highway and onto a road with a sign that seemed to imply we were heading toward the water. "So, Bryant, what about Crete sparks your interest?"

"I..." My heart started racing. I looked to Elizabeth, but she just stared at me wide-eyed and desperate. "Well it's really about"—I glanced toward Devon, but he was already shaking his head in defeat—"I've heard the food's good."

"That's it." Cindy pulled into a curbside parking spot, squeezing between two cars with a slickness I don't think even a Manhattan cabbie could have managed. "I was sent here by Mr. Adams, who happens to be my boss, as in the one who makes sure I have health insurance, to be sure that his son was moved safely from place to place while visiting a foreign country. Now, I don't care if Bryant is interested in art, mythology, foodie culture, or rescuing stray cats, but I did not graduate from an Ivy League school to be duped by this lame ass shit. So, what the hell are you all planning, because this is clearly something Mr. Adams has not sanctioned!"

"*Fransencio*," Eric said.

Cindy's head dipped forward, and she gave a weird little giggle.

"What did you just do?" My hand shook as I reached forward to touch Cindy's shoulder.

"Get your bags. We can walk from here." Eric opened his door and stepped out of the car like everything was normal.

Devon climbed out his side of the car and onto the sidewalk.

I froze for a second, torn between trying to shake Cindy out of her weird spell-induced stupor and running before her mind cleared and she, very justifiably, flipped out at us. The sound of the trunk slamming shut was enough to send me scrambling after Devon. "Eric, what did you just do?"

Eric handed me my backpack and rolly bag.

"Eric," I said, even as I put on my backpack like I was obviously going to follow him whether or not he answered my very important question.

"What did you do?" Elizabeth stood on the street-side of the car, arms crossed as she glared daggers at Eric.

"She'll be fine in a few hours," Eric said. "She may have a headache, but it will buy us time to get to the ferry without interference. I think we can all agree carting Cindy along has been a failed experiment."

"Is she going to remember where we're going?" Elizabeth asked.

"Yes." Eric set Elizabeth's bags in front of her. "Wiping her memory is beyond my skill."

"Then we'd better hope she doesn't come after us." Elizabeth put on her backpack.

"Wait. We're not actually leaving her here," I said as the others all started walking toward the ferry sign.

"That's exactly what we're doing," Eric said. "Now hurry, or we'll miss the boat."

The three of them all kept walking down the sidewalk.

"But we can't do that." I didn't move. I couldn't get my feet to follow them.

"We can, and we are." Eric stopped and turned to face me.

"No," I said. "We can't just leave a lady passed out in a car in a foreign country."

"*Oxailoc*," Eric said.

The locks on the car doors *thumped* closed.

"We must be on our way," Eric said.

"And if a cop comes to see why she's sitting in a car?" I asked. "Or when she wakes up and has to call my dad to tell him she lost us? I have the credit card, not her. What's she supposed to do?"

"That isn't our problem," Eric said.

"But it should be!"

I hadn't even noticed the lady walking past with her kids until she grabbed both of them by the backs of their coats to hurry them away from me.

"She hasn't done anything wrong." I dragged my bag closer to Eric so I wouldn't scare any more small children. "We can't just leave her here. It's wrong."

"Her inconvenience is nothing compared to the suffering the people of Beville have endured," Eric said. "She will have a bad afternoon. We have suffered for years."

"But she has nothing to do with it!" I whisper-shouted. "She hasn't hurt anybody, or sold anybody, or kidnapped anybody. She hasn't even been mean. The only thing Cindy's guilty of is trying to do the job my dad hired her for."

"That job interferes with our aim," Eric said.

"And?"

"Interference is intolerable. We must find the books. I will not allow a human to stand in our way." Eric turned and headed down the street like he'd made a judgment call and the conversation ended there.

"You don't get to do that." I cut around and planted myself in front of him, chin high, shockingly little panic flying through my chest.

I looked between Devon and Elizabeth, waiting for one of them to yell at him for daring to place humans below the books. But they both just stared silently at Eric. Their hurt made everything worse.

"You don't get to trash people's lives because of what you've decided is important." My anger brought heat to my face. "Cindy is innocent. And if you hurt her, you become the bad guy."

"My moral status matters little. There is nothing more important than protecting the books," Eric said. "We have to find them. We have to return the knowledge of ages to its rightful place. Nothing can be allowed to stand in our way."

I let out a breath, and it was like a part of me flew out of my body and something heavier, more mature, took its place. "I bet Thaden said the same thing. And the Ladies. I think it would be impossible to count how many people started off wanting to help and ended up ruining everything because they didn't think about what they were sacrificing to win. You don't get to hurt innocent people. We aren't the villains. I won't let you make us the villains."

"Then stay," Eric said. "Stand beside the car and wait for her mind to clear. And when we lose our chance at rescuing the books, be comforted that you did the right thing."

He stepped around me and strode down the street like he was going to leave without us.

"Eric, stop," I shouted.

I was a little surprised when he actually stopped.

"I'll call my dad," I said. "I'll beg for some favors and make sure Cindy is safe. But you can't keep doing this. You can't keep putting people in danger for what you think is right. Because someday, I won't be able to agree with you. And once you go that far. You might as well be Thaden."

Eric flinched like I'd actually attacked him.

"If you fall that far, none of us will be able to follow you."

Eric stayed frozen for another moment before walking away, following the picture signs that herded us toward the ferry.

I looked back at the car and Cindy staring out the window like a toddler watching a Disney movie before following Eric.

"Bryant." Elizabeth tried to take my hand, but I just kept walking.

"Bry." Devon gripped my shoulder, keeping pace as I followed Eric.

"I will not serve the next Thaden." Heat burned my eyes as I spoke. "I'm not going to sacrifice innocent people for what we've decided is right. If we can't build a system that helps people instead of tossing them out of our way and hoping they survive, I want nothing to do with magic."

"You're right." Elizabeth caught up to me and slipped her hand into mine. "If we're no better than the Ladies, then everything we've done will have been for nothing."

"I don't think Eric sees it that way." My throat was so tight, my words came out raspy.

"Then we'll make him see it that way," Devon said. "If we're supposed to be the good guys, that means it's our job to save people. It means we don't abandon our friends when they get lost."

"What are we supposed to do?" I asked.

"Try and reason with him," Elizabeth said. "Convince him he's better than Thaden could ever have been. If that doesn't work, we lock him up until Lola can figure out how to knock some sense into him."

18

The ferry wasn't too crowded. Elizabeth had booked us seats inside, but I managed to find a quiet place on the deck where I could call my dad. You know, to try and explain why we had ditched Cindy in her car and ask if he could please pull some strings to make sure she stayed safe.

I contemplated being a complete coward and just texting, but it was super early New York time and I didn't want to risk Dad missing my message because he was asleep. Cindy deserved better than that.

"You can do this." I shook out my shoulders like I was about to walk into a fight. "You can do this."

I punched the button to video chat with my dad. I don't really know why, but being able to see his face while I told him how badly things had gone somehow seemed easier.

My phone made a series of weird dinging noises before Dad answered.

"Bryant?" His hair was all messy, and his eyes were only half-open. "Bryant, whass wrong?"

"Nothing," I said. "I mean nothing that bad."

The light shifted as Dad sat up and got out of bed. "Just tell me what's going on."

"Cindy got suspicious about the whole"—I glanced around the deck to make sure there was no one nearby—"magic thing. She started asking too many questions, so we had to leave her behind."

"Leave her behind?" Dad's eyes shifted from sleepy to alert, and he started pacing in front of a pale-painted wall. "What do you mean *leave her behind*?"

"She's super loopy and sitting in the rental car near the docks in Athens. It's not her fault, but you may want to send someone to check on her."

"Come home right now." The path of Dad's pacing expanded. "This is a failed experiment. If you need to study in Greece, it will have to wait until your mother or I can accompany you."

"But Dad—"

He paced past a grandfather clock, and my brain screeched to a stop.

"Dad, why are you in Mom's apartment?" My whole body went sort of numb.

Dad froze. His eyes got wide for a split second before his face went suspiciously calm. "Nonsense. I'm at home, Bryant. I'll book you a ticket—"

"You're sleeping at Mom's!" I shouted loudly enough for one of the ship dudes to peek around the giant tube-ish things on the deck to glare at me. "What the hell, Dad?"

"Bryant, I am not going to allow you to pull me off topic. You, Devon, and Elizabeth are getting on the next flight home."

"I can't come home until our work is done." I held the phone close to my mouth and shouted. "Hope you're getting a good night's sleep, Mom!" into the microphone before hanging up.

I stared at my phone, considering throwing it into the water. Anger, a weird ickyness, and utter disappointment swept through me so quickly, I was too exhausted to throw the phone by the time it started ringing as Mom called me.

I turned my phone off and shoved it into my pocket.

I didn't have time to delve into the possible long-term ramifications of my parents having a slumber party while I was out of the country. I mean, I couldn't deny the obvious. As soon as things went bad between them again, my life would become a nightmare of them not speaking to each other for years, all while sending aggressive messages through their lawyers and passive aggressive messages through me.

"I'm almost eighteen." I dug my knuckles into my eyes. "Once I get to eighteen, it won't be my problem anymore. Except for every holiday and major life event. Oh, this is going to end badly."

With a giant blast from its horn, the boat pushed away from the dock, and we officially left Chaperone Cindy behind.

"You don't get to brood, Bryant." I squared my shoulders and headed toward the cabin. "You're saving the magical world. Teenager-from-a-broken-home brooding will have to wait."

The door to the cabin was heavy enough I had to ram my shoulder against the metal to swing it open, which was harder than it looked since I had to step over a six-inch lip on the ground while doing the pushing, which was way more than my overwhelmed brain could handle and resulted in my stumbling into the cabin while the crewmen stared at me like I was probably drunk.

Giving a little wave and an apologetic smile, I made my way around the rows of seats to the booth Elizabeth had booked for us. There was enough seating for six, which only made poor Chaperone Cindy's absence more noticeable.

"How did it go?" Elizabeth asked.

I opened my mouth to tell them exactly what had happened, decided I didn't have the energy to deal with it, and said, "Dad wants us on the next plane home. I said no. I don't know if my credit card will still be working by the time we get to Crete."

"We'll find a way around it," Eric said. "We could try and persuade Raven to help us keep your card open."

"Great." I sank down into the spot next to Elizabeth. "I can't wait to see what Dad's legal team does with that."

"We can worry about money later," Elizabeth said. "What did Raven tell you about Iliana? Why are we going to Crete?"

I perked up, and thoughts of how badly my parents were yelling at each other over whose fault it was that I'd found out about their sleepover, or whether they'd skipped the blame game to jump straight on to buying tickets to Greece so they could haul me home, slipped away.

"Iliana Dorinda Drakos has a registered address in Crete, and her web traffic seems to confirm that location," Eric said.

"And?" I leaned across the half-circle table to get closer to him.

"She frequently travels to the mainland of Greece," Eric said. "Though once she's on land, Raven cannot track where she goes."

"That's it?" Devon said. "That's all we know?"

"It's a great deal more than we knew last night." Eric pulled out his phone and opened an email before passing it to Devon. "We have an address. We'll start our search there."

"She doesn't look like the *murder you in the woods* type." Devon passed the phone to me.

I looked down at the picture that filled the screen. My brain did a little skip step, like it wanted to be sure that, after all the trauma of the last twenty-four hours, I was actually processing what I was seeing properly. It was the girl from the woods, but older. Closer to my mom's age than mine.

"This is Iliana?" I tipped my head and squinted at the screen, making triply sure I was right.

"It is," Eric said. "There were three other Ilianas who pinged as possibilities in Greece, but one was too young, one too old to be traveling, and one seems to have emigrated to England a few years ago."

"She was in the woods," I said. "She's the girl who was looking for books, *the* books. She still hadn't found them by the time the last of the bookkeepers died."

"That doesn't mean she hasn't found them since," Elizabeth said.

"No." Devon stared at his fists on the table. "But if she hadn't found the books before she forced the phantasms to fight for her, what sort of magic is she capable of with basically unlimited knowledge backing her?"

"No way to know until we find her." Elizabeth leaned on my shoulder.

I'd forgotten I'd been the only one to sleep on the road trip. I wrapped my arm around her, holding her close, ready to keep her steady if she nodded off.

"She might not have even found the books." Elizabeth nestled closer to me.

"She did." Something in my chest clicked into place as I said the words. Like there was a key of certainty fate had been waiting for me to find. "The magical world is too small. For her to have been looking for the books. For her to have set a trap in Meteora where the books were mailed from. No one was even supposed to know the books had been stolen. Ginger William the black-market book dealer couldn't have stumbled onto a completely unrelated woman in Greece who just so happened to like to mail packages from a place Iliana was determined to protect. It would take too many coincidences."

"I agree," Eric said. "Each person who knows about the books, that they're missing, who stole them, where they are, is another gap in defending the secret. If there were that many gaps, I would have heard whispers of a trove of hidden books long before we took the Library from the Ladies."

"At least we have a who." I rubbed my free hand across my forehead. "Now we just have to figure out the where."

Somehow, that didn't make things any less daunting.

I kept one arm around Elizabeth as she drifted to sleep on my shoulder, trying not to wonder how easily Raven could dig into my life as I read through all the information on Iliana.

She was only thirty-five.

She'd been born in Greece, but lived in Canada for a while.

There were pictures of her in New York City. From the clothes, it looked like she'd been there about ten years ago.

Then she went back to Greece and had been living on Crete ever since.

No job listed, but the house in her name was nice enough she'd either inherited it or had money coming in through a nefarious trade like selling priceless books on the black market.

There were no papers filed saying she had married or had children.

It was more information than we'd ever had on Thaden, the Ladies, or Kendrick, but it still didn't seem like enough.

I scrunched my eyes closed and went back to the top of the document from Raven.

Why did Iliana go to New York City? Why did she leave? How did she find out the books were missing, and what led her to Meteora?

I formed the list of questions in my mind, but a little voice in the back of my head screamed it was all useless. Whether we found Iliana or she found us first, there would be no time to ask questions about the why of it all. She'd already tried to murder us in absentia. She would try to kill us again.

And we would fight her.

Hopefully, we would win, which would mean she'd probably be dead. And I would never know the truth of why a girl from Greece had grown up to create an evil enchanted forest.

Nikki,

    Let's say we're taking the laws we've written out and presenting them to the body of people we're intending to govern. How does that work? Do we just show up and say, "Here are some new laws. I have six council positions available. Who do you want to vote in?"

    Bryant

I read the message through four times. Each email had been getting harder and harder to write. Not because I didn't have questions, but because phrasing them in a way that wouldn't make Nikki develop a Cindy-like suspicion became more difficult as we got down to the tiny details.

I added, *Some of the people involved like to argue over petty things, and I want to make sure they don't have a reason to hold the action up.*

"It's the best I could grab."

I tapped *send* and shoved my phone into my pocket as Devon handed me a wrap. I was still trying to avoid reading the dozen or so messages from my parents where neither of them mentioned what had happened but both seemed to be very concerned with how I was doing and when I'd have time to talk.

"Thanks." I'd been left to stand with our suitcases while Eric tried to arrange transport, which I hoped made him regret ditching Cindy, Devon went to find food, and Elizabeth went to buy a guidebook, which I know sounds weird but was actually really important.

"Is it lazy if I really hope the books are near a port?" Devon said. "Or at least an airport?"

"I'm sure they are. They'd have to be. How else could you move thousands of books?"

I ate my wrap, watching the other people on the dock being herded into cabs. Some of them were tired, others excited, a few super angry about something. But I was willing to bet none of them were in the process of overthrowing an evil regime and forming a new government.

My phone dinged with a new email from Nikki.

Hi Bryant,

The player in me says you're the DM, you make the rules.

But if you want to go for realism and practicality, it would depend on how you'd taken control of the area. If you've won a battle, then as the conqueror, you have seized the right to lay out a new code of law. If you're trying to peacefully change things, you would have to put your constitution out there and let the people vote.

In my experience, taking the area by force would move things along more quickly.

Nikki

A squirm of existential dread wriggled in my stomach, making me question if eating a wrap was actually a good idea.

"Are you going to tell me?" Devon asked.

"Tell you?" My voice wobbled.

"I'm your best friend, Bryant. Elizabeth may be the girl-friend. Eric may be the wizard extraordinaire. But I'm the guy who's known you since forever. So what's going on?"

"Aside from being stabbed and ditching Cindy?" I took a bite of my wrap, like chewing could somehow save me.

Devon frowned at me in a disappointed parent kind of way.

"What?" I asked with my mouth full.

"You managed to lie to airport security. That doesn't mean you can lie to me."

"I mean"—I took a moment to actually swallow my food—"Dad had a sleepover with Mom."

"What?" Devon laughed.

"And I've been talking to—"

"I've found us a car." Eric strode up to us. "It's a long ride, but I've promised to tip well."

"We can try my card." I shrugged.

"I found a guidebook." Elizabeth appeared next to me.

"Perfect timing." Eric bowed us toward our new ride.

We climbed into the black car, and the driver, who looked weirdly similar to my favorite cabbie in Manhattan, pre-charged my card, which thankfully went through, which probably had a lot to do with the fact that my parents were worried I was trau-matized by their weirdness, which I totally was, but that had nothing to do with why I was still battling the existential dread monster as we pulled away from the docks and onto the road. The *oh no, I may have waaay overestimated my ability to deal with helping the world instead of just leaving chaos in my wake* feeling was still very much present and interfering with my ability to eat my wrap.

But I couldn't say anything because we had a driver, who definitely spoke enough English to understand words like *magic*, *revolution*, and *lifetime of therapy bills*.

So I spent more time trapped in freakin' transit, not really able to do anything but enjoy the scent of Elizabeth's hair slowly filling the car while being amazed that an island could be so damn big.

———

I f Athens was something out of another world, Chania was something out of a romance novel, with a fancy harbor, which looked weirdly similar to pictures I'd seen of Venice, surrounded by lights and shops even though it wasn't the height of tourist season. There were musicians playing outside restaurants, and men selling flowers. There were restaurant hawkers trying to lure us in, and cats roaming everywhere.

The driver dropped us off at our hotel so we could leave our bags before finding the bad guy, which was not a practicality I had ever had to consider in Manhattan. Then we walked through the harbor district to get to Evil Iliana's house. And ginger librarian William's story about meeting a woman in Greece, having a nice meal with her, and then having her steal the light and sound from the night almost made sense. You've already slipped into a Rom Com setup—might as well add magic. That's just good marketing.

Elizabeth held my hand tight as we weaved away from the harbor and onto less well-lit streets where tiny little restaurants hid between houses.

A very daring part of me wanted to whisk her into the shadows and kiss her until we both forgot about magic, books, and the fate of wizard kind.

But taking time off to make out with Elizabeth while violin music drifted through the windows of a tiny restaurant would have meant risking Iliana murdering us while Elizabeth and I were swirling in a land of bliss and love.

I made a mental note to definitely bring Elizabeth back someday, when our lives weren't in danger, and didn't argue as we left all traces of restaurants and romance behind.

After my legs had gotten tired, but before I'd worked up the nerve to ask Eric if he was lost, he gestured to a bright white house at the top of a hill.

The place was beautiful in a way that didn't seem to fit the old city vibe we'd just left behind.

The walls had been smoothed with concrete and painted pale white. There were two balconies set with chairs so Evil Iliana could have her fiendish friends over to stare at the water far below. A waist-high concrete wall topped with a wrought iron fence, like Iliana had been preparing for the zombie apocalypse, surrounded the grounds, even protecting what would have been a nice garden in the summer and a pool large enough to swim laps in.

"Selling books that should belong to other people may be an awful thing to do," Devon said, "but it looks like a bangin' way to make a living."

I glanced down as a faint *mew* sounded by my ankles.

A little tabby cat blinked up at me.

"Hey, kitty." I looked back to the house. There weren't any lights on inside. There wasn't a car in the driveway either. "Do you think she's already up north trying to kill us?"

"We can hope," Devon said.

"Something doesn't seem right," Elizabeth said.

"Like *seer* doesn't seem right or like *this is way too convenient* doesn't seem right?" I slipped my magical phone out of my pocket.

"Both." Elizabeth walked toward the gate that led to the driveway.

Meow! A new, gray cat stepped on my foot as though wanting to be really sure I knew he was there.

"Sorry, I don't have anything for you." I gave the cat an apologetic shrug before following Elizabeth.

"Do you see any spells?" Eric tented his fingers under his chin. "Any hint of shadows or bone magic?"

"There's something around the front door." Elizabeth tipped her head as she stared into the shadows, letting her curls tumble across her shoulders in a way that made me forget to breathe until a *yowl* yanked me back into the brutal reality of impending larceny.

I looked down to find that the tabby and gray cat had been joined by a massive ginger. "Hey fellas. You're all so pretty."

"There's going to be more than a simple incantation to protect the door," Eric said. "You don't enchant a forest to snare those who might seek information you're protecting only to leave your home open to attack."

"So what's the plan?" Devon gripped his foam/sticky potion blaster in one hand and the tube/hilt of his glowing sword in the other.

"I've no idea." Eric furrowed his brow.

"Well, that's not comforting," I said.

A tiny *mew* sounded by my feet. I looked down to find two little kittens had joined the three other cats.

"So cute," I cooed like a goober, trying to decide if risking ringworm was worth snuggling the tiny calico kitten as she rolled onto her back and showed me her stomach.

"I've told you before," Eric said. "It's never my goal to comfort you. My aim is always to keep you alive."

"Consider me not comforted," I said.

"I think it would be best if Elizabeth and I try to approach the house first." Eric paced in front of the gate. "Once we are sure of the house's safety, the two of you can join us as we search for more information about the books."

"What?" Devon said at the same moment I said, "No way in Hell."

Eric held up both hands to silence us. "As we are traveling into unknown magic, it makes the most sense to leave part of our party on the outside in case rescue becomes necessary. That requires Bryant and me to move separately. Since we will be stepping into spells that could quite possibly involve bone magic"—a shock of dread zapped up my spine—"having Elizabeth with me will ensure our best chance for success."

"She is not going in there without me," I said.

"I believe Elizabeth has autonomy and can go wherever she chooses," Eric said.

"Wait a minute, that's not what—"

"I should go in with Eric." Elizabeth laid her hands on my chest. "He's right. This is how I'm supposed to be helpful, and I'll only be like a hundred feet away."

"But—"

"I'll be fine." Elizabeth kissed my cheek. "Someone has to save Eric from Eric."

"Just be careful." I pressed my lips to her forehead. "If anything happened to you, I think I'd literally lose the ability to breathe."

"You'll catch up to us in a minute." Elizabeth gave me a smile that made the air rush out of my lungs like they were trying to prove that she literally did control my body's ability to consume oxygen.

"What about me?" Devon said. "Should I just chill out here with the cats until you get back?"

"Bryant is staying out here to provide assistance should Elizabeth and I encounter trouble," Eric said.

"And that leaves me...?" Devon glared at Eric.

"Staying with Bryant in case he becomes the one who needs saving," Eric said. "We can't leave him alone."

I was about to snap at Eric for being rude, but Devon stopped glaring at Eric and looked at me.

"Fair." Devon shrugged.

"I..." I deflated a little. "Okay."

"Then in we go." Eric stepped closer to the gate, raising his hands as though testing the air for tension. "Stand back, if you would."

Devon grabbed me by the scruff of my sweater and pulled me away.

I shuffled my feet, making sure I wasn't stepping on the cats, but still a chorus of angry *meows* surrounded me.

"Sorry, sorry." I looked down at my feet to make sure I hadn't hurt any of the five cats only to find three extra cats I'd never seen before. "Why are there so many of you?"

A tiny little black cat gave the sweetest *mew* in response.

"We've got to help these cats," I said. "They look so sad and lonely."

I looked away from the cats as Eric began his spell.

"*Numbare fungilo lui confello. Cliaxo entrunto krifundia!*"

He finished speaking, and an oddness flew through the air. Almost like a ringing I couldn't quite hear. Or a breeze too soft for my skin to feel through my clothes.

"Are you supposed to know that spell?" Devon whispered to me as the gate swung silently open.

"I hope not," I murmured.

Eric swept his hands through the air again before beckoning Elizabeth to follow him.

She gave me a little wave and a smile before stepping through the gate.

"Should we hold the gate open?" Devon whispered.

"I don't think so," I said.

Before I had a second to consider why I didn't think we should keep the gate from closing behind Eric and Elizabeth since I had no freakin' clue how to do the spell he'd used to open the gate, the metal swung shut and closed with *clang*.

Elizabeth flinched, so I knew the sound had carried to the inside of the compound as well. But Eric didn't seem bothered as he stalked slowly toward Evil Iliana's house.

Merwrrow one of the cats at my feet said.

I looked down to find the eight cats had turned into something closer to fifteen cats.

One of the kittens batted at my shoelace.

"If I'm not disowned when we finally get home, do you think I could convince my dad to save the cats here?" I looked back toward the house as Elizabeth took Eric's arm, leading him around one of the paving stones in the walkway.

"Do you mean, like, all the cats?" Devon asked. "Because that might be a stretch even for your dad. I mean, look at them."

I glanced away from Elizabeth to find that closer to twenty cats now surrounded Devon and me.

"Do they not have animal control in Greece?" I asked. "Or a trap and spay program?"

"I don't know the local laws," Devon said. "Look it up after we rescue the priceless books."

"Right." I focused my attention back on the house where Eric and Elizabeth had gone, not to the front door, but to a window on the far side of the entrance. I chewed my lips as Elizabeth slid the window open. "Do you think the owner of the neighborhood cat rescue died and these guys have come to us for help?"

Mew. The tiny little sound came from near my feet as an itty-bitty kitten bumped her head against my ankle.

"I have no idea, dude." Devon took a step closer to the gate.

"But we've got to do something for the cats. I mean, look at them. They need us. They're coming to me for help."

"You probably still smell like dinner."

"I'll find them something to eat once we—"

I never finished my thought.

I was too distracted by the now obvious fact that what the cats wanted to eat was us.

20

It was the tone of the next *mew* that gave me my first warning. What had been an adorable sound that made my insides gooey and my paternal instincts kick in had suddenly become lower and gruffer.

I tore my gaze away from Eric closing the front window of Evil Iliana's house, and looked down to see what big kitty had made such a sound, expecting to find a chonker of a tabby glaring up at me.

I was sort of right.

There was a tabby glaring up at me, but he was not an adorable chonker. He was the size of a Labrador and drawing back his lips to show me his oversized teeth.

"Devon." I gripped his sleeve.

"They're almost in," Devon said.

The other cats started to grow, like they were weird monsters evolving in a video game. Their coats shimmered as their muscles bulged and their bones grew.

"Devon." I shook his arm.

"We can save the cats later," Devon said.

"Devon!" I shouted just as the monster who had been an itty-bitty kitten less than a minute before hissed and launched himself at my side.

"Shit!"

I guess Devon had finally noticed that we'd been surrounded by an über clowder. He grabbed my shoulder, pulling me back as the cat sank its claws into my hip.

"*Primurgo!*" I screamed the spell, but it didn't do anything, probably because I was more focused on the searing pain in my hip than on enunciating the spell.

Another of the feline-ish monsters reared back to pounce on me.

Devon shot a sticky pellet at it.

"You can't do that to a cat!" I pressed my hand to the blood leaking out of my hip.

"It's a demon, not a house cat!"

Three of the demon cats launched themselves at us at once.

Devon stickified one, I shouted "*Stasio*" and trapped another, but the third leapt up and got me, sinking its claws into my ribs as its fangs dug into my shoulder.

"Why?" I knocked the monster off me as Devon grabbed my non-bloody arm, dragging me toward the gate.

The clowder yowled in creepy unison as he touched the metal, but the gate swung open without us having to do any sort of spell.

I watched all the monsters rock back on their haunches as though preparing to pounce, but I wasn't dumb enough to watch them surge forward, choosing instead to just assume they were going to murder me at any moment as we tore up the driveway.

The painful heat of my wounded hip made my stride uneven as we sprinted toward the house.

Devon was right ahead of me, glowing sword in one hand, sticky blaster in the other.

"*Lobula!*" I tried to block the cats/demons because, even

though they wanted to eat me, I didn't want them having to chew Devon's sticking potion out of their fur.

I heard a growl of displeasure but didn't look back to see if the cats were still following.

Devon veered toward the walkway, aiming for the window Elizabeth and Eric had crawled through.

"There's a bad stone!" I shouted a moment too late.

Devon stepped onto the stone Eric and Elizabeth had avoided.

For a split second, I foolishly thought everything was going to be okay, but then a sharp *crack* cut over the *yowls* of the demon cats.

The ground didn't rumble or shake. Chunks of it just started falling away, forming a ravine-style moat around the house.

Not thinking about the probability of our demise, I grabbed Devon around the middle and leapt across the still-growing gap. My toes barely caught the edge of the ground on the far side, but I flung our weight forward, toppling both of us onto the grass.

I lay on the ground panting for a few heartbeats.

"Thanks." Devon pushed himself to his knees, reclaiming his weapons from where they'd fallen.

First, I heard a *yowl*. Then a *hiss*. Then I sprang up just in time to see the cats from Hell pouring around the sides of my blocking spell and charging toward the gap in the ground.

"Run!"

Devon raced toward the window where Eric and Elizabeth had disappeared.

I tore after him, but too much of the ground had fallen away, leaving no path to the window.

Panic flew through my chest as I looked to the door. There was a spell on it. I knew there was a spell on it and was very confident in my inability to break through the spell before being eaten.

I looked toward the next best option, the window on our side of the front door. It was closed and I assumed locked, but the alternative was being eaten by cats.

"*Abalata!*" The black mist of my spell pooled in my palm. I threw it forward with all my might, aiming for the window.

The impact of spell on glass reverberated up my arm, but the window didn't shatter, just formed a spiderweb of cracks.

"Guard my back." Devon turned toward the window while I faced the chasm and Hellcats.

"I don't want to hurt you!" I screamed at the first demon cat that leapt across the gap. "*Conorvo.*"

The tabby shrank as it soared over the crevasse, landing as a less terrifying, Maine Coon-sized cat so it's teeth and claws sank into my thigh instead of my hip.

"Stop biting me. *Stasio!*" A barrier shimmered into being, caging in the fluffy monster.

Three more cats growled as they leapt across the ravine.

A new spell was already forming on my lips when Devon grabbed me and yanked me backward, pulling us both through the remnants of the window.

Ignoring the pain of landing on a bunch of broken glass, I fixed my gaze out the window. "*Milkawa.*"

The ground outside the window twisted and grew, forming a spire of dirt and stone that blocked the opening.

"Bryant." Devon gripped my non-maimed shoulder. "Are you okay?"

"Yeah." I wobbled my way to my feet while getting as little glass embedded in my palms as possible. "Did you get bit?"

"No." Devon looked toward the window where the monsters yowled and growled as they scratched at my dirt barrier.

"*Sinato.*"

Devon breathed through his teeth as bits of glass fell from

his skin as he healed. "You should do yourself, too." He shook out his hands and picked up his blaster and sword.

"Can't." I looked down at the blood seeping through my clothes. "I don't know if the demon cats have venom."

"Right." Devon furrowed his brow as he looked from the blood on my leg to the blood smear I'd left on the floor. "Let's get to Eric and Elizabeth."

I took the lead, crunching my way across the glass on the floor. "How did you break the window?"

"Sliced through it with my sword."

"Nice." I peered out into the hall, expecting to find Eric and Elizabeth, but the corridor was dark and empty. "We made a lot of noise."

"We didn't have a choice." Devon's sword voomed to life.

"But why didn't Eric come see why we were screaming?" A cold trickle of fear wound its way from my neck to my gut. I opened my mouth to call for them but hesitated before whispering to Devon, "I don't want to be responsible for our deaths by calling for them like we're written to be the first to die in a horror movie."

Devon let out a long breath. "Right. We'll just look for them."

The clamor of the demon clowder followed us into the dark hall.

Honestly, if the demon cats hadn't been a thing, the house would have been a great vacation rental. White tiles, an open floor plan for the kitchen and dining area. A glass banister along the steps that led upstairs.

"Do you know any tracking spells?" Devon asked once we'd made a lap of the ground floor, passing through a living room with an epically large TV and finding no trace of Eric or Elizabeth.

"Nope." I eyed the steps to the second floor. "Should you wait down here?"

"Because separating has already done us so much good in this place?"

The yowling and growling outside paused.

"Let's go." I headed toward the stairs, my years of plotting how to survive the zombie apocalypse telling me in no uncertain terms that if we had to fight the demon cats again, higher ground would totally be helpful.

Devon reached the stairs first and started climbing. I let him get three steps up, just far enough for me to follow him without feeling like I was trying to crawl up his butt, lifted my foot to step up onto the first stair, and then it happened.

The steps tipped and smoothed, and then just vanished.

"Devon!" I lunged forward, trying to grab him, but he was already falling into the darkness below. "*Frico.*" I focused on Devon's belt with all my might. My magic latched on to the leather, yanking it toward me, but the stairs shimmered back into being before I could pull him up.

I didn't even hear a *thump* of him hitting the underside of the stairs. He was just...gone.

I stood there, staring at the steps for a moment, like if I didn't move Devon would just magically reappear. Only magic doesn't work like that.

My breath seemed to rattle in my ears as I looked around the empty house.

"Okay." I spoke to myself, because that somehow made it less scary. "You're cornered in a house that's booby-trapped like an old school Christmas movie. But you still have options, Bryant Jameson Adams. You can A) Walk up the stairs and hope you get trapped wherever Devon is and hope you both end up not-hurt enough to find a way out together.

"B) Scream for Eric and hope he comes to save you. C) Try to get out of the house, past the demon cats, and hope you can find someone other than Eric who can help you, except that would make you an awful person since you'd be leaving your girlfriend, best friend, and sometimes asshole-ish mentor behind."

I couldn't handle any of those options. I couldn't leave them behind. I couldn't dive after Devon.

"I'm not supposed to be the one who's left on their own," I whispered. "I'm not the one who stages rescues. I'm a walking master of destruction. I don't save people. I just wreck things."

A weird sensation filled my chest. Not the usual panic, fear, or self-loathing. I poked the wounds on my leg and shoulder, trying to figure out if maybe I'd been poisoned, before realizing what the feeling was.

I felt confident. I felt sure of my ability to contribute to our cause in a meaningful way. Because if my time in the magical world had prepared me for anything, it was causing major structural damage.

"Hope you've got insurance, Iliana. *Aarantha*." The vortex of my spell started out as a funnel surrounding only me. I pushed my hands out to the sides, spreading my spell wider, letting it tear the paintings from the walls.

With a *screech*, the TV ripped away from its brackets, joining the debris of my twister.

I shifted closer to the steps, letting the TV smash through the glass banister of the staircase.

"I'm coming for you, Devon. *Kunga!*" My spell pummeled the side of the steps, but the white concrete didn't shatter.

"*Kunga!*" A dark crack split through the white, but it wasn't enough.

I stepped closer to the stairs, holding my fingers out in front of me like they were some sort of knife. "*Caruson*."

The heat of my spell vibrated my fingers as I sliced through the wall like I was wielding Devon's laser sword. Before I'd even finished the lopsided circle I'd been trying to slice free, the force of my vortex ripped the chunk of wall away.

"Devon!" I shouted over the rumbling of the wind and the crashes of debris smacking into the walls. "Devon!"

I forced my spell forward, leaning through the hole I'd created. "Devon."

A dark space waited under the stairs.

"*Heliono.*" A sphere of light appeared in my hand. I leaned farther into the opening in the wall. There was no cupboard under the stairs where Devon had been locked. The actual space under the steps was bare. "Devon!"

I leaned my entire torso through the hole, ready to crawl into the dark space to search for him. Just before I was going to climb into the dark, I bothered to look down and saw there wasn't actually a floor below me. Just a ten-foot drop and a clear prison where Devon had been trapped.

But Devon wasn't on his feet trying to break out. He was suspended mid-air, lying facedown, like he'd fallen into a mold of clear gelatin and been trapped.

I took a few deep breaths, trying to convince my body that panicking was not, in fact, a helpful reaction.

"I'm really sorry if this goes badly. *Abalata.*" The black of my spell pooled in my palm. I aimed right above Devon's shoulder and threw the black as hard as I could.

The goop of Devon's prison cell shuddered at the impact, but none of it broke away.

"*Exci.*" The force of the spell pummeled the ooze, but the cube stayed intact.

I didn't want to slice into the goop in case it went wrong and I ended up decapitating my friend. I couldn't jump down and try to rip him out by hand in case I ended up stuck so I couldn't free either of us.

"This is such a bad idea." I pulled the force of my funnel into my hand. "Such a bad, bad idea."

The *crash* of falling debris shuddered around the room as I aimed the vortex down toward Devon.

The tip of the funnel met his gelatin mold prison from Hell, and...yeah.

Goop everywhere.

Flying through the air. Covering the underside of the stairs like a food fight straight out of a lunch lady's nightmare. Splatting against the walls with squelching and flooping sounds gross enough to put me off gelatin for life.

Swallowing the sour in my mouth, I pushed the spell down a little farther, letting the vortex burrow closer to Devon. I squinted through the mass of transparent debris, waiting for a glimpse of goopless Devon.

His leather belt, where I'd tried to catch him before, emerged first.

Focusing with every bit of concentration my poor overstressed brain could manage, I fixed my gaze on his belt again. "*Frico!*"

A strain like I was trying to lift a car pulled on my whole body. Every muscle trembled, and a scream tore from my throat.

With a sickening *squelch* and a massive *pop*, Devon squeezed free from the most disgusting cage I've ever seen, soared toward me butt-first, and crashed into my chest, sending us both sprawling onto the living room floor of Evil Iliana's newly wrecked home.

21

"Ow." I coughed out the word.

Devon groaned and slipped/rolled off of me to lie facedown on the floor.

"Are you okay?" My arms shook as I sat up.

"What the hell just happened to me?" Devon panted, not even attempting to move.

"I don't think you want to know. But we have to find Eric and Elizabeth." I stood and surveyed the damage I'd done to the house. The bits that had been covered in drywall had patches torn away. Half the TV had been lodged in the wall beside the front door. The other half seemed to be mixed in with the wreckage that littered the edges of the room.

"Elizabeth!" I shouted. "Eric!" Neither of them answered me.

"What happened in here?" Devon stood, wiping chunks of goo off his sleeves. "What am I covered in?"

"Elizabeth!" My legs wobbled as I circled the room, searching for a place where Eric and Elizabeth might have been trapped.

There was nothing. I mean, lots of wreckage, but not another goo cube prison.

"Elizabeth!" I opened the fridge door and peeked behind the oven.

"What are you looking for?" Devon asked.

"I have to get upstairs." I bolted back to the steps I'd mostly trashed, dragging a cast-aside stool from the breakfast bar along with me.

"But if they'd tried to go up the stairs, wouldn't they have fallen through like me?" Devon grabbed his own stool.

"Not if Elizabeth saw the trap." It wasn't until I'd climbed up onto the bar stool and started scrambling onto what was left of the stairs that I realized I hadn't heard the demon cats yowling in a while. I froze for a moment, torn between finding out if the cats had combined their powers to morph into one mighty demon feline and getting upstairs to hopefully rescue Eric before I had to find out.

Elizabeth.

It didn't matter if the demon cats got me if I couldn't save Elizabeth.

Slicing my hands on the smashed remains of the banister, I pulled myself up and hobbled at top speed toward the second-floor rooms. I darted into three bedrooms, scanning the spaces, hoping for some clear sign of where Eric and Elizabeth might have gone wrong in their search of the house.

The second to last door led to an office that opened up onto a balcony.

Outside the window, the glow of the harbor district reached toward the water. The sight was beautiful, and massively marred by the stone and dirt spire blocking the center of it.

But more importantly, a desk waited off to one side of the room. Not like an evil villain desk. A normal desk with a computer monitor so large there was really no reason a regular person could need it, a stack of papers in a white wire tray, and a flat desk calendar. There was even a little blue coaster waiting to hold Evil Iliana's morning coffee.

I crept toward the desk, testing every step for a trap.

"Do you think she has information about the books on her computer?" Devon asked.

"It seems like she uses it for work." I leaned closer to the desk, resisting the temptation to reach out and wiggle the wireless mouse to see if the screen would light up.

"I bet we could get Raven to connect to the hard drive." Devon took a step closer.

I reached out and grabbed his arm before I really knew why. I blinked for a second, trying to figure out what had made my heart leap into my throat like a sword had been swinging for my neck.

A tiny clump of mostly-blond-but-a-little-black hair stuck out between two tiles on the floor.

"I need you to cut there." I pulled Devon back and pointed to the spot. "Don't cut too deep. Elizabeth is down there."

"So, no pressure then." Devon flicked his wrist and his glowing sword voomed to life. He shook out his shoulders and widened his stance before touching the tip of his blade to the ground. The contact made a *crackle* that would have been really satisfying if Elizabeth's life weren't on the line.

I held both my hands in front of me, ready to shout a spell and rip the section of floor away.

Sweat dripped down Devon's brow as he cut a wide circle. His arms were starting to shake by the time he made it most of the way around.

I held my breath as he sliced through the last few inches of floor.

"*Frico!*" I leapt aside as the section of tile and concrete soared toward me.

"Holy shit." Devon gaped down into the gap he'd made.

The cell was deeper than the space between the ceiling on the first-floor and the floor on the second-floor should have allowed. The compartment was filled with the same clear goo Devon had been trapped in. Elizabeth and Eric floated inside.

"Stand back," I said. "This part is gross."

I formed a vortex and let it suck out the gelatinous ooze.

Devon gagged and stumbled to shelter behind me before I'd gotten deep enough to see the back of Elizabeth's sweater. The weight of the spell pulled against me as I ripped her free, but I only glanced toward her long enough to be sure she was breathing before pushing the funnel farther down.

Devon jumped forward, tossing his nasty coat over the keyboard as the vortex got so filled with slime it started spraying out, covering everything in the office. It splattered across the balcony windows, smacked into the walls with enough force to leave dents, and flooped to the floor with oddly moist sounds that will haunt my nightmares forever.

Finally, I saw it—the front of Eric's coat. "*Frico.*" Using the last bit of energy I had, I tore him from his prison. The vortex goop all splatted to the ground in one squelching *plop* as I fell to my knees, trying to convince my lungs they could still pull in air even though my whole body felt on the verge of collapse.

"Eric"—Devon grabbed Eric's hand, yanking him to his feet—"you need to call Raven."

"Raven?" Eric swayed as he looked around the goop-coated room. "I thought I told you to stay outside."

"Shit happens," Devon said. "Call Raven."

"Bryant." Elizabeth crawled through the slime to reach me. "Bryant, you're bleeding."

"What?" I looked down at my body. Beneath the layers of clear sludge, new blood was still oozing from my cat wounds. "Oh yeah. I couldn't heal them. I don't know if the demon cats have venom."

"Venom?" Eric looked to me, his phone held up to his ear.

"You heal Bryant. I'll talk to Raven." Devon lifted Eric's phone from his hand. "Hi, Raven, this is Devon. The one who bought all the cool toys. I need some help, and we're willing to pay."

"What wounded you?" Eric knelt beside me, his face twisting in disgust as he wiped the goo off my arms.

"The *not cat* cats." I blinked, trying to decide if the room had started swaying because I was dying or if I was just that tired.

"*Not cat* cats?" Elizabeth took my hand, drawing me back to the immediacy of our problems.

"The cats outside," I said. "They got bigger, and evil, and then they attacked us, so we bolted for the house, but now there's a ravine, but we would have had to come in eventually because you got stuck in gelatin jail."

Eric furrowed his brow and started muttering fancy words while hovering his hand over my shoulder.

"I don't have a jump drive." Devon spoke into the phone as he pulled his coat off the keyboard. "Well, I wasn't expecting to have to hack into anything."

A horrible, mind-numbing burning filled my arm. I gritted my teeth against the pain but couldn't stop the groan that rumbled in my throat.

Eric moved on to the wound in my hip.

"Just create a new login?" Devon started tapping on the keyboard.

"I love you," Elizabeth said as the awful burning spanned from my hip to my knee.

I tried to stop the groan in my throat to say *I love you, too* but only managed to make a sound like a pained goat.

"Thank you for saving us." She kissed my goopy cheek.

"How long is this going to take?" Devon said. "I know I'm not actually doing the hacking."

"That should be it," Eric said. "But you've lost a lot of blood. You'll need food, drink, and rest."

"Should we take him to a hospital?" Elizabeth asked.

"And have them ask how he lost blood when he has no visible wounds?" Eric said. "He'd be subjected to more testing than we have time for."

"I am grateful," Devon said, "but we really have to get out of here."

I don't know if the demon cats could understand Devon's words, or if it was just one of those weird magical coincidences fate likes to throw my way, but right after Devon finished his sentence, a shrieking *yowl* split the air.

"What was that?" Elizabeth asked.

"Demon cat." I struggled to my feet, the floor slipping beneath my trembling legs.

Elizabeth stood beside me, wrapping her arm around my waist.

"We need to search the house," Eric said. "I found no sign of the books. But there must be some—"

Another *yowl* cut through the night, and a chorus of screeching demon cats joined in the call.

"I've gotta go." Devon hung up the phone.

The clacking of rock striking rock came from outside the full wall of windows that led to the balcony.

"Do we try for the front door?" Devon raised his sword.

"We go out here." I headed toward the balcony door.

"We have to keep looking," Eric said.

"Trust us," Devon said. "We don't."

"Eric, take the back, make sure they can't follow us." I raised my hand toward the window. "Stay close. I don't know how long it will hold."

Two pairs of glowing eyes peeked up over the edge of the

balcony. The cats spotted me and yowled their triumph to the clowder.

"*Exci.*" The force of my spell smashed through the window. I ran forward before the glass had finished hitting the ground.

One of the demon cats leapt onto the balcony, ready to attack.

"*Kunga.*" I couldn't allow myself to feel guilty as my spell knocked the demon cat over the balcony railing. I didn't have time. I fixed my gaze on the spire of rock and dirt. "*Telinto!*"

The force of the spell leaving my body knocked me back, but Elizabeth grabbed me, hauling me forward as the spire toppled like I'd chopped down a tree.

"*Exci.*"

The glass railing of the balcony shattered just before Elizabeth and I reached the edge.

I've gotten us killed. We're going to fall into the crevasse and die. The horrible thought swirled through my head as Elizabeth and I jumped.

The coward who will forever live deep in my soul screamed for me to shut my eyes as I fell, but I had to protect Elizabeth, so I dared to look down.

The spire had toppled across the crevasse, giving us a bridge to the gate and the road beyond.

My feet slipped as we landed, but Elizabeth gripped my waist, not letting me fall.

One of the demon cats on the far side of the gap growled and sat back on its haunches, waiting for its moment to strike.

I took a breath, rallying the strength to do another spell, but a little *dhoomp* sounded from behind me, and a pellet of grayish goo flew past my shoulder and hit the demon cat in the face.

The cat gave a pathetic *merp* and rolled onto its back, swiping its paws over its face, trying to remove the goo in a way that would have made me feel guilty, but if it's okay to defend a village from a dragon, it's okay to defend your friend from a demon cat.

At the far end of the tumbled-down spire, the dirt crumbled beneath my feet.

Elizabeth jerked me forward and onto solid ground because she's a total badass.

There was more dhoomping, and Eric was shouting spells behind us. But by the time I managed to turn around and look, they'd both made it over the bridge.

Eric had both hands raised as he began to cast a spell. Devon stood beside him, shooting goo pellets at the demon cats who tried to attack.

It was before my knees gave out but after Eric's green barrier had started to shimmer into being that I decided I really missed Manhattan and was very ready to go home.

22

Things I didn't expect to learn while in Greece.

- Washing weird stasis cell gelatin goop from your hair takes an oddly long time.
- Not all cats are friendly.
- Having a hacker on payroll is super helpful.
- My girlfriend is amazing. I already knew it, but her saving me—again—emphasized that fact.
- I may not be the best, most competent, daring wizard the world has ever seen, but I am actually capable of rescuing people if there are no other options and you don't care about structural damage.

Bryant,

I've started compiling the document, and, with the legal language and technicalities, it's already over sixty pages.

Do I need to pare it down? You don't really need all the jargon for your purposes.

Nikki

Nikki,

I want the full document to be loophole free. I don't care how many pages it takes.

Bryant

I sat on my bed in my hotel room in Chania. We'd gone back to wash the goop off while we waited for Raven to do her *non-magical but seems like magic to someone who doesn't know how it works* computer hacking thing.

By the time I'd managed to scrub the gelatin from my purple hair, had a minor freak out when I remembered I still had purple hair, thrown out my goop-covered clothes, realized my suitcase was way more empty than it had been when we'd landed in Greece, had a moment of existential crisis about how much clothing I was sending to a landfill, and finally went to join the others in Eric's room, they were all sitting around his desk completely calm, clean, and eating dinner out of takeout boxes.

"No huge news yet." Devon didn't even look up as I walked into the room. "Raven's been sending information over as she finds it, but most of what she's dug up so far is boring and non-magic related."

"Like what?" I sat on the edge of the bed nearest the desk.

"We know she has an accountant, a landscaper, and her cleaning lady emails her a lot." Elizabeth passed me a box of food. "We also know she really likes online shopping."

"New document." Devon tapped to pull something up on his phone screen.

I stood and peered over his shoulder.

"It's a spreadsheet." Devon opened the file. "Holy shit."

I opened my mouth to say something, but my jaw just hung loose. I couldn't do anything but stare as Devon scrolled down the list of hundreds of book titles, before tapping on the next tab over, which held hundreds more.

"How many tabs are there?" Eric asked.

"About twenty," Devon said.

The tabs across the bottom were marked with titles like *Bone Only, Elite, New York, London, and Do Not Sell*. Some of the titles were highlighted, like Iliana had marked the books that had already been sold.

"Well," Elizabeth said, "at least we know for sure she's the one with the books."

"Does Iliana send all her expenses to her accountant?" I ran my hands through my purple hair.

"I don't know," Devon said. "But we can look."

"Check that and her credit card for any recurring payments," I said. "That many books are going to have to be stored in some kind of warehouse, and that would mean rent or a mortgage."

"Smart." Devon started a text to Raven.

"Yeah, well, Dad used to interrupt a lot of coffee dates to yell at his underlings about their mismanagement of rented space," I said.

"What exactly does your dad do?" Elizabeth asked.

"Make lots of money?" I opened my dinner and was grateful to find none of my food was leaf wrapped.

"What do we do if we find the warehouse?" Elizabeth asked.

"Seize control," Eric said.

"Sounds great," I said. "Just as long as there aren't any cats."

I munched away on my flakey, cheesy pastry as we waited for Raven to send more information. It felt like we were wasting time. Like we should be running for our lives, tearing through the night to find Iliana, or sleeping.

"I must say, I'm proud of you, Bryant." Eric turned in his chair to look at me.

"Whaa fur?" I tried to ask with my mouth full.

Eric didn't even raise an eyebrow at my lack of dignity. "You've saved my life before, in the Battle of Beville, last night in the woods, but tonight was different. Taking on the responsibility of helping someone who is helpless requires courage. You displayed enormous bravery."

I swallowed hard. "Right. Well, I couldn't just leave you, so it's not like I had a choice."

"What I don't think you understand, Bryant," Eric said, "is that a great many people would see a choice."

"We have four abnormal recurring payments and none of them are for a warehouse," Devon said. "Two for different boat docks, one to a woman's name, and one to an inn."

"Please tell me some of those payments go to the same location." I gripped my food box so hard it wrinkled.

"One of the docks, the lady, and the inn are all in the same place." Devon turned around, beaming. "I don't want to push things too fast, but I think Raven might be the love of my life."

"Perhaps you should spend more than an hour in her presence," Eric said.

"Don't need to." Devon grinned. "Some chemistry can't be denied."

"And that's my cue to book us transport." Elizabeth got out her own phone and started working.

Eric pulled out his phone and started reading through the list of books like a guy who was dying of hunger and found a pho place with an extensive menu.

I just kept eating, trying to convince my stomach that it had room for food despite the overwhelming sense of gratitude filling my chest that my friends were alive, not only because they were my friends, but also because I didn't have to be in charge of figuring out how to get us to Iliana's weird dock.

I'd made it through my cheesy pastry and moved on to little balls of I don't know what before Elizabeth started making calls,

Eric started pacing, and Devon sat beside me to pick at what was left of my dinner.

"There's no way we're going to get to sleep here tonight is there?" I whispered.

"Don't worry," Devon said. "We can sleep in the car."

I managed to be brave and not whine as we all grabbed our bags and headed down to wait for a cab in the middle of the night. I even pretended to be excited about the boat Elizabeth had somehow found to ferry us around Crete in the dark. I didn't wince as I handed the boat captain my dad's credit card even though the man had a gleam in his eyes like I'd just paid for his next vacation. I didn't refuse to board the boat when I realized it was a glorified speedboat with no place to sit out of the wind.

But when the boat started bumping through the water and chilly winter mist soaked my sweater, I lost my ability to cheerfully blunder through this adventure hoping we'd end up with the books instead of ending up dead.

"Got any discreet warming spells." Elizabeth took my arm, wrapping it around her shoulder.

Holding her close eased me away from the verge of having an exhausted breakdown.

"*Relanto*," I whispered.

The cold wind warmed, making the air feel more like summery bliss and less like wintery death.

Elizabeth kissed the side of my neck, right beneath my ear.

Warmth that had nothing to do with magic spread through my chest.

"You really are a hero, you know." She nestled closer to me.

I wanted to say something brave like *I'd fight an army of evil cats for you* or romantic like *If I'd lost you, I would have lost my heart.* But it was Elizabeth, so I couldn't stop myself from telling her the truth.

"I don't feel like a hero." I looked over my shoulder, making sure Devon and Eric wouldn't be able to hear me from their seats in the little niche in the back of the boat. "I feel cold and wet and exhausted and weirdly homesick for New York."

"Me too," Elizabeth said.

"What?" I leaned away from her enough to be able to look into her eyes.

"I know I only lived there for a few days, but all I want is to be back in my bed at the Consortium. I want to wake up knowing where I am even if it means having Sniffer McDeadDog hovering over me when I open my eyes. I want to sit at a table in the restaurant, having muffins and coffee for breakfast. I know what we're doing is important and has to get done for the good of all wizard kind, but I just want to go home and sleep for a week."

A genuine chuckle shook my chest. "I thought it was just me."

"Nope." Elizabeth reached up, brushing a bit of my purple hair away from my forehead. "But I don't think being tired and wanting to go home stops you from being a hero. I think it makes you more of one. Because you stay. You keep going even when you don't want to. That takes a lot more courage than living like Eric and being so in love with danger you don't even realize how much you're risking."

"I really do love you, Elizabeth Wick."

"I love you, too." She leaned in and kissed me.

It didn't make me forget how tired I was, but holding Elizabeth in my arms and knowing she thought I was strong enough to keep going made a little voice start speaking in the back of my mind.

You're brave enough to do this.

Fate put you on this boat for a reason.

You're a strong enough wizard to see this through to the end.

By the time the sun began to rise and our destination came into view, I almost genuinely believed I was the hero Elizabeth thought I was. Or at least I could be close enough not to be ashamed of sucking at saving the magical world.

I'd barely been paying attention while Elizabeth had been working out how to get us to the dock where Iliana paid monthly rent for boat space, so I hadn't realized we were going to be landing at the base of a massive gorge.

With the way the rising sun cast shadows across the slice through the earth, it was easy to think we'd found a path to a shadowy underworld.

If it hadn't been for the little village at the base of the gorge, I would have completely believed that headless Thaden and the Ladies had risen from the dead and were going to pour out of the darkness with an army of shadow monsters.

I fixed my gaze on the little cluster of buildings, trying to take comfort in the fact that, if those little houses had been around for years and years with the gorge right nearby, odds were good a Hellmouth wasn't going to open today just because we'd shown up.

But as I studied the little pastel painted buildings, a touch of dread settled in my stomach. There were no warehouses in sight. No giant buildings where Iliana could store the thousands upon thousands of books she'd hoarded.

As the boat stopped at the dock, I could see signs for inns, signs for food, signs for places to buy t-shirts during tourist season, and not one stinking hint of where the freakin' books might be.

23

The sunrise shifted the angles of the shadows in the gorge, making it look less like a pathway to doom and more like an entrance to another world.

I gripped my coffee cup with both hands, trying to anchor my mind to the little inn/café where we'd managed to find breakfast instead of the dark patches in the gorge and what monsters might hide just out of sight. I could hear the rumble of Devon's voice. He was out by the front desk of the inn, being charming as he plied the innkeeper for information about Iliana, the nice woman we'd met in Chania, who'd raved about this spot and told us we *just had* to come.

I couldn't see or hear Eric. Of course, that wasn't surprising as he'd gone for a pre-breakfast stroll around the little village to work up an appetite and hadn't come back to Iliana's favorite inn and café.

I wanted to be strolling, or at the very least not sitting at a corner table in the tiny dining room gripping my coffee for dear life, but Elizabeth and I had been assigned the *look normal* part of the plan.

We were just travelers. We were only looking for breakfast.

We were in no way suspicious. And we most definitely were not looking to steal some already stolen books from the lady whose house we had just trashed after she tried to murder us.

I gripped my cup tighter, resisting the urge to check under the table for demon cats.

"Eat, Bryant." Elizabeth nudged my leg with her knee.

"Right." I pried my hands off my coffee cup and went back to munching on my cream-filled breakfast pastry.

"Relax your shoulders," Elizabeth said. "You look like you're waiting for a fight."

"I am," I whispered.

"Our server doesn't need to know that."

I glanced over to the corner where a guy, who I assumed was the innkeeper's son, glowered at us.

I exhaled and forced my shoulders to relax, then gave Elizabeth a smile I hoped looked flirtatious instead of evil. "How long until we worry?"

"Another ten minutes." Elizabeth looked back to her guidebook.

"I can do ten minutes." I took a bite of my pastry. I have no idea if it was good. My nerves had stolen my ability to taste.

"It's a pity we're not here at the right time of year to hike the whole gorge." Elizabeth pushed the guidebook closer to me. She leaned her shoulder against mine, offering me something to focus on besides wondering if Iliana had found Eric, if Devon's charm was actually going to be enough to get the innkeeper to talk, and how fast my dad could track my credit card transactions here and if he would hire mercenaries to drag me home.

"Do you like hiking?" Elizabeth asked.

"I don't think I've ever tried it." I sipped my lukewarm coffee.

"It's like walking but harder." She winked at me.

"I'd probably fall to my death."

"I'll catch you."

She looked at me with her perfect, sparkly eyes, and I forgot about everything.

"Yeah," I breathed, like a total goober, but she's in love with me so she just smiled and kissed my cheek.

"Thank you," Devon said, loud enough for me to clearly hear. "You have no idea how much I appreciate this."

He strutted back to our table with a gleam in his eye like he'd just picked up two tourist hotties in Times Square.

"Good news." Devon slid into the seat opposite me. "Our lovely hostess recommends we buy a few nice bottles of wine from the little shop down the street to leave for Iliana as a thank you."

"Right." I gripped the edge of the table to keep myself from leaning forward in excitement.

"How long until she gets the wine?" Elizabeth kept a finger in the guidebook to hold her place.

"Iliana usually comes twice a month to go hiking in the gorge." Devon took a sip of his coffee, wrinkled his nose, and set his mug back down. "She was just up last week, and she's not booked to come back for another ten days."

"That's all right," Elizabeth said. "It's wine, not fruit. Wine can keep for much longer than ten days."

I shoved the rest of my pastry into my mouth.

A little voice spoke in my head, sounding like an enthusiastic train as its words rumbled all the way down to my chest, making me feel something shockingly similar to hope.

You're almost there. You're almost there. You're almost there.

A bell *tinkled* on the front door of the inn. I slipped my hand into my pocket to grab my phone at the same moment Devon reached into his own pocket to grip the hilt of his sword.

"A fresh round of coffee, if you could." Eric spoke from the tiny lobby/front room of the inn.

There was something about the tension in his voice that kept me from relaxing my grip on my phone.

He strode into the dining room, subtly glancing to each of the corners before sitting in the last chair at our table.

"Did your walk help you work up an appetite?" Devon slid his hand back out of his pocket.

"No," Eric said. "But as the time for breakfast is nearly gone, I will have to make myself eat anyway."

"So nothing...satisfying about your stroll?" I said as casually as I'm capable of, which was still obvious enough to earn me raised eyebrows from everyone at the table.

"The views are magnificent, but I didn't find any inspiration," Eric said.

We all slipped into silence as we worked our way through breakfast.

I wanted to be planning, or searching the village, or digging to try and find an underground lair.

But the plan we'd agreed on when we'd been dumped on a chilly dock by our boat captain, who seemed to laugh with glee as he sped away like my father's credit card had fully funded his retirement as payment for a few hours' work, didn't allow for any of those things.

Iliana paid people in this village on a regular basis.

Iliana might have paid them to tell her if anyone came poking around the village and seemed suspicious.

If we were lucky, Iliana was still in Meteora, trying to find and kill us.

Iliana getting tipped off to the fact that we were here would bring her sweeping in, ready to slaughter the people who'd escaped her phantasms. Letting her go to her trashed home and then come here to check on the books would give us more time to search.

Our half-assed plan? Pretend we'd met Iliana at a restaurant and she'd told us about the beauty of the gorge. We'd followed her travel wisdom. Hurray for Iliana the travel guru.

Henceforth, tearing through the village in search of the books was a big ole' no-no.

I finished my second pastry and considered ordering a third. Not because I was hungry, just because eating gave me a non-suspicious activity to do.

"I'd like to go for a hike after breakfast," Elizabeth said.

"While the gorge is beautiful," Eric said, "I think we should explore the village to see what's available for our visit."

"But I really want to go hiking." Elizabeth pushed the guide-book across the table.

Devon leaned close to Eric, and both of them read the page.

Eric tented his fingers under his chin, and Devon pursed his lips.

Elizabeth pulled the guidebook toward me and tapped on a section that had been printed inside a little gray square.

The gorge's history is as fascinating as the natural wonders of its rock formations and plant life. In the eighth century, more than four thousand people sheltered deep in the gorge as they hid from Turkish invaders.

In the 1890's, when the rest of Greece fell under the rule of the Ottoman Empire, only the gorge remained free. During World War II, the gorge served as a primary escape route for allied troops.

That one place has sheltered so many across its well-documented history can't help but make you wonder how many others have secretly sought refuge deep within the gorge.

The answer? We'll never know.

As you hike through the gorge, taking in the one-of-a-kind scenery, try to imagine where so many fugitives, refugees, and exiles found sanctuary between the rocky cliffs.

Legends have long told of hidden caves and gullies that protected the people of the gorge, but beware: the rangers will fine anyone found off the designated trails.

I read the passage twice before my heart picked up its pace like I'd already started climbing.

"I think hiking could be fun." I took Elizabeth's hand, threading my fingers through hers. "Help us work up an appetite for lunch."

"Indeed." Eric finished his cup of coffee and stood.

"Oh, like now?" I pounded the rest of my coffee, straightened my scar scarf, and grabbed my sweater from the back of my chair.

"Fate does not favor the hesitant." Eric strode out of the dining room. "We'll be back for lunch. Thank you again for your hospitality."

I tried to match his determined stride as Elizabeth, Devon, and I followed him. It came out more like an awkward scamper, but the innkeeper still smiled and waved at me as we passed her and stepped out into the bright morning.

The air had turned from misty and miserable to crisp and refreshing while we'd been inside. The sun gleamed in the sky like she was urging us on to triumph.

We're almost there.

"Elizabeth," I whispered as we reached the edge of the village, "you're a genius."

"Don't compliment me until we find something worth the climb," Elizabeth said.

If I were smarter, I would have taken that as a warning.

I didn't think much about the steepness of the hill leading out of the village—I'm from Manhattan. I live to climb stairs.

But then we got to the top of the hill and I realized we weren't actually at the gorge, we had to walk two miles uphill to get to the *actual* gorge that had somehow mysteriously protected so many people.

Fine. Whatever. Two miles isn't a big deal. I'm used to walking all over the city.

Then we got to the bottom of the gorge proper, and I realized how tiny and incapable I was. The gorge reached a solid four-teen miles above us, and each of those miles would be climbing uphill.

I whimpered as we began the trek, my legs already screaming at me for being a stupid, cocky, hiking noob. After the first twenty minutes, I pulled out my phone to search for a spell that would make walking easier. It was the only thing I could do to keep myself from crying as my legs began to shake.

Elizabeth stopped every hundred feet or so, staring around us for a few moments before climbing some more. Eric whis-pered spells under his breath. I didn't know what he was trying to do, but I could feel the ambient magic radiating off of him.

Devon slowed his pace to walk with me at the back of the group. "If the books really are hidden in some cave, how do you think they got here?"

"Lots of donkeys?" I winced as my calves seized up like they wanted to be super sure they made their displeasure known. "Honestly, they were probably—"

A ringing from my pocket cut me off.

Eric glanced back to glare at me as I pulled out my non-magical phone.

Two horrifying words showed on the screen.

Dr. Spinnek

I let out a string of curses that made Devon snort.

"What?" Elizabeth glanced back at me, not glaring but with her brow locked in a thoroughly furrowed position.

"I forgot I have phone therapy." Giving in to the anxiety sinking into my chest like poured cement, I pressed the answer button. "Hi, Dr. Spinnek."

"Bryant," Dr. Spinnek said in a cheerful *not at all suspicious* that I literally almost died twice in the past two days which would add up to five recent near-deaths if you counted all the almost dying from the week before we'd left Manhattan way. "I'm so glad we're able to chat even though you're traveling."

"Yeah," I said, "it's great."

"How has your trip been so far?" Dr. Spinnek asked.

Aside from ditching my chaperone in a morally questionable way, all the near-deathness, and having a newfound fear of cats, great!

I swallowed the honest answer I wanted to give and said, "Going really well. I'm learning a lot."

"I'm glad you're learning," Dr. Spinnek said, "but you sound a bit tired. Wanting to take in as much as you possibly can is understandable, but sleep deprivation takes a real toll on mental health."

No, lying to the people you're closest to about maybe the best/worst thing you've ever done, all while trying to find books so you can steal them from a murderer, takes a toll on mental health.

"Well, I'm hiking right now," I said. "So I probably sound more tired than I am."

Elizabeth stopped and took a few steps toward a crack in the side of the gorge. The space only reached back about fifteen feet, shallow enough that bits of moss had grown in the farthest shadows.

"...will make a huge difference," Dr. Spinnek said.

"I'm"—I tried to make my brain remember what Dr. Spinnek had just said. "I'm so sorry, could you say that again?"

"I said eating well and getting enough exercise to help you sleep soundly will make a huge difference in how you perceive your trip when you look back on it."

Elizabeth moved on, walking at a slower pace as she studied the cliff face.

I squinted at the stone, trying to see what Elizabeth was seeing. There were a few trees growing out of the side of the cliff in a gravity-defying way, which was cool, but not really the magical hiding place we were looking for.

"Bryant," Dr. Spinnek said, "I hate to take time out of your trip, but I really think you should pause for a moment so we can chat without distraction."

I can't pause to chat without distraction. We don't know when Evil I've-almost-killed-you-twice Iliana is going to show up.

I took a deep breath and told the best almost-truth I could. "I'm sorry, Dr. Spinnek, I'm just having problems with my parents and I'm not sure I'm ready to talk about them yet."

I looked to Devon who made a *I mean, it might work* grimace before following Eric and Elizabeth across a little log bridge over a creek that sparkled in the sun.

"What sort of problems?" Dr. Spinnek asked.

"I was sort of homesick, so I called my dad for a video chat," I said. "It was stupid early New York time, so I woke him up. He'd been sleeping at my mom's."

"Oh," Dr. Spinnek said.

Elizabeth turned around to look at me, her eyes wide with shock.

"Yeah," I said. "That happened. I don't know if I'm really ready to talk about it."

"It's alright to need some time to process," Dr. Spinnek said.

Elizabeth mouthed *wow* and kept climbing.

The path on the other side of the river wasn't the packed dirt we'd been climbing before that I should have known enough to be grateful for. Our new trail was covered in loose stones that twisted under my feet.

"Let's set aside your parents for a moment," Dr. Spinnek said. "Your father said you were traveling with your friend and girl-friend. How is that going?"

"Great!" A bit of the cement left my lungs as I managed to

answer one question with complete honesty. "Being with them is great."

Trees grew across the path up ahead, leaning low enough that Eric had to hunch over to get under their branches without messing up his ever-perfect hair.

"Having these memories with them is wonderful," Dr. Spinnek said. "Is Elizabeth doing well?"

"Yeah." I ducked under the trees, forgot to breathe for a second as I entered the gully on the other side, remembered my therapist was on the line, and took an awkward gulping breath before continuing. "I think the trip is good for her, too. Getting out of New York has been great for all of us."

Eric looked around the gully, then started along the path again, but Elizabeth didn't follow him. She sort of drifted to the side, like she was on a path I couldn't see, which with Elizabeth was entirely possible.

"I'd like to give you a little project, Bryant," Dr. Spinnek said.

"Uh-huh." I followed Elizabeth, keeping ten paces behind her so I wouldn't distract her from whatever she was seeing.

"Normally, I'd say you need a notebook, but since you're traveling, keeping notes on your phone will work fine," Dr. Spinnek said.

"Great," I said.

Elizabeth reached a sign that read *Most Dangerous! Rock slides!* She stepped around the sign, continuing toward the cliff face.

"Every morning, I want you to take a moment and write down your emotional goal for the day, and three things you can do to help yourself achieve it," Dr. Spinnek said.

"Alright." I crept around the warning sign and took a few quick steps, halving the space between Elizabeth and me.

"In the evening, I want you to look at that goal, and honestly ask yourself if you used all the tools you have to keep yourself happy, grateful, calm—whatever your goal for the day might have been," Dr. Spinnek said.

"I like having tools," I said.

Elizabeth paused for a moment before heading toward two boulders that looked like they might have been two halves of one boulder before they'd fallen in a *most dangerous* rockslide.

"That's good," Dr. Spinnek said. "What we're trying to do is create an emotional tool belt for you so you know how to handle any situation you encounter in a healthy way."

"Wouldn't that be magical?" I said.

Elizabeth tipped her head to the side. Her curls tumbled over her shoulder in a perfect little cascade. She touched the boulder, trailing her finger along a slice in the stone.

"That is the magic we work toward when we commit to giving therapy a genuine try," Dr. Spinnek said.

"That's what I'm doing," I said.

Elizabeth stepped between the boulders and out of sight.

"So, what can your emotional goal for today be? What thoughts do you want use to propel yourself forward?" Dr. Spinnek asked.

"Well, I—"

A flash of light, a rumbling *crack*, and Elizabeth's scream drove every thought from my mind.

24

"Elizabeth!" I didn't even feel my phone fall from my hand. I couldn't see her.

She'd slipped between the two boulders before she screamed.

My heart didn't beat as I dove through the gap. I was numb. There was no sound, no feeling. Nothing in the world existed but getting to Elizabeth.

I reached a little clearing on the far side of the boulders. There was dirt and rocks on the ground, a few scrubby little plants struggling to survive, but no Elizabeth. No monster. No blood. Just a strange shadow that didn't seem like it belonged.

My ears started to work again as I heard a muted scream.

I looked up.

Elizabeth floated twelve feet off the ground, struggling against bonds I couldn't see, lying on her back like someone had lifted her out of bed.

The sight of her still breathing and fighting was enough to allow air back into my lungs.

"Elizabeth!"

She gave a louder muffled scream in response.

"Bryant!" Devon shouted behind me.

I made myself look away from Elizabeth, scanning the trees around the clearing before studying the ground.

Something magical had hoisted her up there. Some spell or trap.

"Bryant, are you hurt?" Devon rammed into my shoulder as he ran into the clearing.

I grabbed his arm before he could move past me.

"Shit," Devon said. "Eric, we need help."

I hated it. I hated that I needed Eric's help, but as Elizabeth struggled, hanging in the air, I would've taken help from the Ladies if it meant getting her down safely.

"Hold on, Elizabeth." I forced my voice to stay steady and sure. "We are going to get you down. You're going to be okay, I swear to you."

Devon's sword voomed to life.

I whipped around as rocks *clacked* under footfalls behind me.

Eric stepped out from between the boulders, frowning as he looked from the clearing to my girlfriend hovering in midair. "Well, Elizabeth, it seems you were right in wanting to go for a hike."

"What?" I shouted.

"Elizabeth wouldn't have stumbled into a spell unless someone had placed one here." Eric frowned as he studied the cliff face. "Why would one risk placing magic so close to where humans tread if there weren't an exceptionally good reason?"

Elizabeth squeaked another scream as she began gliding toward the rock face.

"*Frico.*" I focused on the back of Elizabeth's sweater. My spell yanked on her, bouncing her in the air, but she still kept floating toward the cliff.

"To use such a spell, the reward must be worth the cost." Eric picked his way out into the clearing.

"I don't care about the cost," I said. "Help her."

She was only ten feet away from the rock face. I didn't want to know what would happen when she reached the stone.

"I am helping her," Eric said. "I need to think. I need to know what sort of magic we are facing."

Elizabeth screamed something that sounded like she was trying to speak, but I had no idea what she was saying.

Seven feet.

"You're running out of time," Devon said.

"I'm trying not to make things worse," Eric said.

Five feet.

"I'm so sorry." I took a deep breath. "*Eshan.*"

I focused on her waist with every fiber of my being as I stretched my hand toward her. I'd never tried the spell before. I didn't know to expect the crackling heat on my palm, or the nauseating tugging on my skin as the magic flew from my hand like my flesh was unwinding. Like the glowing gold cord was a bit of magical fishing line made of my own body I'd just cast to try and save Elizabeth.

Two feet.

My spell wrapped around Elizabeth's waist. Part of the gold touched her bare wrists. She screamed as my magic made contact with her skin.

"I'm sorry." I pulled back on my hand, drawing the cord between us tight.

A wave of crackling sparks streaked toward her.

She screamed again as the sparks burned her skin.

"I'm so sorry." I pulled back harder, dragging her away from the cliff. Tears burned in my eyes. I knew the pain I was causing her. I knew how the heat was searing her flesh. Even remembering that pain around my neck brought bile to my throat.

I knelt, dragging her closer to the ground.

"Devon, grab her." I spoke through gritted teeth as I pressed the back of my hand to the dirt.

Devon ran forward and jumped up, catching Elizabeth around the middle.

For a moment, it looked like they would both stay in the air.

"*Eshan.*" Gold flew from Eric's hand, wrapping around Devon's middle.

Devon sucked in air through his teeth, but the spell hadn't made contact with any of his bare skin.

Eric pulled Devon down, getting him low enough that his feet touched the ground, then jerked his hand back, breaking the cord that had bound them.

"*Stasio.*" Eric's spell shimmered into being, surrounding Devon and Elizabeth.

Devon kept hold of Elizabeth, pressing her down even as his own feet left the ground. He only rose a few inches before stopping, like his head had hit some invisible ceiling.

I moved to break the spell connecting Elizabeth to me, but Eric shook his head.

"Keep her tethered." Eric stepped slowly forward. "Until we are sure of what this spell is, we cannot risk her being whisked away."

"I'm so sorry." Tears burned in my eyes as I crept slowly toward Devon and Elizabeth. "I didn't want to hurt you. I didn't know what else..." My words faded away as I saw Elizabeth's face.

Tears streamed from her eyes and trickled down into her hair. Pain had formed creases on her brow. Her jaw moved as she tried to speak, but it was like her lips had been super glued together.

"I'm sorry."

"What happened?" Devon said.

"She was walking ahead of me." My voice cracked. "I was on the phone. I wasn't watching. She went through the boulders before me, and then I heard her scream."

"If she chose this path, she must have seen something to lure her in this direction," Eric said.

Elizabeth gave a muffled sound of affirmation.

Eric tented his hands under his chin. "Was the thing you saw beautiful?"

Elizabeth gave a tiny shake of her head. The movement seemed to cause her pain. Fresh tears pooled in her eyes.

"Was it dark?" Eric asked.

She shook her head again.

"Did it look like regular humans had done it?" Devon asked.

Elizabeth nodded.

People. Normal people had left something that made Elizabeth want to come this way. I tried to think back. I'd been talking on the phone. I'd been an asshat who hadn't been paying enough attention.

I'd been too busy looking at the way Elizabeth's hair swished around her shoulders to really think through the groove in the rock she'd trailed her finger along.

"There's a cut, like a hatch mark on the boulders we had to walk between," I said.

Eric paced beside Elizabeth and Devon's cage, his brow furrowed and lips pursed.

"What?" I wanted to step into Eric's path to stop him, but I couldn't risk hurting Elizabeth more by pulling on the bond between us.

"There are choices to make," Eric said.

"Choices?" Devon said.

"I believe I know how to free Elizabeth without killing either of you," Eric said.

"That would be the ideal outcome," Devon said.

"But there would be no covering our tracks," Eric said. "The moment Iliana walked between those boulders, she would know we'd come this way."

"I'm fine with that," I said.

"It will also take more magic than one wizard should channel in a day," Eric said. "I can't afford to face someone like Iliana in a weakened state."

"You also can't possibly be considering leaving Elizabeth and Devon here." Anger burned past the panic in my chest.

"It may be our best chance of reaching the books," Eric said.

"No." Devon twisted to look at Eric. "Don't go down that road."

"Devon, your safety is simple. All you need to do is step away from Elizabeth. We can leave her here. Come back for her later," Eric said. "There would be no reason to create a trapping spell of this magnitude if one's purpose was to kill. There will be something, like the cells in Iliana's house, that will contain Elizabeth. She can—"

"And if Iliana gets to her first?" My anger shifted to a weird white-hot rage that somehow made my voice creepily calm. "If Iliana questions her? If Iliana hurts her? If you're wrong and there is no trapping, just death?"

Eric didn't say anything.

"If you walk out of this clearing, you go alone," I said. "If you abandon the people you're supposed to care about, none of us will follow you. We're done."

"We are here for the books." Eric spread his arms wide. "They are here. I can feel them. The work of centuries, ready to be restored to its rightful place."

"But it wouldn't be," I said. "How many times has Elizabeth saved us? How many times has Devon fought beside us? How many times have I almost died because I had your back during a battle?"

"And I am grateful for all those things," Eric said. "We will come back for Elizabeth."

"If you walk away from one of your own to find the books, then you shouldn't have them." Pain clawed at the sides of my throat. "If you fall that far, you're not any better than the Ladies or Thaden. You wouldn't be returning the books to their rightful place. You would just be the new bad guy in charge of the treasure."

"You don't understand—"

"There has to be more to magic than fighting and hoping you're not the one who ends up dead!" I shouted. "We have to be better than abandoning our friends to get what we want. If that's all you're capable of, then I want no part in the world you're creating. I won't do it. Because I know we can be better than Thaden, or the Ladies, or anyone else who's come before. We can make the world a better place. We can be happy and peaceful. We don't have to sacrifice people to save the day."

Eric crumpled. Not like fell to the ground, but like a tiny bit of the scaffolding that had been holding up the hero's absolute determination that he was right had been ripped away, leaving a mere man standing in his place.

"Do the spell," Devon said. "You may not have our backs. But you know we have yours."

Eric closed his eyes for a moment before nodding.

I didn't want to be done screaming at Eric. In fact, I would have loved to punch him in the face a few times, but he stepped forward and raised his hands, and it was like a subtle breeze suddenly filled the little clearing.

"*Mea brago indulno*"—Eric tipped his head back as the breeze turned into a wind that whipped around us—"*vinesca endrago*" —the light in the clearing faded as a *crack* sounded from the rock face—"*tearinsca falto*—"

I wanted to glance over to the cliff to see what had made the noise, but I couldn't look away from Elizabeth. Ribbons of light had begun to glow around her like I was finally seeing the magic that bound her.

"—*farita entrasco*—"

The ribbons of light stretched, reaching toward the cliff, and the wind grew into a full-blown gale, stinging my face and slicing through my sweater.

I finally glanced at the cliff just in time to see the shining ribbons slip into the stone like there was something inside the rock face trying to drag Elizabeth away.

"—*tarigo erbracina!*"

The wind vanished. The was no sound that came with the ending of the spell, just a moment of stillness before Elizabeth fell to the ground and Eric collapsed to his knees.

Devon still had her around the middle. He held on, softening her fall and keeping her from bashing her head on the ground. "I've got you." He kept her steady as she opened her mouth and gasped in a breath.

I flicked my wrist, getting rid of the tether that had bound me to Elizabeth.

The golden cord vanished, sending a flare of heat to pummel my palm as Elizabeth took a shuddering breath that ended in a sob as she clutched her hands to her chest.

"You're okay." Devon held her, rocking her as she cried. "It's over."

I wanted to take a step forward, but I couldn't make my feet move. "I..."

Be brave. You owe it to her to be brave.

"I'm so sorry." My words seemed hollow and stupid as Elizabeth looked toward me, and I caught sight of the bright red, indented burns across the backs of her wrists. "I'm sorry."

Elizabeth reached for me. Like she wanted me near her. Like she didn't hate me for torturing her with the spell. Being dragged to auction with that curse around my neck had been bad enough. I'd pulled her whole body, dragged her away from the force of another spell. I'd hurt her, and even Lola might not be able to mend the scars.

I took a step forward.

Elizabeth didn't flinch.

"I'm sorry." My feet fumbled on the rocks as I stumbled to her side and knelt to hold her.

"It's okay." Elizabeth buried her face on my shoulder. "I'm okay."

I wanted to squeeze her to my chest, like I could protect her from any more agony just by locking my arms around her. But I didn't want to cause her more pain by holding her too tight.

"Can you get up?" Devon asked. "I don't think we should stay here. I don't know if the spell could recharge or something."

"That spell is broken." Eric's voice sounded raspy and weak enough that I actually bothered to look toward the asshat who'd suggested we abandon my girlfriend.

He knelt on the ground, sweat slicking his brow, the blue of his veins fighting through his pale skin.

"Though I do agree we need to keep moving." Eric planted his hands on the ground, his whole body shaking as he lurched to his feet. "If Iliana set one trap on this path, there will be more. We can't afford to waste time."

"Saving Elizabeth was not a waste of time," I spat.

Elizabeth squeezed my arm before I could start shouting all the names I wanted to call the nasty, abandoning Eric Deldridge.

"I could see something." Elizabeth pressed on my shoulder, using me to steady herself as she got to her feet. "It was like a tiny shimmer on the ground, or a sparkly little rock. It was over there." She pointed behind Eric. "I didn't even get within ten feet of it before I got sucked into that spell."

Eric's head sagged forward.

For a second, I thought he'd passed out, but he just let out a long breath before speaking. "The traps in the house were worrying. Well-disguised and each less visible to Elizabeth than the last. But to set a trap designed to lure in a seer, that leaves us more vulnerable than I had feared."

"Do you think this isn't the way to wherever the books are hidden?" Devon said.

"I'm quite sure the books are this way," Eric said. "I only worry what else awaits us."

"Come on then." Devon lifted Eric's arm, draping it over his shoulder, and wrapped his own around Eric's waist.

"I can manage without assistance," Eric said, his voice wavering in a way that made me sincerely doubt he wasn't about to keel over.

"We're the good guys," Devon said. "We don't leave our own behind, even if they make a shitty mistake. Now come on. Let's go finish this thing."

25

As a general rule, feeling useless is pretty standard for me. But as we crept down the tiny path that cut along the bottom of the cliff face, somehow not being able to help felt way worse than normal.

I couldn't hold Elizabeth's hand, because it might hurt the wounds I'd left on her wrists. I wasn't going to be the one to help Eric shamble down the path, because he could go screw himself for all I cared. We may have needed him to get to the books, but I was not prepared to forgive him. Not by a long shot.

So, Devon had taken up the duty of keeping Le Grand Asshat on his feet while the asshat and Elizabeth examined every stone, twig, and shadow for the next trap. Which was the smart thing to do but made moving along the path a very slow process, so all the hairs on the back of my neck prickled like Iliana was already watching us and just having too good a laugh to be bothered with jumping out to kill us.

We'd given a wide berth to two more sparkly things only Elizabeth could see, skirted around a patch of shadows that darkened the ground even though there was nothing any of us could find that should have been blocking the sun, and fully ignored a cry that was either an abandoned baby or mating animals, before we finally came to a little waterfall cascading down the side of the cliff.

The water looked clean and beautiful. My first instinct was to reach out and touch the pool at the bottom to see how cold it really was, but there was something in the way the water glimmered in the light that made me fairly certain touching the falls would end badly.

"Well"—Elizabeth tipped her head as she studied the water. I looked away before her movements could distract me—"I guess she gave up on subtlety."

"Or this spell is of an older making." Eric stepped away from Devon's support to stare at the pool below the falls.

And, as a mark of how truly hopeless I am, I didn't actually notice how weird the base of the falls was until everyone around me was staring at it.

The water falling from the cliff was a little too beautiful to be normal, but the super weird bit was the fact that the water fell into a ten-foot-wide, shallow pool with no outlet. No stream running out of it. No marks where the pool sometimes overflowed.

"Huh," I said, like the genius I am.

"This is where the path ends." Elizabeth moved like she was going to dig her fingers into her curls before wincing and lowering her arms. "If the books are hidden in this gorge, they've got to be here."

We're almost there!

"So," Devon said, "do we dive in or walk through the stone wall?"

"I say we move the water and see what it's hiding." I stepped as close to the edge of the pool as I could and stared down.

"Move the water?" Devon said.

"I mean, we're way past the point of subtlety." I shrugged.

"I'm afraid I haven't the energy to manage it," Eric said. "You'll have to do the spell yourself."

"I don't remember asking for your help." I flexed my fingers a few times as I stretched my hands out over the water. "*Stilgarna.*"

If you've ever seen a fire hydrant explode, just magnify that amount of water and gushing force by about ten thousand. If you've never seen a fire hydrant blow, then picture all the water from the waterfall and all the water from the pool shooting out toward the middle of the gorge like a badly aimed rocket.

The blast of water knocked over trees, shoved aside boulders that probably hadn't moved in a few thousand years, and washed enough dirt away in three seconds that I'd probably changed the terrain forever and really confused future geologists.

"See anything!" I shouted over the continuing roar of my water cannon.

"There's a gap in the cliff." Elizabeth crept closer to the rock wall. "It's big enough to fit through."

"I'll go first." Devon looped around, her pulling out his sword.

"I can go," Eric said.

"You're barely standing, we need Elizabeth to spot traps, and Bryant's our only functional wizard." Devon's sword voomed to life. "I'm the spare. Don't worry. I know you won't abandon me."

"Devon, you aren't the spare." I took a step toward him, but he'd already slipped through the crack in the rock.

My water cannon wavered as fear filled my chest, not because the spell still actively needed my magic to work, more like the spell was a part of me and my whole being tensed as I waited for Devon to scream.

"First five feet are clear," Devon shouted.

The water cannon restabilized as Eric slipped into the crack.

I moved to scoot around Elizabeth to go into the darkness, but she held a hand up, blocking my path.

"I'm having a really bad day." Elizabeth gave me a strained smile. "Don't make me watch my boyfriend walk into the dark."

"That's supposed to be my line."

"We're a modern couple, remember?" Elizabeth stepped into the slit.

I ran a few steps and darted between the stones right behind her, the terror in my chest that screamed the rocks would close and I'd never see any of them again batting aside my reason.

The rough texture of the stone pulled at the fabric of my sweater as I sidled into the black.

I'd thought it would be like walking through a door, but the stone path was long enough I'd started to wonder if claustrophobia was going to join my list of issues before I managed to make it out on the other side.

The glow of Devon's sword was the only light to be seen. The red gleam cast shadows that towered over us, which somehow didn't feel more comforting than being in the dark.

"Heliono." The glowing sphere appeared in my palm, giving more light to the space, but not offering much more comfort.

The chamber was about fifteen feet wide. Someone had carved stacks of large ledges into the side walls. I hoped the shelves were meant to be stone beds, but they could easily have been made to hold corpses.

On the far side of what I really hoped was a sleeping room, another tunnel led deeper into the darkness.

"Can we cross?" I looked between Eric an Elizabeth.

"A stone please, Bryant." Eric held out his hand.

I looked around the floor, but there were no loose stones I could see.

"From the wall, Bryant." Eric kept his hand raised.

"You could have started there." I turned toward the wall and raised two fingers like I was making my own knife. "*Caruson.*" The magic buzzed through my hand as I carved out a chunk of stone that I really hoped wasn't necessary for the structural integrity of the chamber. The rock radiated warmth as I passed it to Eric.

His legs trembled as he lowered himself to kneel. He took a moment, actually aiming the stone, before sliding it across the floor toward the tunnel beyond.

I held my breath, waiting for spells or spears to shoot from the walls like I'd gone from being a wizard to being a whip-wielding archaeologist.

Nothing happened.

"Elizabeth?" Eric asked.

"Nothing," Elizabeth said.

Eric started across the chamber, Devon keeping close behind with his non-sword hand hovering near Eric's back as though ready to catch the attempted abandoner if he fell.

"*Abalata.*" I let the black of the spell pool in my hand, ready to throw it at whatever waited for us in the tunnel.

Elizabeth picked up the rock I had carved from the wall, tucking it into her pocket before entering the narrow passage.

The light from my spell wavered against the chamber walls as I headed toward the tunnel, keeping to the same path the others had tread, not running from the ghosts my gut seemed really sure were staring at me from the shadows.

The passage sloped down. Not at a severe angle, just enough to make you wonder how deep the person who'd dug the tunnel was brave enough to go.

I studied the walls as we moved slowly farther away from fresh air and freedom. The passage was magic-made. Even if the walls hadn't been so smooth there was no way a human could have done it, I could feel the ambient magic in the air, pressing against my skin.

Who made this place, and why did you have to hide?

I knew I'd never get an answer even as I thought the question. The people who'd dug this tunnel were long dead and the history of magic too buried by violence and secrets.

A gasp sounded from up ahead.

"Eric." I tried to keep my voice calm, but I sounded freaked out anyway.

"He's okay," Devon answered.

Another light joined the glow of Devon's sword.

"Wow," Elizabeth breathed just before stepping out of the tunnel and into the room beyond.

"Whoa." I stood at the end of the passage for a moment, trying to get my brain to process what I was seeing.

A round room was a good place to start. Gold inlay swept through the stone walls, making a massive image of the gorge and the falls outside.

Silver shapes, like oversized steppingstones, had been set into the floor.

Thousands upon thousands of jewels sparkled from the ceiling, their gleam brightening to an unnatural glow as I stepped into the room and added my light to the space.

I wanted to walk along the wall, trailing my fingers across the bits of gold, but the others stood clustered together, so I stepped into the pack before I could start a cave-in by touching the wrong thing.

"This isn't right," Eric said.

"It's amazing." Elizabeth tipped her head back. The jewels set into the ceiling sparkled their dazzling glow across her face.

"But it can't be the end," Eric said. "The books aren't here."

"Right." I looked around the room, searching for the books, feeling like a boob for having momentarily forgotten about the things I'd almost died a few times trying to save.

"I don't think this is the end." Elizabeth took a tiny step away from our group.

I shifted with her, keeping so close my arm brushed against her back.

"Do you see any exit?" Eric said.

"No. It's..." Elizabeth turned in a slow circle. "I can see where magic melded the metal to the stone on the walls. I can see the power it's taking to hold all the jewels in place on the ceiling. It all has a faint glow, almost like a visible hum. But there aren't any cracks in it, no places where a part of the wall should push away."

"Then it's gotta be down." Devon inched a step forward.

Elizabeth furrowed her brow as she studied the floor. "There's nothing joining the magic that formed each of the stepping-stones, but they all look the same."

"Then we must take our chances," Eric said.

"What?" I let the black in my hand fade so I could take Elizabeth's arm, drawing her away from Eric.

"One of these stones must open," Eric said.

"Which means touching the others will probably do something that might get us killed," I said.

"Exactly." Eric carefully picked his way across the floor, avoiding stepping on any of the silver stones.

I shook out my shoulders, fighting my surprisingly on-point instinct to flee. "The entrance would have to be large enough for a person to fit through."

"That would be imperative." Eric stopped to study the stone at the center of the room.

"So don't pick a small stone," I said.

"A very wise point," Devon said in a mock Eric voice.

"I've never said Bryant was unwise." Eric moved closer to the left-hand wall. "He, like all of you, lacks experience. That is neither a personal insult nor a permanent state. It is merely an honest fact."

He moved toward the right-hand wall and leaned over a stone that would have been large enough for a person to fit through as long as that person had no fear of covered playground slides.

"This seems to be the clear choice." Eric tented his fingers under his chin.

"But how does it open?" Elizabeth said.

I studied the floor, trying to see why that particular bit of silver on the floor was a clear choice. They all looked the same to me.

"I'm not sure." Eric reached his foot forward like he was going to press the stone with his toe.

"Don't!" Elizabeth took a careful step toward Eric and pulled the rock from her pocket. "Let's try not to get stuck in anymore traps." She bounced the rock in her hand for a moment before tossing it onto the bit of silver.

The rock hit the steppingstone then tumbled aside with a *clatter* that echoed around the room.

I think we all held our breath as we waited for the floor to open up, so we all got to hear the *click* from the ceiling.

"*Primurgo!*" I grabbed Devon and Elizabeth, covering them with my shield spell, extinguishing the light I'd held in my hand.

Pops came from above as a shower of jewels shot toward us and pinged off the floor.

I pulled Elizabeth and Devon closer to me as the hail of priceless projectiles pounded against my shield with enough force to penetrate a human skull.

"Eric!" Elizabeth shouted.

I looked toward him.

Devon's sword gave the only light in the room, but through the shimmering of my spell, I could see Eric's outline—hunched over as his own shield crackled and sparked under the impact of the room's attack.

"It'll be done soon," I called over the noise of the jewels bouncing off the stone, like I actually knew what was going to happen. "Just hang on."

Eric fell to his knees like something had hit him.

My heart tightened and flew up into my throat as the crackling of Eric's shield began to fade. I wanted to help. I needed to help. But I didn't know how to do anything without dropping the barrier that was protecting the three of us.

"Let me out." Devon looked to me.

"What? No!" I tightened my grip on Devon's arm.

"Just let me out." Devon pulled a tea saucer-sized, silver disk from his pocket. "Trust me, Bry."

I let go of Devon and held Elizabeth close to my chest, pulling my shield away from my best friend.

My spell pulsed as Devon pressed a tiny indent on the silver disk, making it grow from the size of a saucer to a full shield. He shouted as he shoved his way out of my barrier and the spell sizzled against his skin.

The pinging of the jewels against the metal rang around the room as he bolted toward Eric. He stumbled, his feet slipping on the jewels, but kept his shield over his head.

A groaning rattled my spine, like I had literally been consumed by my fear and was standing in its rumbling stomach.

Devon screamed and stumbled again. "I'm okay!" he shouted as he knelt beside Eric, holding his metal shield over both their heads.

Eric's shield spell faltered as he slumped toward Devon, who caught him around the middle, keeping him from falling out of the safety created by the Raven-made shield.

26

There are some death-defying situations in life that start to get a little boring because they're just too drawn out. You're there, almost dying, in fight or flight mode. And then you're still there, still almost dying, but there's nothing else to do about it besides what you've already done and your adrenaline starts to fade and suddenly the whole mess is just exhausting.

I was about halfway to exhausted by the time the jewels stopped raining down on us. First, it slowed from a barrage to a patter, and then, with a weird swishing *tinkle*, all the stones that had pelted our shields soared back up to their places on the ceiling.

Devon gave a yelp and a groan as a jewel ripped out of his calf and flew up to join the rest of the stones that had already nestled back into the ceiling.

I waited for a long moment before letting go of the shield spell that surrounded Elizabeth and me.

"Do you need me to heal you?" I looked to Devon as he pressed the indent on his shield to shrink it back to being pocket-sized.

"As long as jewels don't have venom." Devon spoke through gritted teeth.

"*Sinato.*" I bit my lips together, hoping I wasn't accidentally murdering my friend.

Devon hissed through his teeth as my healing spell knit his skin back together.

"Thank you." Eric's voice sounded hollow and husky. "Thank you for protecting me."

"That's how we do." Devon let out a long breath before pushing himself to his feet. "Let's try another bit of floor and see what fun things happen."

"I think you already did." Elizabeth pointed to a silver steppingstone Devon had run across as he'd bolted to help Eric.

The silver had sunk an inch into the floor, leaving shadows around its edges.

"Maybe we should stand together in case I have to make a shield to cover all of us." I reached for Elizabeth.

"Good idea." She held loosely on to my fingers as we wound our way between the steppingstones toward Devon and Eric.

"So, do we just poke it?" I planted myself closest to the sunken stone, ready to cast whatever spell I could to protect us from the next doom that decided to attack.

"I'll do it." Devon stepped up beside me, reaching his toe toward the stone.

"You aren't expendable," I said.

"But you're so good at healing me." Devon slammed his foot down onto the stone and leapt back just before a weird shimmer passed over the silver.

Primurgo balanced on my lips as the stone began to glow, but instead of blasting us with high-end shrapnel, the light faded and the stone disappeared, leaving a hole leading into the darkness below.

I formed a light in my hand and reached toward the opening. The shadows shifted, revealing a worn stone staircase leading down into the black.

"That's not creepy at all." My voice wobbled as I spoke.

"After me, I think." Eric stepped up to the edge of the gap, swaying slightly from the effort.

"You're barely standing," Devon said.

"All the more reason for me to be the first to meet my fate if any of us should fall. *Heliono*." The light that blossomed to life in his hand was half the strength it should have been, but none of us argued when he stepped onto the top stair. "I think it's only right after the mistakes I've made."

"Death is permanent," Elizabeth said. "Mistakes can be forgiven."

"And atonement carves that path." Eric gave a sad smile before heading down into the darkness. Once his head was below floor level, Devon started down the steps.

My heart raced. I wanted to say something profound and meaningful in case we were all about to die, but I couldn't think of anything as Devon climbed down, leaving the red glow of his sword as my only assurance that he still existed.

Elizabeth squeezed my fingers before starting after them.

I knelt beside the stairs, lighting her path for as long as I could. But her shiny blond hair disappeared into the darkness, so there was nothing I could do but follow.

"You can do this, Bryant." I clenched my jaw as I stepped onto the first stair. The stone beneath my feet stayed solid. "You can totally do this."

I started down the steps, trying not to grind my teeth to the point of cracking them and making a mental note to talk to Dr. Spinnek about relaxing my jaw while under intense stress if I survived the creepy stairs and if she was still willing to schedule me for an appointment.

From above, I'd thought the steps just went straight down,

but really it was a wide spiral staircase reaching deep into the earth.

"You can't scare me with going belowground." I spoke to the stone around me. "I've been to the tunnels below Beville. This is nothing."

"Are you okay?" Elizabeth took a step back to look at me.

"Yeah." Heat crept into my cheeks. "Just talking to the stairs."

"Ah. Totally normal." Elizabeth winked at me and stepped forward, shifting out of my view around the spiral.

The temperature of my cheeks still hadn't returned to normal by the time the end of the stairs came into view.

It didn't look like anything special. There was no grand entryway. No singing angels or sparkling lights. Devon didn't whoop in triumph, and Eric didn't say anything snarky.

A desperate disappointment stabbed at my stomach. I shoved the feeling aside and squared my shoulders, ready to give a rousing motivational speech if that was what it took to keep the others going as we searched for the books.

I stepped off the last stair, my mouth already open in preparation for saying something deep and meaningful about the salvation of knowledge, and then I just froze. Like I'd been trapped in one of Iliana's gelatinous prisons.

Books.

Everywhere books.

Thousands upon thousands of books.

Tables laid out with stacks of books. Trunks so packed with books, they couldn't be closed.

Shelves along the walls had been filled with books, and the room stretched farther back than my light could reach.

I stood there, staring as my body went completely numb with awe.

Even knowing what we'd been looking for, I hadn't realized how beautiful the sight would actually be.

I took a step forward, wanting to race into the dark just to know how far back the room reached.

"There are so many," Elizabeth said.

"Who the hell got them all down here?" Devon said.

"We won't be able to move them quickly enough." Eric's hands trembled as he reached for the nearest table. "Even if Iliana doesn't come for days, we won't have enough time to get all the books safely away. We need help."

"We need a shipping container," I said.

Eric picked up one of the books and ran his fingers along the cover. "The most precious wisdom our people possess. Hidden belowground for generations."

"We should take what we can carry," Devon said. "Get it up and out of here while we come up with a plan."

"We can't leave any of the books," Eric said.

"We can't risk ending up with none of them if Iliana decides to get vengeful and destroy them all," Devon said.

Two sounds carried from the back of the space. A sharp, slow clapping and low relaxed laughter.

"How very smart the boy is." A female voice spoke as the *clack* of footsteps on stone came closer to us. "You've come all this way, to try and take my books. I can't let you have them. I would rather they burn."

A flare of fire burst to life, crackling in Iliana's palm. She held the flames in front of her, casting their flickering glow across her face.

I could tell she was the girl from the forest. She had the same features, the same hair. But there was a malice about her the phantasms hadn't shown me. Or maybe she hadn't sunk to that level of evil before she'd gone to visit the bookkeepers in the woods.

"You would burn the books?" Eric stepped forward. "After all you did to find them?"

"You're right." Iliana smiled. "I did find them. I spent years hunting for this place. Tracking the footsteps of a long dead thief to find his lair. If it weren't for me, the books would have moldered down here. I found the treasure. The books are my prize, and I will not let you steal them. Better burned by my magic than ripped from my hands."

"There's something glowing behind her," Elizabeth said, her voice loud enough to bounce around the space. "It feels like death. I think it's bone magic."

Bile stung my throat. She'd used bone magic where she kept the books. It felt like a double desecration.

"A seer," Iliana said. "You really did try your hardest. That should bring some comfort to you before you die."

"There will only be one death here today," Eric said. "And I will not lose one of mine."

"*Erunca!*" I shouted the spell, not waiting for Eric to perform his own. Streaks of lightning shot down from the ceiling.

Iliana raised her hand, swatting the bolts aside in a way I didn't know was possible. But the lightning still touched her skin, and her face betrayed her pain. "How cute. Attack me again, and your deaths will be painful."

I froze, stuck between my need to fight and my unwillingness to be the cause of my friends' suffering.

"*Lobula.*" Eric held his hands to his sides, staggering as the magic of his spell shot out of his palms, forming shimmering shields on either side of Iliana, blocking her from reaching the tables.

"Bryant," Eric said. "If you would."

I stepped forward and everything inside me got creepy calm. Like I was just in the ballroom at Eric's house in Beville, ready for another sparring session, and he'd given the order to begin.

"*Parapus.*" The thin, black lines of my spell soared toward Iliana, clanging against her hand as she batted them aside.

"*Exci!*" I shouted my second spell before she looked away from the first.

She coughed and doubled over from the blow. Then her head snapped up and she glared at me. She didn't even mutter a spell, but a stinging radiated through my hand and dragged a scream from my throat.

Devon bellowed as he charged forward, his sword raised.

The stinging in my hand faded as Iliana turned her attention toward Devon.

His steps faltered, but he still swung his sword, nicking Iliana's arm.

"*Kalitza,*" Iliana spat.

Devon screamed and fell onto his back.

"*Abalata.*" I threw the black from my palm, shouting, "*Tudina!*" before the first spell even reached her.

Iliana ducked, and a shield of light blossomed from her arm, protecting her from my magic.

Devon gasped on the ground.

I glanced down. Blood had started dripping from the corners of his eyes.

"Eric!" I shouted. "*Hieata.*" I glanced back toward Devon as Iliana knocked my spell aside.

Eric knelt beside Devon, eyes closed as he whispered.

Iliana looked that way, too.

"*Erunca.*" I tried the lightning spell again. Not because I thought it would work, just to get Iliana to stop looking at Devon.

She used her shield of light to shove my attack back at me. I dove to the ground, reaching for Elizabeth, ready to pull her out of the way of the lightning, but she was gone.

I wanted to call out and see where she was, but I didn't have time.

Iliana snapped her fingers, shoving Eric and Devon aside.

Eric's spell that had been protecting the books flickered and faded away.

Iliana laughed as flames reappeared in her hand.

"*Ilmatiot.*" I hated the feel of the spell in my mouth, hated the fact that I had to use it.

Iliana's breath hitched in her chest, but she still stalked toward me. She inhaled deeply then blew on the flames in her palm, making the fire grow.

"How many books will I have to burn before you give up and die?" She tossed the fire onto the nearest table of books, letting the flames consume the priceless pages.

"No! *Aarantha!*" I formed a vortex, syphoning the flames away from the books and toward the ceiling.

"You are not going to win this fight," Iliana said.

A red light flashed through the corner of my vision.

Iliana saw it, too. She turned toward Devon as he lunged, reaching his sword for her gut. Her shield of light blocked the blow, then solidified and lengthened, her magic forming a gleaming blade of her own.

I hadn't even really registered what was happening before she stabbed Devon in the chest.

"Devon." Panic froze my veins as Devon crumpled to the ground. The vortex I'd made vanished, and the flames trickled back down onto the books. I didn't care.

"One down." Iliana grinned.

"Devon!" I scrambled toward him.

Iliana swung her spell-formed sword, blocking my path.

"*Milkawa.*" I curled my fingers toward the ground, begging the stone to grow to my will.

Iliana sliced her sword, aiming for my neck.

I barely ducked away.

I couldn't run. I had to keep her still. I had to get to Devon. I had to protect the books.

I couldn't do all those things. I could barely keep myself alive.

I was failing, and the people I cared about would pay the price.

The air in the room shifted as the flames rose back away from the books, not in a funnel, but as though someone had lifted dozens of torches.

Eric knelt beside Devon, blood on his hands as he forced the fire up with some spell I'd never learned.

"Are you volunteering to go next?" Iliana looked toward Eric, lurching as the stone I'd grown around her feet held her in place. She laughed. She actually looked down at her trapped feet and laughed.

The sound of it brought bile to my throat. "*Erunca.*"

Lightning flashed down from the ceiling.

She knocked my magic toward me again.

I leaned out of the way, already focusing on her legs. "*Turso.*" The streak of white light hit her in the knees. She buckled forward.

That little movement changed the course of the deep green, jagged arrow that flew from her hand.

I felt myself scream as her spell hit me in the shoulder, felt my arm go limp. But the pain couldn't break through the anger that had swallowed my whole being.

"*Telinto*," I spat the spell.

Blood sprayed from a cut on Iliana's cheek.

"How cute." She flicked her finger toward her feet, shattering the rocks that had bound her. "I had expected more from wizards who came so far to steal my books." A blazing sheet of orange shot toward me.

I dove under a table. The heat of the spell blistered the skin on my arm. I screamed and rolled farther away.

"You really do disappoint me." Iliana's boots crunched across the shattered stone.

I forced myself to my hands and knees.

Eric knelt on the ground twenty feet in front of me, sweating, swaying, and crumpling beneath the weight of his own magic.

Devon lay still beside him. Blood stained his eyelids.

Pain that had nothing to do with my injuries shot through my whole body.

I screamed as I scrambled back out from under the table. "*Frico.*" My spell grabbed onto Iliana's jacket, yanking her toward me. I didn't bother formulating a spell as I swung and punched her hard in the face.

Something stung my side. The warmth of my blood trickled down my ribs.

"*Erunca.*" I grabbed onto Iliana as lightning streaked down from the ceiling.

The spell finally found its mark. The surge of it traveled through my hands, knocking my heart out of rhythm as Iliana tossed me to the ground.

I tried to get up, but my limbs couldn't hold me.

"I'm tired of playing." Iliana raised her hand. Bits of carved, white shrapnel flew from the back wall to land in her palm. She grinned as she blew on them. The bits of bone glowed red.

"*Primurgo.*" The word stole the last bit of air my lungs had to give.

She threw the bones at me like they were nothing more sinister than confetti.

Sparks crackled across my shield, the weight of other, long dead wizards' power pressing against my weakened magic.

Iliana screamed and turned away from me. Blood dripped from a wound in her back.

"Leave my boyfriend alone." Elizabeth gripped a bone-tipped spear whose point had been slicked with red.

"Is it time for me to hurt you now?" Iliana raised her hands.

"No." Elizabeth smiled as she glanced toward me. "It's time to end this the way it all began." She leveled her spear, ready to charge forward.

I wanted to shield her. I would have thrown myself in front of her if I could move. But I had nothing left. No magic. Not even enough air in my lungs to tell Elizabeth I was sorry for failing her.

Iliana shouted a spell I couldn't hear over my pulse thundering in my ears.

Elizabeth staggered before thrusting the spear again.

Iliana laughed as she leapt aside.

Elizabeth didn't cringe. She didn't back away. She was brave and strong and everything I'd loved since before she'd actually spoken to me. Since before it all began. Since the day I started a fire in a stupid scene shop and fate dragged Elizabeth into my life.

She swiped the spear at Iliana's ankles.

I grabbed my phone, pressing my thumb to the scanner before I'd even gotten it out of my pocket. A little icon of cartoon fire popped up on the screen. I tapped the app. A picture of flames appeared, along with a level bar.

I aimed the phone at Iliana's back.

She lifted her hand. Jagged shards of white surrounded her fist as she shifted her weight to aim for Elizabeth.

I dragged the bar all the way to the right.

A pillar of flames roared to life in the middle of the room. There was no screaming. Just fire.

One, two, three.

Elizabeth dropped the spear and backed away from the flames.

Eight, nine, ten.

I dragged the bar to the left, and all the fire, from the pillar that surrounded Iliana to the blaze Eric held in the air, just disappeared.

The room went silent.

I coughed a sob and dragged myself across the ground toward Devon.

Eric sat back on his heels, covering his face.

"I'm so sorry." I reached my best friend's side and clasped his still-warm hand. "I didn't...I'm so..." I couldn't speak through my tears.

"Devon." Elizabeth knelt beside him. "Devon, wake up."

"Elizabeth, he's..." I couldn't make myself say that my best friend was dead.

Elizabeth tore open the front of his sweater and shoved his shirt up.

I started to close my eyes, not wanting to see his wound, but Devon's skin was the wrong color. Something silver covered him, and there wasn't any blood.

"If Raven's armor stopped the blow, why isn't he awake?" Elizabeth shook Eric's shoulder. "Why isn't he awake? Think, Eric." She yanked his hands away from his face.

"She manipulated magic, concentrating the force of it to form a blade." Eric rose back up to his knees, new life filling his eyes as he touched the thin fabric that covered Devon's torso. "Raven's invention stopped the blow from penetrating Devon's body, but the dispersed magic still struck him."

"Okay, so how do you heal from that?" Elizabeth said.

I reached my hand out, laying it on Devon's chest. It didn't move. "He's not breathing."

"The lack of inhalation is a side effect, not the true problem. He is suffering the receiving form of a burn out. Too much magic where it should not be." Eric swatted my hand aside and laid both his palms on Devon's chest. "*Crantella stasina bracenta erbracina!*"

The most radiant glow I'd ever seen floated up from Devon's body like Eric was separating spirit from flesh.

Eric raised his hands, lifting the light, drawing it toward himself. The gleam wrapped around his arms and traveled up his neck before surrounding his whole body. He gasped as the last of the light peeled away from Devon.

Before I could start to panic, Devon took a great shuddering breath.

"Devon." I squeezed his hand.

A weird *hum* pulled my attention from my now not dead best friend.

The gleam surrounding Eric had condensed, forming a solid light like a suit of armor that blocked his actual body from view.

"Eric?" Elizabeth reached toward him.

With a *crack*, the light flashed as it shot into Eric's body.

"Eric!" Elizabeth threw herself toward him as he fell, catching his head before it struck the ground.

Devon squeezed my hand.

"You're alive." I leaned over him.

"What the hell was that?" Devon blinked the blood from his eyes.

"You were a little dead, but you're better now." I laughed, not caring that my tears were literally falling onto Devon's non-punctured chest.

"Go slow." Elizabeth wrapped an arm behind Eric's back as she helped him sit up.

"Thank you, Eric," I said. "Are you going to be okay?"

"A wizard's body can handle more magic than a human's." Eric swayed as he looked to Devon. "I'll have a few bad days. But I'll survive."

"At least you can read a good book while you recover," I said.

"Where's Iliana?" Devon sat up.

I grabbed his shoulder, keeping him from tipping over.

"She's gone," Elizabeth said. "All we have to do now is sort the books and see which ones need repair."

"And figure out how to get all of them back to America." Devon looked to me.

I cringed, remembering my abandoned therapy session,

tossed aside phone, and having broken the one rule my parents had laid out for the trip.

"Maybe it's a good thing my parents are having slumber parties," I said. "Nothing like a little emotional blackmail to get someone to pay for international shipping."

"That's the spirit." Devon laughed. "Everything happens for a reason."

And for a little while, I thought he was right. I'd fulfilled my destiny. The four of us were meant to work together because it took all of us to find the books and defeat Evil Iliana.

We were done. Fate could find someone else to twist her web around and leave me alone.

But fate wasn't done with me. Not yet.

28

I t was already dark by the time we got back to the inn and I finally ran out of excuses for not calling my dad.

I bounced up and down on the little street that led to the water, like a boxer getting ready for a fight.

"You are not a coward, Bryant Jameson Adams." I took a deep breath and tapped on my phone's now super-cracked screen to call my dad.

He answered on the second ring. "Bryant, where are you? Why the hell did you go to Crete?"

"I guess the credit card tracking is working well for you." I shoved down my anger at being stalked by my own father.

"Bryant, you need to come home right now," Dad said.

"I want to." I looked out over the dark water.

There was no trace of people existing beyond the island. A pang of homesickness joined the fatigue that filled me. I missed Manhattan's light pollution and constant ambient stink. I missed ticket scalpers and sketchy food vendors. I missed angry tourists and packed subways and toxic street sludge.

"You have no idea how much I'd love to hop on a plane and be back in New York."

"Tell me exactly where you are, and I'll find a way to have someone pick you up," Dad said.

"I can't come home yet. I still have something I need to do, and I need your help." I rocked back on my heels. "Do you happen to know someone who could help me get about nineteen-thousand-ish irreplaceable books from Crete to Manhattan?"

———

E xplaining to your dad that you lied about why you needed to come to Greece? Not the best time.

Figuring out how to get thousands of books out of a hidden cave of death? Enough to make your head explode.

Dealing with renting donkeys to haul the books? Stinkier than you'd think.

Finding secure local storage while you wait for the book ferry to arrive to carry your massive shipping crates? Gonna give you an ulcer.

Having both your parents show up to *help*? Adding to the therapy bills.

Having your parents sneak around together while you pretend not to notice? A small price to pay if your dad's footing the vomit-inducing shipping bill.

Getting books regular humans should never see through customs? I have no idea. Dad hired someone, and I decided not to ask how legal it was.

Packing your almost empty bag to accompany the books home? Priceless.

Having your magical I-never-ring phone ring in your pocket for the second time ever? Gonna make this story just a little bit longer.

I know, shipping the books to Manhattan and restoring

generations worth of knowledge to its rightful place should have been the end of the story, but like I said, fate wasn't quite done with me.

———

The sun was already bright enough to burn the little bit of my pasty neck that peeped up over my bohemian-chic scar scarf by the time the crates were all on the medium-size boat that would carry us to the larger boat that would take us home.

I stood on the dock, holding Elizabeth's hand while Dad chatted with the captain, and Eric intimidated the crew that had been charged with securing the crates.

"I can't believe we're heading back." Elizabeth leaned her head on my shoulder.

"How far behind do you think we're going to be in school?" I'd been avoiding the question for the two weeks it took us to figure out how to get the books out of the cave of deadly wonders and to Manhattan.

"I don't know," Elizabeth said. "But we're going to have nine days on a cargo ship to figure it out."

I rested my cheek against her hair, reminding myself of the primary reason—besides protecting the books—that nine days stuck at sea sounded like a really good idea.

"We're ready," Eric called from the deck.

"Coming," I said.

"The faster we're gone from this place, the better." Eric swept inside what passed as a cabin on the ship.

I could understand his loathing of the gorge. I don't think he'd really gotten over the fact that Iliana had come super close to actually murdering all of us. I'm not sure he ever will.

I didn't blame him. Iliana had given me issues of my own. I'd had two phone therapy sessions with Dr. Spinnek where I meticulously didn't mention the fact that I'd torched a person, and I still didn't really want to look at my magical phone.

It wasn't like I thought it was the phone's fault I'd added to my deeply disturbing body count. If I hadn't been able to use the phone to stop Iliana, the four of us would probably be dead. But I still felt icky about touching it, like a favorite kitchen knife you'd used to stab a murderer who'd broken into your home. Only magical. And one of a kind. And tossed into your path by fate herself.

I let my fingers graze my pocket, checking to make sure I hadn't somehow lost my magical mobile, as Elizabeth led me toward the boat. I pulled my hand away, and a ringtone sounded. Not a normal ringtone. A weird song I had only heard once before.

Elizabeth and I both froze.

The phone rang for a few seconds before Elizabeth met my gaze. "Bryant, why is that phone ringing?"

"I don't know." I didn't even look at my pocket. I kept my eyes locked on Elizabeth's like if I didn't acknowledge my phone, it would stop.

The song ended.

My shoulders relaxed just a touch before the song started again.

"Come on guys." Devon stepped out onto the deck. "Eric's going to lose his shit if we don't start moving." He tipped his head to the side. "What's that?"

"My phone's ringing." I cringed, flexing my fingers as I worked up the nerve to fish out my phone.

"Wait, like, the special phone?" Devon jogged down the ramp to the dock. "Answer it, Bry."

"Right." I reached into my pocket. "That's what one does with phones."

I held my breath as I looked at the screen, hoping against hope it would just go blank and I could pretend it hadn't rung at all.

Unknown Number

My hand trembled as I pressed the answer button.

"Hello?" My voice shook.

"Hi, I'm calling to make sure you've finalized your ticket purchase for The Event tomorrow night," a chipper voice on the other end of the line said.

"The Event?" I said.

"It's not to be missed!" the voice said. "And no one will be allowed into The Event without a pre-booked ticket."

"I'm sorry," I said. "I think you may have the wrong number."

"I don't think so," the voice said. "This number is definitely on my call list, and Mr. McDonald handed the list to me himself."

"McDonald." A chill trickled from the back of my neck to the base of my spine.

"Absolutely," the voice said.

"How did he get this number?"

"That's above my pay grade, sir," she said. "Would you like to book your tickets now?"

"I'll take four," I said. "I'll give you my credit card number."

I pulled my wallet from my back pocket and ran onto the ship, reading the numbers to the woman on the line as I shouldered open the cabin door.

"Perfect. What name should I have the tickets waiting under?" the woman asked.

"Umm." I froze, staring at Eric who glared at me like making the boat wait a few minutes to leave was clearly the most disappointing thing I'd ever done.

"Put them under Mr. Wick."

Eric wrinkled his brow at me.

"First name?" she asked.

"John?" My voice wiggled.

"Perfect Mr. Wick," she said. "We look forward to hosting you for the premier of The Event."

I tapped the button to end the call.

"Who is John Wick and why are Devon and Elizabeth still on the dock?" Eric frowned at me.

"We have to get off this boat." I grabbed Eric's arm, dragging him toward the door.

"Absolutely not." Eric yanked his arm free. "The books are on this boat. We are staying on this boat."

"Yeah but my *phone* rang"—I held up my magical mobile for added emphasis—"with a call from someone who works for *Mr. McDonald* making sure I had my tickets for the premier of *The Event* tomorrow night." I opened my eyes awkwardly wide at Eric as my parents sidled around to our side of the cabin.

Eric tented his fingers under his chin. "We cannot leave the books unprotected."

"We can't ignore a literal phone call from fate," I whispered.

"Bryant honey," Mom said. "Are you okay? You look a little flushed."

"If someone were to find out what these crates contain, it would be a disaster." Eric shook his head. "We've come too far."

"Dad, I want to fly home." I looked to my dad, who had no idea I'd just put an unknown amount of money on my credit card.

"Fly?" Dad wrinkled his brow. "I thought you wanted to ride with the cargo?"

"Yes." My intestines clenched as I tried to come up with a reasonable lie. "But I'm starting to panic about being behind in school. If we fly home today, I can hop right back into class."

Mom pursed her lips and crossed her arms, diving deep into full parental suspicion mode.

"I appreciate your wanting to get back to school—" Dad began.

"Your father and I can tutor you on the trip," Mom cut across him.

"But that's not the same as being in class?" My voice pitched up at the end like I was asking an actual question.

"You'll get individual attention," Mom said.

The cabin door swung open, and Devon and Elizabeth came to stand behind me.

I'm a badass wizard. I can pull this off.

"Ok. So, the man who tried to have me kidnapped is having a party. I want to go and identify him so the *people who deal with those things*," I said like it was code for the magical police that in no way existed, "can get him once and for all. They aren't going to hold him for nine days waiting for me to get back. And if they don't grab him at his party, I don't know when we'll get another chance to finally stop him."

Dad looked to Mom.

"We could get rid of him once and for all," I said. "I'd be free. I wouldn't have to look over my shoulder anymore."

"We cannot abandon the books," Eric said.

"I can stay," Devon said. "I'll keep an eye on them."

"I am not leaving a minor alone on a cargo ship," Mom said.

"I'll hire a plane," Dad sighed.

"Leo, that costs as much as a house." Mom gripped his arm.

"I already own a house." Dad pulled out his phone and walked onto the deck.

Mom buried her face in her hands.

My heart felt like it was going to explode with panic at the mere thought of dumping the money on a private cargo plane.

Elizabeth slipped her arm around my waist like she knew damn well I was about to pass out.

"Well," Mom said. "I guess I should email the school and tell them I won't need a sub for next week."

"If we ever decide to get married," Elizabeth whispered in my ear, "we're eloping before your dad decides to drop that much money on a fancy ceremony."

My panic disappeared in a flush of absolute joy as Elizabeth threaded her fingers through mine, and the medium-size ship finally left the little village at the bottom of the gorge, heading to a place where we could catch our last minute cargo plane to New York.

The next bit of the story is really just blah, blah, blah, boat, blah, blah, sketchy customs official who lets us through way too easily. Blah, blah, blah, flying in a cargo plane is not actually fun. Blah, blah, I bet you forgot about the time the New York City police had pictures of us wreaking magical havoc. Too bad for us, the police didn't forget.

29

By the time we landed in New York and got to the weird offshoot of customs where people on non-commercial flights are sent to feel special, all I wanted was to sleep in my own bed. I'd dozed on the uncomfortable plane, but between all the traveling and Eric's freak out about having to step away from our precious cargo to go through customs, my whole body felt like it had gotten packed full of sand.

Even my eyes were gritty as the customs official asked me his questions.

"Do you have anything to declare?" The man barely looked at me as he spoke.

"No." I dug my nails into my palms, forcing myself to not wince at the not-quite-a-lie. Technically, Dad was the one with an entire plane full of things to declare.

"Reason for travel?" The man flipped through my passport.

"Vacation." I turned my voice wobble into a pretty convincing yawn.

"Where do you live?"

"Manhattan."

I got through and dragged my rolly bag to meet Mom on the other side.

"Can you come home to rest for a bit?" She pushed my purple hair away from my face.

"I don't think so," I said. "I have to meet *the people* soon."

By *soon* I meant *I don't actually know what time The Event is or where it is, but Devon texted Raven and offered to pay her if she could send us the information because I'm an asshat who didn't bother to ask either of those questions when I was on the phone with the bad guy's sales rep.*

A group of people entered through the sliding doors that were very clearly marked *Exit*.

"I don't think you should go back to school tomorrow," Mom said. "Take a day to rest and catch up on your work. Running yourself into the ground won't do you any good."

"Yeah. That would be nice."

The door people just hovered near the exit, not blocking it, but not seeming to have had any reason to have entered either.

"I could help with unloading the books," I said.

"I want you resting and doing schoolwork." Mom stepped in front of me, blocking my view of the hoverers. "Unloading those books could take weeks. You'll have plenty of time to help."

"With the way the Library's filing system works, it'll be done a lot quicker than you'd think."

"I can't wait to not have a suitcase with me anymore." Elizabeth rolled her bag next to mine and took my hand. "Also a hot shower and one of Lola's muffins."

"I'm sure she's been lonely," Mom said. "Her guards aren't exactly keen on conversation."

Devon set his suitcase next to mine as Dad gave Mom a smile before stopping ten feet away from us to make a call.

"I wonder if we could grab some muffins before we head down," Elizabeth said.

"I'm starved," Devon said.

I was going to say something along the lines of *I three crave nourishment*, but the hoverers moved away from the door, their whole unit coming straight for us.

Letting go of Elizabeth's hand, I took a little step sideways, just enough to keep any spells from hitting her before I knew what kind of wizards had come to attack.

"Elizabeth Wick," was not the thing I expected the lady at the front of the pack to say.

"Umm, yes?" Elizabeth pressed her hand to my back, though which of us she was trying to keep from panicking, I really don't know.

"Devon Rhodes?" A man stepped up beside the lady.

Until then, I hadn't realized the lady looked kind, like a superhero's aunt. The man's stern expression and harsh voice made me appreciate the lady a lot more.

"That would be me," Devon said.

The man pulled a shiny badge out of his pocket. "We're going to need you to come downtown. We have some very interesting questions for you."

We're going to need you to come downtown. He actually said it like that. Like on a cop drama.

"About what?" Devon didn't even sound shaken.

"You're wanted for questioning regarding a disturbance at a retail location," the cop said.

"Just for that?" I cut in. "Nothing else?"

Devon stepped on my toe. "I don't know what you think I did wrong—"

"Devon, don't say anything without a lawyer." Dad stepped forward and took Devon's shoulder.

"Mr. Adams," the cop said. His knowing my dad's name sent a shiver down my spine. "We'd also like to speak to your son. If we could schedule an appointment for you to bring him down to the station—"

"Why don't I get an appointment?" Devon said.

"We don't have Bryant on camera using an unknown weapon." The cop nodded, and two men with handcuffs stepped toward Devon.

"What do you want with me?" Elizabeth prodded me to move so I stood mashed up next to Devon.

"I'm from Child Protective Services." The lady gave what could almost be considered a sympathetic smile.

"Why?" Elizabeth asked.

Devon pressed a metal cylinder into my hand. I slipped the hilt of his sword into my pocket.

"Your parents have been looking for you," the lady said.

"My parents have nothing to do with me," Elizabeth said. "I'm petitioning to become an emancipated minor. I can live on my own."

"The court has yet to hear your case," the lady said. "A minor leaving the country without parental consent is—"

"You don't have to grab me." Devon glared at the cop who had him by the arm.

"—worrying enough that your parents contacted our office," the lady finished.

"First of all, how did they even know where I was? They have no right to track and harass me like that," Elizabeth said. "Second, I'm not going back to their apartment, and I'm sure as hell not going back to Soaring Horizons."

"Elizabeth, just go with her," Dad said. "I'll have Nikki take care of it."

The CPS lady frowned at Dad.

"What's going on?" Eric strode toward us, his voice almost bored even though there was a pack of cops facing us.

"You," the head cop said, "we've been looking forward to

speaking with you as well. Finding your name has been an interesting chore."

"And I'm afraid it will have to remain a mystery." Eric gave them a nod. "Shall we?" He looked to me.

"I don't think we're actually allowed to leave right now," I whispered.

"We don't have time for this," Eric said. "*Fransencio.*"

All the cops' faces went a little slack, and the CPS lady giggled.

"That's not good," I said.

"What did you just do?" Dad said in a cool tone before looking up toward the security camera in what he seemed to think was a casual way but totally proved where I get my awkward-under-stress habits from.

"We need to be going," Eric said. "As it is, we'll barely make it to The Event on time."

"I don't know if I can go," Devon said. "I'm pretty sure I'm being arrested for having a magical sword."

"I'm not going back to my parents," Elizabeth said.

"It'll be temporary." Mom laid a comforting hand on her shoulder.

"No." Elizabeth stepped away from my mom. "I'm not going back at all. Not even for a night. I'm not going to live with them and pretend magic doesn't exist. I can't. I've seen too much, and I can't pretend to be the girl who doesn't know there's more to life than my parents' petty drama."

"Elizabeth is coming with us. Devon?" Eric looked to Devon.

"I don't think I have a choice," Devon said.

"He can't go anywhere," Dad said. "If he walks out of here, I don't think the police will be very friendly next time they find him. My lawyers are good, but resisting arrest is not a charge you're going to want to fight."

"And if I let them take me, how am I supposed to explain

what happened when we fought the Lancre?" Devon said. "What answers am I supposed to give them?"

"None, until you've spoken to a lawyer," Dad said.

"I can't tell a lawyer the truth either. Not without betraying the wizards we've been fighting to protect," Devon said. "I think I'm really pretty screwed here."

"I give you both two choices." Eric looked between Elizabeth and Devon. "Stay here, take Mr. Adams's kind offer and allow his lawyers to assist you. Lie as well as you are able, and hope that will be enough. Bryant and I will go tonight and do what we can without you."

"Get to the option that doesn't involve you and Bryant going after Kendrick without us," Devon said.

"Going after?" Mom said.

"We walk out of here," Eric said. "And you accept the fact that a human attempting to live a life that bridges the gap between the normal world and ours is unsustainable. That many secrets and lies are too great a burden for anyone to bear. You have to choose a path. Were it my choice to make, you'd come to Beville. You belong with the magical community."

"Sounds great," Elizabeth said. "I can go to cyber school until I'm eighteen. After that, my parents can—"

I won't type out what she actually said.

"Being a wanted man," Devon said. "Not quite the take on desirable I thought I was going to end up with."

"Devon, absolutely not," Mom said. "You have your whole life to think about."

"I've got some pretty cool friends belowground," Devon said. "I think a little flirting might be able to get me wiped out of every database."

"I won't pretend I have the power to stop you." Mom planted herself in front of Devon like she very much thought she had the power to stop him. "But you are throwing away a very promising future. You're both invested in your lives at school and—"

"And how many people want to run away to a place filled with magic?" Elizabeth hugged my mom. "We actually get to live it. This is what's right for me."

"Shall we?" Eric wheeled his suitcase around the still-dazed cops.

"Bryant, honey"—Mom let go of Elizabeth to grab my arm—"I will not lose you to the underground."

"Of course not." I hugged Mom. "Can you take our bags to the apartment and I'll come get their stuff later?"

"Yeah." Mom gripped me tighter. "You had better be home by morning, Bryant Jameson Adams."

Dad stepped in to wrap his arms around both of us.

"I will." I gave them an extra squeeze. "But maybe look into the cyber school paperwork for me, too."

"You need to go to university," Dad said. "I already have interviews lined up for you at—"

"Let's figure out how to get rid of the purple hair and then I'll apply to college," I said. "After the year I've had, I'll have some really interesting experiences to mostly lie about in my college essays."

"See you at home." Mom laced her fingers through Dad's.

"Love you." I took Elizabeth's hand. "Let's go."

The three of us followed Eric outside.

The biting cold of New York greeted me, slicing through my coat as its own little welcome home.

"Are you really sure about this, Devon?" Elizabeth whispered. "My parents can't get to me after I turn eighteen, but if Raven can't hack you out of this, the police could be looking for you for a really long time."

"I may be able to charm my way out of just about anything," Devon said, "but convincing cops they shouldn't worry about me using a magical sword to stab a guy with venomous fangs in the smart watch section? Even I'm not that good. I knew the risks when I started carrying the sword. That's the problem with being a non-wizard in a magical fight. Your weapons are way more obvious than spells."

"I'm sorry," I said.

"Don't be," Devon said. "Just get the handcuffs off. They do not live up to the hype."

"*Cliaxo.*"

The locks clicked open.

Devon shook out his wrists. "So much better."

A cab pulled up to the curb, and the driver rolled down his window. "I haven't been to this part of the airport in ages." The world's best cabbie gave us a wave.

"How did you know?" I would've hugged him if it wouldn't have been almost weirder than leaving my parents in a pack of dazed cops.

"I called him," Eric said. "Lola's guards are seeing to the books. We are going to Columbus Circle. And, with any luck, order will be restored to the people of Beville before morning and we'll never have to hear the name Kendrick McDonald again."

30

The sweet scent of car exhaust and overcooked hotdogs filled the air as we stepped out of the cab at Columbus Circle. A glorious slosh of freezing sludge lapped into my shoe as a car raced by. An angry tourist shouted at a street musician for being too loud.

I was home.

"I love New York," I whispered to myself as my whole heart filled with such joy, I would have sat down and wept if there had been a semi-clean place to sit.

"Come on." Elizabeth ran back up the stairs to collect me. "We're on a schedule."

"Right." I shook my head, knocking my thoughts into an order that didn't center on how much I loved the chaos and grit of my hometown.

We weaved through the crowd, my purple hair attracting shockingly little attention, and toward the strip of wall where no one ever seemed to look.

"Where exactly are we going?" Devon asked.

"To Beville." Eric glanced casually around before muttering. "*Portunda.*"

"Where in Beville?" Elizabeth asked.

"No idea." Eric opened his newly formed door. "All the chatter Raven could find simply said The Event could not be missed."

"Hopefully they meant that literally." I slipped through the door after Elizabeth.

Even though she'd started walking down the tunnel, she held her hand behind her, waiting for me to catch up.

I ran a few steps to reach her hand and kissed the scar I'd left on the outside of her wrist before lacing my fingers through hers.

She gave me a smile that reached her perfect, sparkly eyes as I walked beside her.

My heart swooped around in my chest so hard I almost forgot we were on our way to do deadly and important things.

"Any chance of Lola's guards joining us?" Devon held his sticky blaster up to the dim light of the tunnel's ceiling, checking the...I don't know, but it looked like he was checking something important.

"They're needed to get the books safely into the Library," Eric said. "I think we can all agree leaving the books waiting in a truck is an unacceptable risk."

"There are too many wizards in Manhattan who would kill to get them," Elizabeth said.

"Can they save us at least one crate to file?" I pictured myself dumping a crate of books over the railing on the top floor of the Library and watching the books drift down to their places on the levels below.

Eric raised an eyebrow at me.

"We can always reload a crate to dump." Devon clapped me on the shoulder. "We can make a daily game of it."

"While you're hiding from the law in the basement of the Consortium?" Eric said.

"The Consortium's not a bad place to be," Devon said. "And if things get too dicey aboveground, I'm sure your house could find space for me. You know you love company." He winked at Eric.

"And if we get cornered at the Consortium?" Elizabeth asked.

"We know a back way out." Devon shrugged. "We'll even bring goggles this time."

"On the plus side, life won't be boring." Elizabeth laughed.

I made myself give a few chuckles of support, but I honestly couldn't wrap my head around it.

None of us were going back to school.

It wouldn't be safe for Devon to sit in Times Square trawling for girls.

He and Elizabeth were dropping out of the spring play.

It wouldn't be safe for me to take Elizabeth on dates aboveground for a long time.

Worries about college and job possibilities and how I was going to explain switching to cyber school to Dr. Spinnek all swirled around in my head.

Life was never going to be anything close to what is was before we'd stumbled into magic.

But the thing was, I couldn't find a *but* that made it not worth it.

"Should I bother asking if we have a plan?" Devon asked as we neared the end of the tunnel to Beville.

"We always have a plan," Eric said.

"Find the trouble. Pretend we're going to scope out the trouble so we can form a plan," Elizabeth said. "Forget we were supposed to form a plan and dive into the mess. Sound about right?"

"Yep," I said.

"I do appreciate consistency," Devon said.

"This isn't the time for sarcasm," Eric said.

I was on the verge of saying something sarcastic and funny when a familiar noise caught my ear.

At first, I thought it was a rumble like a subway train racing overhead. Then I noticed the consistency and rhythm. Like people stomping on the bleachers at a basketball game.

"What is that?" Devon handed his sticky blaster to Elizabeth and pulled out the hilt of his sword.

The end of the tunnel opened in front of us. On one side, the stone spire that reached up to Times Square pierced the ceiling. But where we should have had a clear view of the houses on the other side, the area had been blocked off by a white-and-black circus tent someone had erected in the middle of the street.

"They did say we wouldn't be able to miss The Event," Devon said.

"It's strange." Eric took the lead as we headed toward the tent of doom. "On a personal level, I find the lack of subtlety distasteful. But as someone who needs to find Kendrick—"

"Kudos to him for making it easy," Devon said.

"At what point are we going to acknowledge that the giant tent set up by Eric's house is probably a trap?" Elizabeth tightened her grip on my hand like she thought Kendrick was going to try and swoop out of the sky to kidnap me again, and she wanted to protect me because she's the most amazing girlfriend in the world like that.

"I figured we were just going to ignore it," Devon said.

"Trap or not, we can't afford to forgo this chance," Eric said.

"Nope." I slipped my non-Elizabeth claimed hand into my pocket, pulling out my phone. "If fate let the magic phone ring, we answer the this-is-totally-a-trap call."

"Tell me you have someone lurking in the shadows as backup," Elizabeth said.

"I've already told you Lola's guards are unloading the books," Eric said.

"And Charles?" I asked.

A loud guitar lick came from inside the tent.

"Charles doesn't communicate through technological means," Eric said. "He doesn't even know where we went, let alone that we're back in the country."

"Awesome." Devon ran a hand over his hair, somehow making tousled and jetlagged look cool.

The entrance of the tent came into view. More instruments joined the guitar, blasting out music so loud I was worried the vibrations might shake the ceiling apart and send Times Square tumbling down onto our heads.

The same beefy dude who'd been the bouncer at The Game stood at the entrance. He'd traded his awkward kilt and top hat combo for a black-and-white spandex and latex combo that would have totally worked in a production of Pippin.

The tiniest hint of a menacing smile curved the corners of the bouncer's lips when he saw us approaching.

The music paused for a moment, and a roar of joy filled the tent.

"That's probably a bad thing." Fear wiggled its way down my throat to squirm in my stomach.

"Welcome to The Event." The bouncer gave a sanctimonious bow. "I hope you purchased tickets in advance. Our performance tonight is sold out."

"We have tickets," I said.

The bouncer snapped his fingers, and a girl stepped out of the tent, tablet in hand. She wore a glittery body suit, which failed so badly at actually covering her body Elizabeth sidestepped to plant herself between me and the girl.

The worry in my gut paused for a moment to do a happy little jig because Elizabeth wanted to defend her territory, which made me her territory because the most perfect girl in the world had actually claimed me.

"Name?" the girl said.

"Mr. Wick." The joyful dance shifted back into worry as an *Ohh* like people were wincing at someone else's pain came from inside the tent.

"Welcome, Mr. Wick." The light sparkled on the girl's shiny lipstick as she smiled at me. "We have your booth waiting for you."

She bowed us toward the open entrance of the tent.

I could tell the tent flaps had been tied open but could see only darkness inside.

I shook my shoulders out and tipped my chin up, because if I was going to walk into a trap and potentially be murdered in a really horrible way, I didn't want tales of my demise to center around how I'd been a coward as I faced my doom.

"Come along. After the month we've had, I could use a bit of diversion." Eric strode into the darkness.

I held tight to Elizabeth's hand as we stepped into the tent, expecting to be shrouded in black. But as soon as we passed through the canvas opening, dazzling lights surrounded us.

We weren't on the ground anymore. Somehow, we'd entered a box on the highest of the three tiers of the audience. Wooden walls formed the two sides of our box, with black velvet across the back blocking our way out, and the open front giving us a perfect view of the inside of the tent and the things I really didn't want to see.

It was like we'd entered a modern-day version of a gladiator's arena.

Off to one side, a band played on a little platform. On the other side, another platform had been set up with a board displaying betting odds.

But most of the lights were focused on the center of the arena and the two fighters who faced each other on the blood-stained ground.

The crowd cheered as the boy charged the girl, his knife raised.

She shouted something and dove to the side.

The boy's shoulder lurched back like someone had punched him. Blood dripped from his fresh wound, but I had no idea what spell the girl had cast to do the damage.

And suddenly, the cops not handcuffing Eric or me for the trouble at the electronics store made a lot more sense.

The girl attacked first the second time. She raised her fist like she was going to bop the boy on the head, and a rolling wave of light, like sound made visible, pounded from her fist as she leapt high.

The boy staggered but stayed standing and sliced his hand through the air to strike her in the back of the knees.

From the way her mouthed moved, it looked like she was screaming as she fell to the ground, but I couldn't hear her over the pounding music.

The boy smiled as he stalked toward her, raising his arms, asking for the crowd to cheer for him.

The roar from the audience brought bile to my throat.

The boy looked down at the girl. His mouth moved as he began a spell, but the girl sprang to her feet, digging her fingers into the boy's chest like she was going to rip his heart out.

The boy stiffened. His hands started to shake, and the trembling spread up his arms until his whole body was twitching.

"We have to stop her." I stepped toward the railing of our booth. "Eric, we have to stop her."

The girl yanked her hand back, and the boy crumpled to the ground. He lay on the blood-stained dirt and didn't twitch anymore.

The crowd cheered.

"He's dead," Devon said. "He's dead, and they're cheering."

The music from the band swelled as the girl raised her arms high.

She bowed as two men entered the arena to carry the boy's body away.

"What a match!" A horribly familiar voice echoed around the tent.

A spotlight blinked on directly opposite our booth.

Kendrick McDonald stood on a glistening black stage. His black-tipped white Mohawk practically glowed in the light. He wore his black, fur-collared cloak and had added black lipstick to complete the Ren Faire Goth vibe.

"I promised you this would be an event to remember," Kendrick said. "Have I kept my word?"

The crowd cheered.

Kendrick raised a hand to quiet the masses. "And the excitement is only beginning. This night is not merely one of entertainment. The end of an era has arrived. It is time to say goodbye to the fly that buzzes around our ears. Please welcome Eric Deldridge and his crew of interfering, do-good misfits. Tonight, we end their reign of nuisance and see how easily their blood is split. Let's get a round of applause for our guests of honor."

31

A new spotlight flashed on, shining down on our booth, blinding me to the crowd who roared their approval.

"So definitely a trap then," Devon said.

"I didn't know you were this unpopular," Elizabeth said. "An entire tent full of people cheering for your death?"

"People will cheer for anything if you present it with the right enthusiasm." Eric stepped up to the rail and waved at the crowd below.

"So, are we going to try for a plan?" I pulled my thumbs out of the holes in my sleeves, placing my hand scars on full display. I hesitated before taking off my scarf and letting my neck scar show, too.

Maybe I imagined it, but it almost seemed like the pitch of the cheering changed as the audience saw all the spell damage I'd managed to survive.

"We get to Kendrick," Eric said. "Without a ringmaster, The Event ends."

"Better than we usually have," Devon said.

Eric raised his hand as Kendrick had to silence the crowd.

They all went quiet, but in a different, eager sort of way.

"Flies, Kendrick?" Eric said. "You've been defeated by *flies* twice. What sort of wizard does that make you?"

"The sort who will be responsible for your deaths." Kendrick shrugged, the fur shoulders of his cape almost eating his face with the movement.

I don't know if it was jetlag, desensitization from almost dying so many times, or the fact that he looked like a furry puppet, but I just started laughing. Like full on tears in my eyes, belly laughing.

"Bryant," Eric said with a hint of warning in his voice.

"I'm sorry." I wiped my tears away. "Sorry. Keep going."

Eric kicked the waist-high wall at the front of our balcony and it tipped forward, unfolding and lengthening to form a ramp that reached all the way down to the center of the arena.

"You have to teach me that one," I whispered.

Eric raised one black eyebrow at me.

"I don't mean right now," I said.

"I must admit, Kendrick, I didn't think you'd be so bold." Eric strode down his ramp. "Pulling all these people together. Congregating in the open to commit such dark deeds. Do you really believe there will be no consequences for your actions?"

"Let the Ladies come for me," Kendrick said. "I don't fear them."

For the first time, a sound came from the crowd that wasn't excitement. It was like every person had looked to their friends and murmured *he shouldn't have said that* at once.

I squared my shoulders and followed Eric, trying to look like a second who was ready for a duel. Pretending to be a badass got a lot easier when I heard Devon's and Elizabeth's footsteps following me.

"The Ladies missed us at The Game," Kendrick said. "We

were already gone by the time they arrived. We slipped right through their fingers. It's been months, and they haven't come for me. Not even a whisper of the Ladies coming to exact their justice. Do you know what that says to me?"

I bit my lips together to keep from saying *They're all dead?*

"That either they are too weak to confront you"—Eric stepped down onto the ground—"or they agree with your cause—creating the strongest possible wizards by letting the weak be slaughtered in battle."

"You must think you're so smart." Kendrick stomped on his stage. His ramp unrolled like a long black carpet.

"Intelligence is one of my finer attributes." Eric bowed. "Would you like to know why you're wrong about the Ladies?"

"No." Kendrick started down his ramp. "I'd like you to be dead so I never have to hear you speak again."

"Are you sure?" Eric said. "It might change your plan."

"At least Kendrick has a plan," Devon murmured.

I glanced toward him, but he wasn't looking at me or at Kendrick. His gaze was fixed on the aisle between the tiers of booths where three people lurked in the shadows.

"I want you dead," Kendrick said. "I want my patrons to watch your apprentice die. The fact that you dragged two humans to the slaughter? That just gives the crowd a better value for their ticket."

Ignoring the fact that Kendrick had almost reached the bottom of his ramp, I looked around the tent. Four shadowy aisles hid eleven fighters.

Twelve against four didn't sound like the worst odds in the world, but they didn't really make me feel any better either.

"Then I will reveal the truth that could have saved you after you're dead," Eric said. "Bryant, try and buy Kendrick and me some time alone."

"Sure." I bounced on my toes. "Sounds exciting. *Milkawa.*" I focused my magic on the nearest aisle where the girl who'd killed the boy lurked in the shadows.

The ground rumbled and started to grow, twisting and morphing to block the entrance, like I'd created a stone door that could rise up from the ground.

As I was marveling at the fact that I'd learned to somewhat control the spell, two of Kendrick's minions leapt over the top, leaving one behind.

"Not a bad start." I turned toward the next entrance. "*Milkawa.*"

Eric began a spell, but the band started playing again, and I couldn't hear anything over the music.

All three of the wizards made it out of the second aisle, but at least I'd made it so more couldn't come pouring in to join the brawl.

Devon flicked his wrist, his sword vooming to life as I sealed off the other two entrances.

A fountain of sparks flew from Eric and Kendrick's fight, but I didn't have time to see why the audience was cheering. Ten of Kendrick's minions were closing in on Devon, Elizabeth, and me.

Elizabeth aimed the sticky blaster and shot one of the boys in his bare chest. He looked down in disgust and tried to wipe the goo away, sticking his hand to his own skin.

"Nice one!" I shouted, not knowing if she could hear me but needing to praise my girlfriend anyway because she's freakin' amazing.

One of the minions raised his hand like he was grabbing a spell out of the air to hurl at Elizabeth.

"*Erunca!*" The lightning streaked down from above, striking two of the spotlights before hitting the minion. The two lights flashed out as the minion screamed and fell to the ground.

Not what I had wanted to happen, but whatever.

A girl dove at me, brandishing a black knife.

"*Stasio.*" The clear cage formed around the girl. She looked like she was screaming in rage, but I'd already turned to my next opponent.

Half of his face had been covered in sticky potion, but he'd been smart enough not to touch it.

"*Abalata.*" The black of my spell pooled in my palm. I tossed it at the gray goo on the minion's face. I hit my mark and the spell stayed stuck to his cheek as I jerked my hand back, yanking him forward. I cringed as he hit the ground hard. "*Stasio.*"

"Bryant!" Elizabeth shouted.

I whipped around, ready to defend Elizabeth, but she'd stuck one of the minions to the ground by her bare feet.

"*Stasio.*" I trapped that one, too.

I spared a glance for Devon, who swung his sword with such speed, the light of it blurred in my eyes and I couldn't get a clear aim to trap his opponent.

A scream from behind me barely carried over the music.

The girl who had killed the knife boy leapt toward me, her hand raised as the weird wavy spell pooled beneath her fist.

"*Exci.*" My spell hit her in the stomach, knocking her off course just enough to let me dodge out of the way.

I caught a glimpse of Elizabeth. She pulled the trigger on the sticky blaster but nothing happened. She'd run out of pellets.

One of the minions raced toward her, knife raised.

"*Frico!*" I yanked the knife out of the minion's hand.

The blade flew toward me. I dodged the knife, knowing full well I had no chance of catching it without hurting myself.

A grunt sounded from right behind me.

I spun around.

The girl who'd killed the boy stared down at the blade lodged in her chest.

"Oops." I raced for Elizabeth. "*Erunca!*"

Lightning streaked toward the girl who'd been charging Elizabeth. She dodged, missing the full blast of the spell, but it was enough to draw her attention to me.

She grinned as she stalked toward me.

Devon raced behind her, running from someone who wasn't the minion he'd been fighting before.

"*Turso*," I shouted.

White light whipped out, catching Devon's foe. The minion fell to the ground.

The girl who'd tried to stab Elizabeth muttered something as she came closer to me.

"*Parapus!*" Thin, black lines flew from my hand and soared toward the girl.

She sliced her arm down, batting my spell aside.

I backed up a step. The music had started to make my brain go muddy. I just wanted everyone to be quiet while we fought, but that's not exactly a thing you can ask for when you're stuck in a death match.

A giant *crack* sounded from the far side of the arena where Eric and Kendrick fought. The crowd gasped.

"*Hieata.*"

The girl coughed as my spell knocked all the air from her lungs.

"*Stasio.*" I stumbled as the clear cage wrapped around the minion.

I glanced down to see what my feet had gotten tangled on. The girl I'd accidentally stabbed lay dead on the ground.

I yanked the knife from her chest and bolted toward where Devon and Elizabeth stood back-to-back, each facing a minion.

"Leave them alone!" I shouted.

The music stopped.

The sudden quiet rumbled in my ears.

"Go to Eric." Devon passed Elizabeth a fresh clip of sticky pellets.

There was something in his tone that shot fear into my spleen.

I looked toward Eric for the first time.

His face was stained red with blood, and I could tell from the way he had his feet planted he was barely staying upright.

"He can hold on."

A wave of heat lapped toward us from the guy who was facing Elizabeth.

"*Stasio.*" I made the split-second decision to trap him before protecting us. On the one hand, I got him stuck in a cage. On the other hand, his spell stung my skin like I'd swum into a cloud of jellyfish.

I gritted my teeth against my own scream even as Elizabeth's cry dug into my heart. I looked toward the last of Kendrick's minions.

A storm of silver clouds grew above her, flickering with bolts of lightning that glowed electric blue.

A stream of the bolts hurdled toward Devon.

"*Lobula.*" I blocked the bolts' path.

The minion looked toward me. I could see hate in her eyes, but there wasn't any fear. Like Kendrick had somehow drained that bit of humanity from his fighters as he trained them to kill in his stupid show.

"*Stilgarna.*" I felt heavy as I spoke the spell. Exhausted from the cycle of fighting and killing.

A stream of water flew up from the ground, dousing the minion and bringing her own lightning down to strike her.

She fell to the ground, screaming in pain.

"*Stasio.*" I trapped her before she'd stopped twitching.

I scanned our part of the arena. Two dead, seven trapped. The dude with the goo on his bare chest had somehow stuck both his hands to himself and glowered from the shadows.

"*Stasio.*" I locked him away before running to the far side of the tent.

32

The band stayed silent as I sprinted toward Eric. I could see the audience watching me. Some of them looked enthralled, but most seemed disgusted or sad or scared, like they'd realized they'd been watching real people fight and die. None of this was a game. It was a deadly battle we'd been trapped in for months, even if the reality of the blood and pain had been hidden beneath the shining façade of entertainment.

Every part of my body hurt and I wanted nothing more than to curl up in one of the fancy audience boxes and sleep, but their disillusionment gave me comfort and made me run faster, because if they could see how far they'd fallen, maybe they'd want to help build something better.

A massive cloud of deep gray mist formed in front of Kendrick, billowing toward Eric, who had one hand pressed to the blood that leaked from a gash on his cheek.

I opened my mouth to start a healing spell, remembered the *no venom* rule, and stayed silent as I skidded to a stop by his side.

"You made quick work of them," Eric said.

"Yeah, well," I spoke loudly enough for Kendrick and the audience to hear, "maybe Kendrick should have taken a little more time training his new flock of minions. Did you even want them to win?"

"Their fate is not my primary concern." Kendrick's cloud raced toward us.

"*Primurgo!*" I grabbed Eric's arm as my shield spell blossomed over us. "So you're admitting in front of everyone here that you were willing to let all those kids die?" I shouted as the cloud surrounded us.

The weight of Kendrick's spell pressed against my shield.

I took a deep breath, calming my nerves and forcing my magic to hold strong.

"They are a sacrifice I am willing to make to rid Beville of the pestilence of Eric Deldridge," Kendrick said.

"Let me out." Eric spoke softly.

I dropped my shield.

"*Habelo.*" A wave of wind erupted from Eric's hand, blasting Kendrick's cloud away, carrying with it all the debris from their battle in a storm of wreckage.

"Kendrick McDonald," I said, "you recruited underage wizards with the promise of training them to be strong enough to build a better future. Using illegal Lancre, you captured underage wizards and forced them to fight to the death. You have just admitted to willingly sacrificing all of their lives to your vendetta against Eric Deldridge, a man you have only hated since he destroyed your restaurant after you tried to kidnap me."

A blaze of wavering, deep blue light *screeched* like a bird of prey as it streaked toward us.

Eric shouted something I couldn't hear over the earsplitting noise. Purple flames flew from his hands, consuming Kendrick's spell.

Kendrick waved a hand, sending the flames up toward the roof of the tent.

"Kendrick McDonald," I shouted, "will you confess to your crimes?"

"The only true crime is weakness." Kendrick sneered.

The purple flames spread out over the roof of the tent, reaching toward the top tier of the audience. Frightened screams filled the shadows.

"Then you are guilty." Eric held out his blood-coated hands. "*Tudina.*"

Kendrick lunged to the side, a smile twisting his lips.

"*Ilmatiot.*"

Kendrick didn't stop smiling as Eric's spell squeezed all the air from his lungs. He stayed on his feet for a moment, raising his hands as though he thought he could still fight back.

"*Aarantha.*" I formed a vortex, syphoning the purple flames away from the roof as Kendrick fell to his knees. "*Stasio.*" The cage formed around Kendrick as he clawed at his throat. "Let him live, Eric."

"Let a monster live?" Eric asked.

"We have a chance to build a better world. Shouldn't that world be built on justice and mercy?"

The radiance of Eric's flames hovered above my hand.

"What you ask can't be done," Eric said. "To let a monster walk free—"

"He won't walk free," I said. "Just trust me. I actually have a plan. This is our chance to change everything."

Eric held my gaze for a long moment before nodding. He waved a hand, and Kendrick gasped in a breath.

"How shall we change the world?" Eric asked.

The crowd in the stands began to murmur, growing restless since imminent death was no longer a concern.

I froze for a moment, realizing that literally hundreds of people were watching me. Then I heard my mother's voice in my head.

A good production comes down to staging.

"Come on." I headed toward the ramp that led up to Kendrick's stage, waving across the arena for Devon and Elizabeth to join us.

The walk up that stupid ramp was the longest climb of my life. I could feel the gaze of everyone in the place on the back of my neck.

"Bryant, what's going on?" Devon whispered.

"We're forming a new magical government," I said.

"We're what?" Elizabeth slipped her hand into mine.

"Don't worry, it's all very legal. I had Nikki write us up a constitution and everything," I said.

"You did what?" Devon whisper-shouted.

"Kendrick's imprisonment will fall under section twenty-seven, paragraph six," I said. "There's already a criminal indictment procedure laid out."

"What?" Elizabeth asked.

"It's fine," I said. "As far as Nikki knows, she's being paid overtime to help me plan the most detailed Dungeons and Dragons campaign of all time."

"She fell for that?" Devon laughed.

"Lying is a lot easier through email."

We reached the top of the ramp, and the spotlights swiveled to beam onto our backs, silhouetting the four of us across Kendrick's shining stage.

I didn't need Elizabeth's little gasp to know I'd seen the image before. The hero, the adventurer, the apprentice, the seer. The four of us together. All part of the same picture. All necessary to make it to the end of the journey.

I took one more deep breath and turned to face the crowd. Cold dread trickled into my fingers.

"Shall I begin for you?" Eric said.

"Uh-huh."

Eric stepped in front of our group.

"Witches and wizards," Eric said, "too long have you lived in a darkness filled with secrets, lies, and the constant threat of danger. Today we move forward. Today we take the first steps toward a better world. The Ladies are dead."

A rush of gasps and whispers flew around the arena.

"We conquered them and took control of the Library and the Consortium, only to find the books, the very knowledge the Ladies claimed to possess, had long since been stolen from them. We have journeyed across the ocean to reclaim what rightfully belongs to the wizards of Manhattan.

"We have fought, and bled, and killed to give you hope for a future where knowledge is the right of every child born with magic. Where digging in the shadows for scraps of magic is no longer needed. Where hiding from the wrath of dictators is nothing but a grim memory from our dark past. Today, we step into a new world. Join me, for our future will be glorious." Eric turned to me.

"Right." I glanced to Elizabeth and Devon.

They both smiled at me, like they knew I'd be okay.

I looked around the arena. At the bottom, where there shouldn't have been any people moving, ten women stood together. The keepers of the dead, watching me with joy filling their faces.

Tears burned in my eyes as I gave my fairy godmothers a nod.

"Our new society must have a structure that can last for generations. That's what we want, a peace that will outlive us all." I tipped my chin up, letting my voice fill the arena. "There will be laws and consequences for those who break them. Kendrick will be tried and punished for his crimes. A council of six seats will be formed to run our community. We won't be outcasts hiding underground anymore. We will be a magical world, thriving just out of sight."

The people of Beville cheered, and a weight broke away from my shoulders, like the golden strands of fate that bound me had loosened just a bit. Devon clapped me on the back, Elizabeth squeezed my hand, and hope that maybe it really had all been worth it bubbled inside me.

We had reached the brink of a new era of magic. And I, Bryant Jameson Adams, teenage wizard, hopeless geek, and daydreaming misfit had survived to see the start of the most prosperous years Beville had ever seen.

But that's a tale for another time. I'll end my story standing with my friends as the fate of wizards in Manhattan changed forever.

EPILOGUE

Post Credits Scene (You know, like the little flashes of extra story that pop up once they've scrolled past the stars' names in the end credits at the movie theatre.)

I know I said I was done, but I don't think it would be fair to walk away without telling you how things turned out.

Chaperone Cindy got a promotion and is now the assistant to the head of HR for my dad's company. He said her ability to handle difficult people with grace made her the perfect candidate for the job.

Nikki has started DMing her own regular Dungeons and Dragons game. I've played a few times. There are a lot of rules involved.

Dr. Spinnek is writing her first novel. It's about a boy who's a part of a secret society that lives under Manhattan.

Charles and his people gladly took over the role of jail keepers for Kendrick and other criminals of the magical variety. Charles is on the council of six.

The keepers of the dead are still below the Library. I tried to visit once, they laughed, told me it wasn't my time, and sent me away.

Lola sits at the head of the council of six. She's still in charge of the Library, and Sniffer McDeadDog and the rest of her guards do a great job keeping the books safe.

Mom and Dad get a little more complicated. Since I'm gone so much, Mom moved in with Dad *so she wouldn't be too lonely.* They have two separate bedrooms. We all pretend I don't know it's a sham.

Mrs. Mops is really happy living in Dad's giant house where she has lots of places to nap.

Eric is still Eric. He's on the council, sprints around Manhattan seeking adventure, and is the one all the bad guys fear. He's been keeping Charles in business as he rounds up the wizards who have been breaking the laws of Beville.

Elizabeth is still living at the Consortium with Devon and Lola while we all work on cyber school. Nikki managed to get her emancipated from her parents before college applications had to be sent in. She's applying for a double major in musical theater and classic literature with an emphasis on mythology. She's clearly going to get in everywhere she's applied because she's the most brilliant and perfect girl in the world. And she loves me. Which is the best thing that's ever happened.

I'm applying to all the schools she is, but as a political science major. Dad got way more chill about me not going to an Ivy League for undergrad when I told him I want to be a lawyer. He hasn't figured out it's because I'm on the council. I've decided not to tell him that little tidbit. Also, my hair still grows in purple, which is a fun thing I get to deal with. On the plus side, I'm easy to find in a crowd, and Elizabeth swears she thinks it's cute.

And Devon...well, technically Devon Rhodes no longer exists. Raven had to wipe out all digital traces of his name to get him off the police radar. No past. No paper trail. My best friend's life is a completely blank slate. Mom's making him finish high school under a fake name, but he's not applying to college. He's been making a list instead. Pinpointing every place where Lancre might be hunting. Raven's been helping him search and building him all kinds of crazy stuff, and...

That's his story. So I better let him tell it.

THE WORLD WANTS A HERO. THE CURSE NEEDS A THIEF.

Six of Crows meets Heist Society in this New Paranormal
Fantasy.

Read on for a sneak peek of *The Cursebound Thief.*

BEFORE

Ari,

You are hereby invited to a heist of the highest order. Danger, deception, and the salvation of the feu are promised to those who commit to attendance.

Please R.S.V.P. at your earliest convenience,

Jerek

Jerek,

Sounds thrilling. Who could say no to a party that delivers salvation?

Are you sending a car?

Ari

Ari,

I'm coming to you. Need your help collecting a partygoer before you fly east.

In the meantime, bring our boy home.

Jerek

JEREK

J erek squeezed the bridge of his nose between his knuckles, closing his eyes as he waited for his computer to ding with Ari's response.

The first rumble of a spring storm shook the windowpanes. He didn't spare the glass a glance. The house would hold against any storm. The roof would stay sturdy even as everything else crumbled.

Minutes ticked past. An ache crept up the back of Jerek's neck. He stared at the red-stoned ring on his left hand, trying to distract himself from the gnawing pain in his head. His bag was packed, the plane tickets bought—the time for turning back had long since passed.

A faint mew carried up from the floor as a furry head pounded against his ankle.

"You can't come, Cas," Jerek said. "Cats and burglary don't go well together. You'll have to stay behind."

Casanova dug his claws into Jerek's calf.

"I promise I'm sending you someplace nice." Jerek shut his eyes and kneaded his temples. "The height of cat luxury. You'll never even think of missing your life here."

Jerek opened his eyes to find the white cat sprawled across his keyboard.

Purring rumbled in Casanova's chest.

"I understand." Jerek scratched between the cat's ears. "But we both know there's no other choice."

The computer dinged.

Jerek,

He's on his way. To your house by morning. The Maree aren't happy. Don't think they're just going to send him to you and forget about it. There will be hell to pay for this.

Ari

"Hear that, Cas?" Jerek lifted the cat off the keyboard. "Our brave knight Lincoln is finally coming home."

Jerek kissed the cat on the top of the head before setting him down on the armchair beside the library's fireplace.

No fire crackled in the grate.

He pushed aside the imagined chill that lapped at his neck and allowed himself one long moment to look around the room.

The shelves were packed with texts that held information many would kill to possess. The records and files that didn't need to be hidden had been sorted into an order that would be easy for others to interpret. The pictures of his family had been dusted and perfectly aligned on the mantle.

"Don't mind the sound, Cas. It'll be over soon."

Taking the box of matches from the mantle, Jerek walked through the front door and out into the rain. He didn't need to bother with placing any charges—he'd already run the fuse right up to the stone steps of the entryway.

He touched a match to the fuse and went back inside, not bothering to stay and watch the black car explode. There was too much to be done. Windows to destroy. Glass to scatter.

This was only the beginning of the necessary chaos. Saving everything he loved would require much greater sacrifices than wreaking havoc on his own home.

Jerek Holden didn't even flinch as the boom of the explosion shook the floor beneath his feet.

GRACE

Cheers filled the packed stands. The umpire rolled his eyes as a flock of girls shoved their way onto the front row of bleachers.

Each of the girls carried a handmade sign.

Go all the way Steven!♥!

Homerun for the Homecoming King.

Swing your bat Steven.

Grace tucked her feet under her seat as the girls pushed past, unwilling to tear her focus from the batter long enough to tell the now giggling girls to sit down and pay attention to the game.

Steven strode up to the plate, rolling his shoulders and testing the weight of the bat in his hands.

"Come on, Steven," Grace murmured.

As if he had heard her, Steven glanced up, tossing Grace a wink.

She smiled back, her thrill of joy barely breaking through the surface of her panic as the pitcher drew back his arm.

Her heart throttled into her throat as the ball soared toward Steven's perfect face.

A crack rang around the baseball diamond as Steven hit the ball.

Her lungs forgot how to draw in air. A tingle shot through Grace's chest as the white leather seemed to glow for a moment before becoming nothing more than a pale dot as the ball soared past the outfield, over the roof of Sun Palms High School, and out of sight.

LINCOLN

"We're booked on a commercial flight?" Lincoln asked as the cab stopped in the long line of cars waiting at the departure gate.

"Did the hills of Italy turn you into such a snob that peasant travel is now beneath you?" Jerek passed the driver twice the money the trip had cost and stepped out of the car, leaving Lincoln in the back seat.

Lincoln climbed out on his side, letting his gaze sweep over their fellow travelers as he looped behind the car to stand beside Jerek. "I'm a Maree, Jerek. I'll sleep in the mud, wade through swamps of blood—"

"And only fly in private jets?" Jerek grinned.

"It's not funny." Lincoln placed a hand on Jerek's backpack, guiding him toward the sliding doors in a less than gentle manner. "You may be my best friend, but I swear you can be such an idiot sometimes."

"Glad to see my top position wasn't stolen while you were away." Jerek walked past the ticket counters and toward security.

"There is someone trying to kill you," Lincoln murmured.

"Have you considered that traveling on a plane packed with people could put hundreds of lives at risk?"

"They'll be fine." Jerek pulled out his phone, accessing their digital tickets as they joined the security line. "Just take a breath and act like a normal person who doesn't want to be at the airport."

"I will never understand you." Lincoln clenched his jaw, biting back the lecture he longed to spew as he presented his ID to the dozy-eyed guard.

The guard glared at Lincoln before letting him pass, allowing him to join Jerek in the next segment of the line.

"I just flew across an ocean to protect you," Lincoln said. "We should be in your home keeping you out of sight while we figure out who's trying to murder you."

"No one's trying to murder me." Jerek gave a maddening wink as he placed his backpack on the belt to go through the x-ray machine.

"So the bomb in your car and shots through your dining room window were just some assassin's way of saying hello?" Lincoln dropped his bag onto the belt, worsening his feeling of terrible nakedness.

I should have a sword. And a bow. A damn dagger at the very least.

He held his breath as he walked through the scanner, not exhaling until he'd retrieved his bag on the other side.

"There is no assassin trying to kill me." Jerek slipped his pack back on. "I blew up my own car, so just relax and try to have a nice flight."

Jerek strolled down the terminal, leaving Lincoln behind.

Lincoln blinked at his best friend's backpack disappearing into the crowd.

"Dammit, Jerek." Lincoln ran after him.

A blond girl with a pixie cut grinned at Lincoln, trying to step into his path as he reached Jerek's side.

"You blew up your own car?" Lincoln ducked his chin, avoiding meeting the blond's gaze as he stepped around her.

"And shot out my dining room windows." Jerek stopped in front of the departure board, scanning the gate assignments. "An assassin wouldn't have been able to harm Holden House. I thought you'd have known that."

"Have you lost your mind?" Lincoln's words came out louder than he'd intended.

"Of course not." Jerek gripped Lincoln's elbow, leading him toward the gate. "I blew up my car and shot at my house while of sound mind and body and without breaking any laws."

"Why?" Lincoln yanked his arm free. "What the hell would possess you—"

"I needed a reason for the Knights Maree to assign you to protect me. What better reason for requiring a personal body-guard could someone present than multiple attempts on their life?"

"You staged two assassination attempts so I would get sent to visit you?" Lincoln dragged his hands over his face. The ridges of his palms caught the faint traces of stubble on his chin.

"No," Jerek sighed.

A hint of relief eased the tension in Lincoln's shoulders.

"You were already on your way before I blew up the car and shot out the windows," Jerek said. "I had to make sure if the Maree sent anyone to check on us, they would find adequate damage."

"You've actually lost your mind."

"And, as wonderful as it is to see you, I didn't blow up my car so you could come for a visit. I *do* need your help, and by being here you *will* be saving lives. But the Maree would never have let me borrow you without explaining why, and there are some things the Knight's Council just can't know."

"Talk. Now."

"What do you want me to talk about?" Jerek weaved through the rows of seats at their gate, skirting around the rubble of luggage left haphazardly at the feet of weary travelers. "I've decided I don't like melon anymore and have matured into a greater appreciation of fish."

"You are such an impossible asshole." Lincoln sank into a seat in a row of empty chairs.

Jerek stared at him for a long moment before sitting beside him.

Lincoln scanned the crowd as he waited for Jerek to talk, his training telling him to search for any person that could be a threat, his instincts telling him to shake his friend back into sanity—or to punch Jerek if the shaking didn't work.

"I found a way to fix it," Jerek said.

A stone settled in the pit of Lincoln's stomach.

"You may think I've lost my mind, and that's fine," Jerek said. "But I've hauled you here, and you're going to listen to me. I can mend the Fracture."

"Ladies and Gentlemen, Flight 407 to Las Vegas will begin boarding momentarily." An overly bright female voice filled the gate. "We will begin our boarding with Elite Diamond members, families with small children, anyone needing extra time on the jet bridge, and, as always, members of our armed forces on active duty."

"Too bad normal people don't recognize the Knights Maree," Jerek said. "It would be nice if the sombs let us settle into our seats."

"The point of being a secret society isn't to get priority seating," Lincoln said.

A woman with three small children made her way to the

gate, her face almost as red as the cheeks of the sobbing toddler who gripped the back of her pants leg.

A man with an oddly shaped backpack stayed close behind the woman until an elderly couple stepped between them.

The four-year-old began to wail when his mother stopped to present their tickets.

"Jerek," Lincoln said under the cover of the toddler's hiccupping cries, "I know you want to fix the Fracture. We all want things to go back to the way they were before, but it can't be done."

"It can."

"No, it can't. There is no more magic left in the world. It's gone. Destroyed. You should know that better than anyone. Some things can't be fixed. Pretending they can is just a more efficient way of getting yourself killed than blowing up your own car. Which is really, incredibly stupid, by the way."

"Anyone fiercely dedicated to a cause will be considered insane by those who don't believe in their mission," Jerek said. "I can do this, Lincoln. It won't be easy, and I need help. But I can put things right. I can give the feu back the world we were meant to live in."

"I know you want to believe that, but it's not possible. People tried for years."

"I know people tried. But the failure of others does not prohibit my success."

Lincoln shoved aside the bubble of pain in his chest. "I won't let you risk your life for a doomed cause. If that means I have to haul you to Italy and lock you in a cell to keep you safe, so be it."

"You won't even give it a chance? You won't give *me* a chance? The Maree are pledged to protect the feu. Mending the Fracture, restoring magic, what could be more important to the oath of a Knight Maree than that?"

"Nothing. I would gladly give my life if fixing magic were possible, but it can't be done."

"It can." A glint shone in Jerek's eye. "I know how, I know what tools are required, and I know who I need to help me get them."

"Jerek, I..." Lincoln searched the crowd again, wishing for the first time one of his brethren would be amongst the throng, watching him. Judging him.

Ready to tell me how I'm failing and snatch Jerek away from my incapable hands.

"Even if you don't believe me, you're going to come with me. You've been ordered to protect me, and I'm walking into much more danger than I faced while setting the charges in my car." Jerek stood, joining the line waiting to board the flight to Las Vegas.

He looked so rational and normal standing in the queue of travelers. Nothing in Jerek's slim shoulders or unruly brown hair hinted at madness bordering on a death wish.

Gritting his teeth, Lincoln stepped into line right on Jerek's heels. "You do realize that protecting you includes protecting you from yourself?"

"Absolutely." Jerek grinned. "I would expect nothing less of you. But I want you to make me a promise."

"A promise to a madman? And here I thought this trip to the states might be boring."

"When I convince you I can mend the Fracture, you'll do whatever it takes to help me, and you won't tell the Maree what we're doing until it's already done."

"That's a lot to ask."

"Not if you truly think I'm wrong." Jerek passed his phone to the gate agent, smiling silently until they made their way onto the jet bridge. "And if there's any chance I'm right, wouldn't it be worth risking everything to succeed?"

Lincoln stared at the worn carpet under their feet, trying to imagine a time that had disappeared when he was very young. When flying across the country meant searching out some glorious new adventure filled with the danger and wonder of magic, not playing babysitter to a potentially deranged feu.

"Fine," Lincoln said. "I promise, on my honor as a Maree, I will help you if you've found a way to fix the Fracture. I will stand with you until the work is done. But if you're wrong, if you've lost your mind and developed a penchant for property damage, you have to promise not to fight me when I haul you in front of the Council of the Feu and swear to take whatever help they give you to fix your messed up head with gratitude and a smile."

"Done."

Jerek's confident smirk sent a tingle of fear across the back of Lincoln's neck.

Preorder The Cursebound Thief *today.*

ESCAPE INTO ADVENTURE

Thank you for reading Five Spellbinding Laws of International Larceny. If you enjoyed the book, please consider leaving a review to help other readers find Bryant's story.

As always, thanks for reading,

Megan O'Russell

Never miss a moment of the danger or hilarity.

Join the Megan O'Russell mailing list to stay up to date on all the action by visiting https://www.meganorussell.com/book-signup.

ABOUT THE AUTHOR

Megan O'Russell is the author of several Young Adult series that invite readers to escape into worlds of adventure. From *Girl of Glass*, which blends dystopian darkness with the heart-pounding danger of vampires, to *Ena of Ilbrea*, which draws readers into an epic world of magic and assassins.

With the *Girl of Glass* series, *The Tethering* series, *The Chronicles of Maggie Trent*, *The Tale of Bryant Adams*, the *Ena of Ilbrea* series, and several more projects planned, there are always exciting new books on the horizon. To be the first to hear about new releases, free short stories, and giveaways, sign up for Megan's newsletter by visiting the following:

https://www.meganorussell.com/book-signup.

Originally from Upstate New York, Megan is a professional musical theatre performer whose work has taken her across North America. Her chronic wanderlust has led her from Alaska to Thailand and many places in between. Wanting to travel has fostered Megan's love of books that allow her to visit countless new worlds from her favorite reading nook. Megan is also a lyricist and playwright. Information on her theatrical works can be found at RussellCompositions.com.

She would be thrilled to chat with you on Facebook or Twitter @MeganORussell, elated if you'd visit her website MeganORussell.com, and over the moon if you'd like the pictures of her adventures on Instagram @ORussellMegan.

ALSO BY MEGAN O'RUSSELL

Ember and Stone

Mountain and Ash

Ice and Sky

Feather and Flame

Guilds of Ilbrea

Inker and Crown

Myth and Storm

Viper and Steel

Heart of Smoke

Heart of Smoke

Soul of Glass

Eye of Stone

Ash of Ages

Fracture Pact

The Cursebound Thief

Sorcerers of Ilbrea

Spell and Secret